# THE
# LOST
# PLANET

# THE
# LOST
# PLANET

## Rachel Searles

FEIWEL AND FRIENDS
NEW YORK

A Feiwel and Friends Book
An Imprint of Macmillan

Feiwel and Friends books may be purchased for business or promotional use.
For information on bulk purchases, please contact the Macmillan Corporate
and Premium Sales Department at (800) 221-7945 x5442 or by e-mail at
specialmarkets@macmillan.com.

Library of Congress Cataloging-in-Publication Data Available

ISBN: 978-1-250-03879-1 (hardcover) / 978-1-4668-5695-0 (ebook)

Book design by Véronique Lefèvre Sweet

Feiwel and Friends logo designed by Filomena Tuosto

First Edition: 2014

10 9 8 7 6 5 4 3 2 1

mackids.com

*For my parents, who always believed in me,*
*and for Bülent, who takes on the world with me.*

# CHAPTER ONE

The boy opened his eyes to a sky the color of melted butter and a sense of inexplicable terror.

He sucked in a ragged gasp of air and sat up. The pain followed a second later, smacking the back of his head like a club. The world swam around him in a blur. He grasped for simple facts: where he was, how he'd gotten here. Why he hurt. Why he could barely see.

Nothing.

Shoving aside his confusion, he pushed himself to one knee with a grunt. The muggy air seemed to vibrate, but he couldn't tell whether it was real or whether he was imagining it. He squinted hard enough to make out the gray shape of a nearby building, and something vast and green behind it. What was this place?

A hand landed on his shoulder. With a cry of surprise, he

turned and saw a blurry figure crouched beside him. It took a moment to unscramble what the person was shouting.

"Who are you? How'd you get past the fence?"

*Fence?* He shook his head. Something had begun to rise in his chest, a bubble of vital information—what was it? His mouth worked silently, trying to pin down the words dancing at the edge of his tongue. The pain swelled, crowding everything else out, and he felt himself slipping away.

"Guide the star!" he shouted, just before the blackness closed in.

✳   ✳   ✳

"Hey! Hey, wake up!"

He opened his eyes. The blinding sunlight was gone—he was somewhere dim and quiet, breathing processed indoor air. A dark-haired boy leaned over him, studying his face. "There you are."

For a moment he struggled to form a slurred question. "Where am I?"

"I brought you inside. You're safe. You're in my house."

He stared at the pale, sharp-faced boy. Was this the same person who'd spoken to him outside? "Uh . . . who are you?"

"Okay, you're welcome. I'm Parker. Now who on Taras are you? Where did you come from?"

Letting the questions fly over his head, he looked past

Parker to take in his surroundings. He was lying in a bed, inside a small, empty bedroom. The only light came through an open door. He turned his head to see what lay beyond the door, and winced as throbbing erupted behind his eyes.

Parker had crossed his arms as if he were waiting for something. Did he know this Parker? He didn't think so. His eyelids grew heavy and began to droop.

"No you don't. Stay awake." Parker reached down and slapped his cheek lightly, but he may as well have swung a hammer. Jagged bolts of pain raced across the boy's skull, and he cried out.

Parker raised his hands. "Whoa, sorry! Good lords, what happened to you?"

"What happened?" he repeated, looking for the answer himself. The confusion he'd felt outside started to rise again.

"Um, yeah. How did you get through the fence?"

"Fence?"

Parker shook his head. "What is wrong with you, kid?"

"Kid?" He felt like a bleating idiot repeating everything, but it was as if his brain had shorted out. Why didn't he know the answers to these questions? Why didn't he know anything?

"Yeah, what are you, thirteen?" Parker said, with the authoritative air of someone much older. He couldn't have been more than fourteen himself.

*How old am I?* "I don't know," he admitted.

"Don't know how old you are? Are you some kind of runaway?"

"I . . . I don't know."

"What do you mean you don't know? Who are you?"

*Who am I?* He stared into Parker's gray eyes, and his confusion began to twist into fear. "I don't know," he repeated a third time, his voice dropping to a whisper.

Parker's face lit up with a grin. "Are you kidding me? You must've really gotten your brains scrambled. I know what to do—hold on a sec." He left the room and returned a minute later, thrusting a mirror into the boy's face.

Wincing, the boy hoisted himself up on one elbow and grabbed the mirror with the other hand to steady it. His stomach plummeted and his heart began to race. A sandy-haired, ashen-faced stranger stared back at him from the mirror with wild eyes.

A low gasp diverted his attention from the mirror. "Oh lords," said Parker, staring past the boy at something behind him.

Tingling panic raced over his skin. "What is it?"

Parker was already backing toward the door. "I'm gonna call the doctor," he said quickly. He turned and ran, his pounding footsteps echoing down the hall.

Frantic, the boy on the bed wrenched his head around. Fresh explosions of pain knocked him back into unconsciousness, but not before he glimpsed the bright red stain spreading on his pillowcase.

✳   ✳   ✳

Warm, firm fingers pressed on his neck, probing it gently. One hand cupped his head while his upper body was lifted away from the bed. The fingers moved to meander through his hair. Someone was speaking in a low, calm voice, but his brain only processed snippets of words: *the fence, run a pulse, huge risk.*

He felt himself starting to drift away again and forced his eyes to open. A man in glasses with a gray-speckled beard leaned over him. When their eyes met, the man smiled.

"Hello, there. I'm Dr. Silvestri. I'd like to take a closer look at this wound you've got on the back of your head, so I'm going to need you to roll over on your side. Can you do that for me?" He lifted the boy's right shoulder and helped him turn. An agonizing bolt of pain shot from his head down through the middle of his shoulders, and the boy groaned.

"On a scale of one to ten, how much pain are you in?" the doctor asked.

"Nine?" the boy gasped, his voice muffled by the pillow. The pain spread out in waves, blotting out the rest of his thoughts. His fingers curled into the sheets.

"Alright, hold on a moment." There was a rattling sound,

and the doctor placed a hand along the boy's jaw and pressed something against the back of his head. A cold sensation spread out from the area, and the pain cut off instantly, like flipping a switch. The boy sagged into the mattress with relief.

"Can I get you to roll forward a little bit more?" Something beside the boy's ear made a series of clicks. "We'll get you all cleaned—" Dr. Silvestri drew in a sharp breath.

The boy's pulse sped up a notch. "What?"

"Hey, is that—?" Parker's voice rang out across the room.

"Get out of here, Parker," the doctor snapped.

"Oh, come on!"

*"Now."*

There was a huff and the door slammed.

"I'm sorry," Dr. Silvestri said. "I'm going to talk with you in a second about this wound, but I think I've already found something that may help us out."

The boy waited, feeling nothing, his ears filled with the rushing of his heartbeat.

"Parker told me that you can't remember your name," the doctor murmured as he worked.

"No," said the boy in a tiny voice.

"Well, let's see what we can do about that. Okay, you're all bandaged up. It was just a flesh wound; the steamgel I used should heal it up in about twelve hours. You can roll over now."

When the boy turned back around, Dr. Silvestri was squirting clear liquid into a flat glass dish. He swirled it around a few times and held it out to show a tiny black fleck resting in the bottom of the dish. "I suppose you didn't realize you had an ID marker implanted under your scalp, did you?"

Leaning over to get a closer look, the boy shook his head. "Does that mean you can tell me who I am?"

"The chip's been damaged, but it looks like there's some readable data on it. I'll run a scan on it right now." The doctor fished a hand-size device from a case on the floor and held it over the tiny marker for a few seconds. "It'll take a few minutes for the frag analysis to run."

The boy sank back into his pillow. In a few minutes, this confusing nightmare would be over. He looked around the small, windowless room, which contained little more than the bed he lay in and a blinking console by the door. "Where am I?"

"You're in Asa Kaplan's estate, in the Wesley District. We're on the far outskirts of Rother City." The doctor paused for a reaction, and added, "We're in the Eastern Territory . . . on the planet Trucon."

The doctor could have been speaking gibberish for all the boy knew—none of the names were familiar to him. He remembered the strange yellow sky he'd seen outside and shook his head.

"You were lucky to make it here safely." Dr. Silvestri inhaled as if he were about to say something else, but stopped himself. "Parker told me you said something to him before he brought you inside?"

He remembered the words he'd spoken and the urgency he'd felt, but had no idea why it had seemed so important to say them. "'Guide the star.' I don't know what it means." He stared at the foot of the bed, and his vision shimmered and doubled as tears filled his eyes. Why couldn't he remember? What kind of a mess had he gotten himself into?

Dr. Silvestri placed a hand on his arm. "Just relax. How does your head feel now, Chase?"

"Fine," the boy mumbled, looking away as he wiped his face. When he realized what the doctor had said, he looked up. "Chase?"

Dr. Silvestri had pursed his lips in the beginnings of a smile, but he stopped when he saw the boy's confusion. "That doesn't sound familiar to you?"

The boy raised his eyebrows doubtfully. "My name is Chase?"

"Yes." Dr. Silvestri peered at the screen on his device. "It says here your name is Chase Garrety."

Chase lowered his head, swallowing back disappointment. He had hoped that his own name would sound familiar, would open up his memory like the key to a safe. Instead it sounded like two arbitrary words, no different than if he'd been told his name was Blue Shirt or Wooly Fantastic.

"You found that on the chip?" Chase asked, once he could control his voice.

"Yes. There's more coded on the chip than just your name, but it's pretty badly damaged. I'm going to take it back to my lab and see if I can recover any information from it. I took a tissue sample as well, in case we need to use DNA records to track you down."

"What should I do?"

Dr. Silvestri regarded him with a sober expression. "I'm going to tell you the truth. The wound on your head is not something I see often, particularly not on someone as young as yourself. It looks like . . ." He paused for a moment, glancing down at his hands. "It's a blast mark. I can tell by the small radius, and the burned edges. It looks like someone fired an annirad blaster at the back of your head. Low frequency, obviously, or you wouldn't be here, but still . . . it looks like you were attacked."

*Attacked?* A flicker of the earlier urgency surfaced, but with no details attached, it felt meaningless.

"And you really don't remember anything at all?" the doctor asked. "Not even a partial memory or an image?"

Chase closed his eyes and willed himself to remember, but his mind was maddeningly empty. He shook his head.

"I'd like you to stay here for the time being. We don't know what happened to you or who did it. If there's one place I know you'll be safe, it's here at the Kaplan compound. Sound good?"

Chase hesitated. "Isn't there someone that I should contact for help? To see if anyone's looking for me?"

Dr. Silvestri held Chase's gaze for a long moment. It looked almost like there was something important that he wanted to say, but he gave a quick sigh and smiled. "Let me handle everything for now. I'll run a search on your name in the local databases, see what I can find."

He dug into his equipment, pulling out a clear vial. "I'm going to give you something that'll make you feel a lot better. Get some rest, and I'll be back in touch as soon as I know anything." He slipped the vial into a slim metal cylinder with a flat disk on one end, and pressed it against the inside of Chase's right elbow.

A peaceful sleepiness rushed over Chase as the medicine kicked in. He was safe. The chip held the answers. The doctor would help him.

"I'll see you very soon," said Dr. Silvestri as he stood. "Don't worry. You've survived the worst already. We'll figure this out." He walked out of the room, turning off the light as he went.

With every beat of his heart, Chase could feel himself floating farther away. The last thing he saw was a silhouette standing in the door frame, and then he slipped into the blackness.

# CHAPTER TWO

In the darkened room, Chase drifted in and out of aware-
ness, oblivious to time or worry. Was it hours that passed?
Days? When the pieces of his consciousness began to reassemble, he stared at the ceiling in blank confusion for a few
moments. Then he remembered: Parker, the doctor, the microchip . . . and his missing memory, an unanswerable question
looming before him.

He climbed out of bed and fumbled his way through the
darkness, groping along the wall until he found a door. The
room opened into a hallway, bright with daylight from high
frosted windows. Squinting, Chase looked down and noticed
he was wearing soft gray pajamas.

He headed down the hall, and at the end he came to a
wide room filled with sleek, comfortable furniture. More
frosted windows filled the room with airy light, and like the
hall, it was silent and empty. Where were the people who

lived in this house? Chase sat down on one of the couches for a moment to think. It occurred to him that he could find the front door and leave, but where would he go? He wondered where Dr. Silvestri had gone, and how soon he could talk to him again.

"Finally, you're awake."

Chase whirled around in surprise. Parker stood in the doorway, pushing his dark hair out of his eyes. "I thought you were going to sleep forever. How's your head?"

Chase's hand crept up to the bandage on the back of his head. He couldn't believe he'd forgotten about his injury, but he had. The pain was completely gone. "Feels okay, I guess."

"Do you remember who I am?"

"Um, Parker, right?" For a second, Chase doubted his answer.

Parker nodded. "So who are you?"

"I'm . . . Chase."

"And where are you from?" The question followed quickly, as if Parker was testing him.

Chase opened his mouth to reply and closed it with the confused expression it seemed he was constantly wearing. "I don't remember."

Something like a smirk crossed Parker's face. "Well, that sucks. But at least you can remember my name." Seeing Chase's frown, he added, "What I mean is, whatever brain damage you've got, at least you're able to make new memories. That's good, right?"

This was true, but there was something annoying about the way Parker mentioned brain damage, like it was only a sprained ankle. And why was he talking like he was some kind of memory expert? Chase crossed his arms in front of his chest. "Where's everyone else?"

Parker had started toward a shiny black panel on the wall, but he glanced back and raised his eyebrows. "Everyone who?"

"The other people who live here, I don't know. Your parents?"

"My parents are dead."

Chase ducked his head, cheeks burning. "Oh, sorry."

"Don't be. They've been dead a long time. I live alone."

"Alone? You're, like, thirteen."

"Fourteen," corrected Parker. He shrugged and turned back to the panel.

That had to be a lie. No way was a kid that young living by himself. "Dr. Silvestri said this was someone else's home. Asa something."

"Kaplan." Parker tapped something on the panel, his back to Chase. "Yeah. Technically it's his estate here on Trucon."

"He doesn't live here? Is he your uncle or something?"

Parker sighed, and after a minute Chase thought he was

going to ignore the question. Finally he turned around. "Asa owns some big tech corporation. My parents used to work for him. They died in an accident when I was a baby, and Asa took me in as his ward and sent me to live at this compound. But he's never lived here."

"How can you just stay here by yourself? What do you do all day?" asked Chase. "Do you go to school?"

Parker made an exasperated face. "No. There's plenty of stuff to do. I study, I play games. I eat, I sleep. Whatever normal people do." He leaned against the wall and narrowed his eyes. "What do *you* do all day?"

Chase's mind automatically reached for the answer to that question, and again hit a blank. He frowned and shook his head.

"So what does 'guide the star' mean?"

"I don't know." Chase felt stupid admitting that he had no idea what it meant when he was the one who'd said it.

"Try harder. Can't you dig up any personal memories at all?"

Did Parker think he wasn't trying hard enough? "No. Where's Dr. Silvestri?"

"At his home, I assume. How about any type of strong feelings? Do you remember any fear? Anger?"

"No," snapped Chase. "Will you let up? I don't remember anything at all, and you're not helping."

Parker looked surprised for a moment, and then his face closed, as though he'd drawn a curtain over it. "Fine," he muttered. He punched a button on the panel, and a screen lit up on the wall and started playing a video feed of a crowd of people in a packed street.

A black sliver appeared directly below the video screen, widening as a large panel of the wall slid upward. Chase watched in wonder as a tabletop, set for two and covered with platters of food, extended out into the room. On either side of it, sections of floor rose silently to form two benches, flipping their tops to reveal a cushioned side.

Parker took a seat on one of the benches. "Don't you want any breakfast?"

Chase gaped at the feast spread out on the table. "Where did it come from?"

"Autokitchen. Sit down."

Chase sank onto a bench, breathing in the rich smells from a tower of hot buttered bread rings, platters of syrup-drizzled fruits, and a bowl of small red jelly-like balls. "But who made it?"

Parker gave him that examining look again, and Chase couldn't tell whether his expression was incredulous or irritated. "It's from a food synthesizer. Are you going to eat?"

His stomach suddenly roaring, Chase grabbed a bread ring and crammed the whole thing in his mouth in two bites.

Crispy and sweet, it dissolved into buttery richness in his mouth. He reached for another.

"Whoa there, animal, don't choke yourself." Parker leaned over his plate and stared as Chase attacked the food like he hadn't eaten in weeks. He touched the video screen beside the table, and the volume increased. On the screen, a sharp-faced man gesticulated behind a podium, speaking in a strange, fluid language.

"What are you watching?" asked Chase through a mouthful of tart green berries.

"I like the news," said Parker defensively. "Why, would you prefer cartoons?"

Chase rolled his eyes. The video changed, and a blond anchorwoman stood in front of an ornate building. "Leaders from several planets are already commending the new Lyolian president-elect for his strong stance on shutting down interplanetary trafficking networks," she chirped. "Here in the capital it's a happy day, but in the wake of this surprising election, many are holding their breath as they await the response of the planet's Karsha Ven militants. This is Parri Dietz reporting live on Lyolia. Back to you, Boris."

"What's Lyolia?" asked Chase.

Parker's head snapped around so fast Chase could practically hear the air crack. "What?"

"I—I just haven't heard of . . ."

Parker stared at him intensely for a moment. He pointed at the newsfeed. "What's that called?"

"Um, a video screen?"

"What rises in the morning and sets in the evening?"

"You mean the sun?"

"Is a fork an animal or a utensil?"

Chase scoffed. "A utensil. Why are you—"

Parker held up a hand to interrupt him. "How many planets are there in the Federation?"

"What Federation?"

Parker's eyes widened. "Fifteen. Is Trucon a colony planet or an origin planet?"

Chase shook his head.

"Colony. What's the capital of Earth?"

"Earth?"

"Good lords! Earth, your origin planet. You're Earthan, Chase—come on, you've gotta know that."

Chase shook his head, the names and information whirling around inside it. How did Parker know that he was Earthan, whatever that was? What other options were there?

Parker stared at him. "Last night after you passed out, I was reading up on amnesia. If you know what a video screen is, what a fork is, that means your semantic memory—your memory of facts and information—is intact. You should be able to answer the most basic questions about the galaxy.

How could you not know this stuff? How could you not even know that you're Earthan?"

Chase flushed and started to stammer something about memory loss. The gaping void in his brain was bad enough, but somehow it made things worse to know that the only clue he had so far was that he didn't know much about anything. "How do you know I didn't just forget that too?"

Parker narrowed his eyes, shaking his head. "After you showed up here yesterday, Dr. Silvestri and I figured you probably escaped from one of the slave traffickers. They're always moving shipments of slaves around in the deserts here. But even a slave would know what Earth is, unless you're just really dumb. Did you grow up in a wormhole or something?" A smile stretched across Parker's face. Was he *enjoying* this?

"Obviously I don't have any idea where I grew up," said Chase through clenched teeth.

Parker opened his mouth to say something else, but his eyes flickered past Chase, and abruptly the smile vanished. His expression darkened into a scowl.

Chase glanced over his shoulder. To his surprise, a teenage girl with long brown hair had walked into the living room. Her bright eyes locked on Chase, and she walked right up to his chair and extended a hand.

"Hello, Chase," she said.

"Um, hi?" He turned around and shook her hand. Behind him, he heard Parker snort. Why hadn't Parker mentioned this girl?

"Welcome to our home. My name is Mina." Her face was calm, almost expressionless, but her blue eyes rested on him with an unsettling intensity.

So Parker had lied about living alone. "Nice to meet you, Mina," he mumbled.

"Where did you come from?"

Did she really not know about his amnesia, or was this another attempt to trick his brain into giving up the answer? "I don't know," Chase said after a strained pause. "I can't remember."

"Okay." She stared for a few more uncomfortable seconds, analyzing him. What kind of weirdo was she? A normal teenager might try to make conversation, or at least blink.

Parker flicked at a piece of bread on the table, shooting a crumb across the room. "What do you want, Mina?"

"I'm going out to run some errands." Her eyes never left Chase. "Don't leave the house." She turned around and walked away as suddenly as she had arrived.

"Who was that?" Chase asked after she had left. "Is she your sister or something?"

Parker's eyes widened. "Are you—? You've got to be kidding me." He got up from the table, shaking his head.

"Honestly, I'm starting to think maybe you *were* raised in a wormhole."

Chase stared at the video feed, grinding his teeth. Obviously there was a lot he didn't understand. Parker didn't need to make him feel so stupid. "When is Dr. Silvestri going to come back?"

"I don't know. Hey, get up." Parker jabbed him in the shoulder. "Come with me. You want to play a piloting game? I've got a pretty good virtual deck downstairs."

"I don't want to play any stupid games," said Chase angrily. "I need to figure out who I am, did you forget that?"

Parker raised his hands, backing away. "Fine, freak. Whatever. Do what you want."

Feeling guilty for his outburst, Chase added, "But thanks for breakfast. And for letting me stay here."

"Like I had a choice," Parker said over his shoulder as he walked away.

Chase watched the video feed, where people were dancing in a street somewhere. As far as he could tell, they looked the same as he did. Did that mean they were all Earthan? What was the opposite of an Earthan?

If he couldn't remember where he was from, the best thing to do would be to retrace his steps from yesterday. If he'd really come in from the desert, maybe the desert was where he should start looking for clues.

*Don't leave the house.*

*Yeah, right,* Chase thought, jumping up from the table. He headed down the hall, away from the living room and past his bedroom, until he reached a foyer with a large metal door. He yanked the door open, and a wave of heat washed past.

The sky was a strange bright yellow, casting a warm glow over the landscape. Chase stood for a moment with his eyes half closed, soaking in the warmth on his face. He tried to look around, but it was difficult to see in the blinding sunlight. A pale green lawn stretched out before him, dotted with a few gnarled trees. Beyond the lawn, all he could see was a bordering jungle of leafy plants that looked like giant blades of grass, each one as wide as a man's shoulders. He took a step to the left, planning to circle around the house.

Something shot up out of the grass forest into the sky, a large, dark shape moving at incredible speed. Chase took a wary step backward, raising his hand over his eyes as it vanished against the glare of the sunlight. Then he saw it—a scaly black creature at least twice his size, with wings spread like a fan and far too many reaching limbs. He froze, holding his breath.

It was headed straight for him.

A loud electric crackle vibrated through the air, and the creature suddenly rebounded, tumbling inexplicably backward, away from the house. Chase tasted metal, and the hair on his arms stood up. The creature fell into the grass forest and vanished, but a second later, three more leapt up into the sky.

Chase stumbled backward into the foyer, slamming the metal door shut. A siren was blaring inside the house, though he hadn't noticed when it started. He turned around to call for help and found himself face-to-face with Parker.

"What are you doing?" Parker shouted. "Are you insane? Defense, lock sequence!"

The siren cut off as the heavy *thunk* of a deadbolt falling into place sounded in the door behind Chase. His heart still hammered in his chest. "What was that?"

"You mean the Zinnjerha?" Parker ran a hand through his hair. "Good lords. If you don't know what those are, there's no way you're from Trucon. If anything, *anything*, is burned into your memory, that would be it. The whole planet is full of those underground monsters. They could rip you to shreds."

"Why did—it couldn't get to me—"

"There's an electrified dome protecting the house," said Parker, waving his hand in a circular motion. "But you still can't go walking around out there like bait. One or two or five can't get through, but get two hundred of them riled up and I can't promise we'll be okay. Especially with the way they've been acting lately."

"Everyone here lives like this?" Why would anyone live on a planet where they couldn't go outside?

"No, in the cities there's a perimeter fence. But we're pretty far from any city out here."

An image formed in Chase's mind of where they were, in a solitary house out in the middle of nowhere. On a planet he wasn't even from, apparently. "Where did you first find me yesterday?"

"Out there in the yard, setting off all the perimeter breach alarms. And, yes, the Zinnjerha were trying to break through and tear you apart."

"How did I get there?"

Parker shook his head. "I don't know. Nobody knows. That's why Dr. Silvestri told me not to let you leave."

Chase looked back at the door. "Could I even go any-where if I wanted to?"

"Not really." Parker shrugged. "Sorry. You're stuck here for now."

Anxiety teased at Chase's stomach. Dr. Silvestri had seemed so friendly when he told Chase it was safer for him at the compound. But that wasn't the real reason he'd asked him to stay put. He was suspicious of how Chase had gotten inside.

Nobody told the truth here, it seemed.

# CHAPTER THREE

Sitting alone in his room, Chase felt like the walls were closing in on him. After locking him in the house, Parker had once again offered to play the same dumb piloting game with him, and then stalked away when Chase turned him down. It was starting to infuriate Chase that Parker treated him like a funny houseguest and not someone with a major problem.

He reached back and tore the bandage from his head. Unable to see his wound, he pulled aside the hair that fell over it and gingerly touched the area at the base of his skull. The doctor's healing gel had done its job—the wound was already covered in a layer of smooth, tender skin.

Whatever had happened to Chase, whoever had given him this injury, the biggest question bothering him was how he had gotten to this place. Parker said nobody knew, but he could have been lying. Clearly he had no problem with dishonesty, since he'd lied to Chase about living alone.

The house was a frosted prison, surrounded by a forest of monsters. The doctor had deceived him. Mina, whoever she was, was a weirdo who'd barely spoken to him. And Parker was, well, Parker. There had to be a way to contact the outside world from this house. Even if he couldn't get out, he could try to look for help from someone.

Chase slipped out of his room and down the hall. He returned to the foyer, where a second hallway branched off, but this hall only lead to an empty dining room. Hadn't Parker said something about there being a downstairs?

When Chase walked back from the dining room, he noticed a closed door that he hadn't seen the first time. It opened onto a flight of stairs leading down.

"Hello?" He stood at the top of the stairs for a moment and descended, taking light steps. Would he be in trouble if someone caught him coming down here?

Another long hallway stretched out before Chase at the bottom of the stairs. The first door he came to was locked, as was the one after that. He didn't expect much from the third door he tried, but it swung open on a small room that held little more than a trio of video monitors and a keyboard. There were some other items in the room that he barely glanced at, wall panels and storage cabinets. He went straight to the monitors.

Maybe Parker was on to something with his semantic

memory talk, because Chase navigated easily enough through the video screens, and the keyboard felt natural under his hands. He found his way to a messaging console and started looking for emergency contacts. A notification blinking on the side of the screen caught his eye: *Transmission pending.*

Chase clicked on the notification, and a message popped onto the screen.

> Code Maartens—immediate response required
> Unknown Earthan boy, approx. 13 years,
> appeared within compound yesterday with
> blaster wound to back of head and damaged ID
> marker. Bypassed all level 1 and 2 defenses by
> no explicable means (see attached video);
> destruction countermeasure initiated but
> deactivated by P. Current status: Silvestri
> examining marker, boy being held pending your
> instruction. Threat level: uncertain.

Pending whose instruction? Who had written this message, and why were they calling him a threat? He had to scan the words *destruction countermeasure* several times before their meaning sank in. The compound's defenses would have annihilated him if this P, undoubtedly Parker, hadn't stepped in.

With a growing sense of dread, Chase opened the

attachment. A video window opened, playing a recording that must have come from a security camera outside the house. It showed the pale lawn outside the compound, with the grass forest waving gently in the background.

A prone body suddenly appeared on the lawn. Was that him? How had he just shown up like that? He winced as he watched himself sit up and curl over in pain. There was a flash of black in the background, and then another: the Zinnjerha.

Parker raced across the lawn, sliding to a stop beside him, throwing his arms in large gestures. The black shapes of the bounding Zinnjerha grew in number, darkening the back of the screen. Chase saw himself speaking and then collapsing in front of Parker. After a moment of looking around in a panic and shouting, Parker hooked his hands under Chase's arms and dragged him back toward the house.

When the video clip ended, the screen went gray. Chase leaned back in the chair. So Parker had saved him. For a moment he was impressed, but he reminded himself that in bringing Chase inside, Parker had merely been protecting himself and his home.

"What are you doing here?"

Chase jumped out of the chair, heart thumping. Mina stood in the doorway with a sober and somehow menacing expression. "Who are you trying to contact?" she asked.

"What? No one, I was just—"

She took a step toward him. "Who sent you? What are you doing here?"

"No one." Chase's voice shook as if he'd been caught stealing. "I wanted to see the video. I'm trying to figure out what happened to me."

She advanced another step, backing Chase into a corner. "I won't hurt you if you come with me." Her hand fell on his shoulder like an iron weight.

"Let me go!" Chase twisted out from under her hand and tried to dart past, but she sidestepped, blocking him. His panic skyrocketed and his legs felt so shaky, he wasn't sure he'd be able to run anyway.

"What's going on?" Parker appeared in the doorway, looking confused.

"Go back to your room, Parker," said Mina. Still blocking Chase, she opened a cabinet on the wall, from which she pulled out two silver rings. She slid one on her finger and held the other out to him. "Put this on."

"No!" Parker rushed into the room and snatched the ring from her palm. "You can't take him away! I won't let you."

"He's becoming a threat. I'm removing him from the house."

"I wasn't doing anything!" insisted Chase.

"You were spying on our network and interfering with

our communications." Mina took another ring from the cabi-net. "Put this on and come with me."

Parker grabbed her wrist. "Stand down, Mina. Stand down, you stupid—"

"Where are you taking me?" Chase interrupted.

"To Dr. Silvestri."

Chase paused as a spark of hope ignited inside him. While he still didn't know how much he trusted Dr. Silvestri, he did have Chase's microchip, and possibly more answers for him by now. "Okay," he said, holding out his hand. "I'll go with you."

"I'm coming too," said Parker, slipping the ring he'd taken onto his finger.

"You're staying here." Mina's tone was flat and final.

"No!" Parker shoved her shoulder as she turned to the terminal on the desk, but she barely moved. "You can't leave me out of this."

"It's safer if you stay here." She entered something on the terminal, and then glanced at him. "Do I need to lock you in your room?"

Two bright red spots had risen in Parker's cheeks. "I hate you," he spat.

Mina kept her eyes on the monitors. "Let's go, Chase. Stand on one of those." She indicated a trio of metal disks stamped into the floor.

Stepping onto the nearest circle, Chase avoided looking at Parker, embarrassed by his outburst. He still didn't understand how Mina could act like his guardian but not be his sister. Was she some kind of teenage bodyguard? But he was too excited about the prospect of seeing Dr. Silvestri to waste any time asking about her. "How are we getting there?"

"Just stand still," said Mina. She entered something onto a panel on the wall and held her hand against it for a moment.

"What's—" Chase began to ask, and then the entire room faded out.

A horrible, icy sensation rushed over Chase, as if every nerve in his body had gone dead. He would have shouted had he not been utterly paralyzed. A moment later, the numb feeling passed and he buckled to one knee with a cry. A pinging sound came from the ground below him. He opened his eyes to see that his ring had slipped off and fallen to the asphalt.

They were standing on a city street, in what looked like an abandoned warehouse district. Mina looked down at him. "Are you okay?"

"That felt awful! What was that?" He picked up the ring and rubbed his arms, his skin still crawling.

Mina arched an eyebrow as she helped him to his feet. "Teleportation. It's not supposed to feel like anything."

"You didn't feel it?"

"Of course not."

As Chase looked around, adjusting to the new location, he realized that this must have been how he'd appeared so suddenly on Parker's lawn—he'd teleported. Tall, dilapidated buildings surrounded them, and there were no other people or vehicles anywhere in sight. The sky overhead had faded to a grayish violet color, the white disk of one sun lingering near the horizon.

"Where are we? I thought you said we were going to the doctor's," he said, trying to hand the teleport ring back to Mina.

"No, keep the ring on, we might need to leave quickly." Mina glanced around. "The doctor has an anti-inport device installed at his home. No one leaves their home open for anybody to teleport into without a return ring. It's the same as leaving your doors unlocked."

"He lives around here?" The desolate neighborhood didn't look like the kind of place where anyone would live.

"He has an apartment above his lab." Mina rushed down the street, glancing at the tops of the buildings like she was looking for snipers.

"Is this place dangerous?"

"This is an abandoned district. There's no perimeter fence here. Normally when the sun is setting, the Zinnjerha are no danger because they go underground at night. But they've been acting against their nature for the past two weeks. Keep moving."

After a minute they stopped in front of the boarded-up window of a dilapidated building. Like many of the others, it was decorated with a patchy mosaic of rust and spray-painted symbols.

"Dr. Silvestri, will you let us up?" Mina asked the solid wall. Chase gave her a dubious look, but moments later a segment of wall swung inward like a door. Ahead of them was a dark stairway leading up. The air inside had a sharp chemical tang.

Dr. Silvestri appeared in the doorway at the top of the stairs. "Mina, what's wrong?"

"I had to remove him from the compound." She spoke confidently, addressing the doctor like an equal. "He was becoming a threat."

"I wasn't threatening anything!" Chase protested.

Dr. Silvestri came down and met them midway on the landing. "Let's go into my lab. Hi, Chase." He opened a door on the side of the staircase, giving Chase a squeeze on the shoulder, but his worried smile made Chase's stomach plummet. It didn't look like he had good news.

"David, is everything okay?" came a woman's voice from the apartment.

"It's fine, Anna," he called back up the stairs, closing the door gently behind them. Track lights flickered on overhead.

His lab was a long, narrow room lined with high tables. Strange machines filled the space, some whirring, others silent and covered in plastic sheets. A scattering of medical devices and flat metal screens covered the tables.

"I wasn't doing anything wrong," Chase blurted out before Mina could say anything. "I was just trying to . . ." He realized he couldn't say, *trying to look for a way to escape the house.* "I found the video of how I showed up outside."

Dr. Silvestri nodded in a distracted way. "I don't think you need to worry, Mina. I don't think he's a threat to us." He leaned against a table and rubbed his forehead, frowning.

"What is it?" she asked.

"His microchip."

The word brought Chase a mix of excitement and fear. "Did you get more information? Do you know where I'm from?"

The doctor kept speaking directly to Mina as if Chase weren't even in the room. "The data on it is fairly corrupt, and also highly encoded, so I'm having trouble retrieving any information. But the technology . . ." He paused and glanced over, like he didn't want to say this in front of Chase.

"What is it?" asked Mina in a low voice.

"It's extremely similar to Parker's," the doctor told her quietly. "The design is . . . I'm almost certain it's Asa's work."

A connection to Asa? Maybe this was why he'd shown up at the compound. Chase's mind immediately began twisting and testing the name, trying to find any memories to fit it into, inventing an entire history with a stranger named Asa Kaplan. It was impossible to imagine, but so was everything else with a blank memory.

Mina hadn't responded, fixing the doctor with her implacable stare, although it didn't seem to bother him as much as it did Chase.

"Have you been able to contact Asa yet, to tell him what's happened?" he asked.

She shook her head. "I've queued up a message, but he's out of range this week—I'm not expecting him to be reachable for two more days."

Dr. Silvestri crossed his arms. "Do you think . . . could he have another?"

"No. Not that I'm aware of."

"Another what?" asked Chase.

The doctor barely spared him a glance. "You'll have to hold on to him at the compound until we reach Asa. I don't know what this all means, but with his injury, I have a bad feeling that this is only the beginning. And we still don't know how he got inside the compound."

"I teleported, right?" said Chase. "That's the only way I could just show up outside like that."

Dr. Silvestri shook his head. "That's impossible. The entire perimeter is ringed with scramblers."

"With what?"

"Anti-inport devices. That compound is locked down like a fortress. For you to just turn up like that—it's very strange. And very worrying."

"Why?" asked Chase.

Dr. Silvestri pushed his glasses up on his nose and glanced at Mina. "Because Asa Kaplan has a lot of enemies."

A million possibilities opened up in Chase's mind, none of them good. All of them blocked by his missing memory. The freshly healed wound on the back of his head prickled, and he rubbed it. Had that been the work of Asa Kaplan's enemies?

Mina was watching him with her creepy analytic stare. "I'll take him back to the compound and keep him under close surveillance for now."

"Give him the same level of protection you give to Parker."

Mina nodded. "I'll send the message to Asa as soon as I see his signal come back in range."

Dr. Silvestri drew a deep breath and turned toward his work table. "I'll keep working on the chip. I've also got a tissue sample I took from Chase's wound. I'll see if I can find any matches on his DNA. Be safe."

"Be safe," said Mina, taking a step away from the doctor. Chase reached for the door, but she stopped him. "No, we can leave from here. Just hold still."

From the corner of his eye, Chase saw her touch the ring on her finger. This time he squeezed his eyes shut as the horrid sensation rushed over him, numbing his entire body. Instinctively he jerked backward from the discomfort.

Before he opened his eyes again, he knew something had gone wrong. A strong breeze blew on his face, and he heard a whistling, rustling sound all around him. Chase looked out into the darkening twilight, and his heart began to race. He was standing in the middle of a grass jungle, outside an electrified dome.

And he was alone.

# CHAPTER FOUR

Chase stumbled backward through the tall stalks, his heart galloping in his chest. The grass grew so thick that he couldn't see more than a few feet. "Mina?" he called in a shaky voice. No one answered. She wouldn't have sent him here on purpose. Had the teleport failed?

Suddenly he lost his footing and went sprawling down, slicing his arms on the sharp edges of the grass. His left foot had slid into a wide, deep hole. He yanked it out in a panic, scuttling away on his hands and feet.

An ominous whirring sound echoed up from the hole. A moment later a pair of scaly black limbs reached out, followed by the dark, angular head of a Zinnjerha. Its protruding, glittery eyes swiveled toward him, and it clicked the curved pincers jutting from its mouth.

As the dark creature emerged from its tunnel, Chase sat paralyzed with terror. *RUN!* his mind screamed, but his legs were two dead weights. The Zinnjerha tilted its head and started toward him.

Chase finally forced his legs into action, scrambling backward until he could jump to his feet. The creature clicked, closing the distance between them in two long strides. More clicking cut through the air, coming from every direction. Another Zinnjerha pushed through the grass, and then a third.

Chase backed through the jungle of plants, not daring to turn and run. One of the creatures lunged forward, its scaly limbs raking against his skin as it knocked him to the ground. Then it pounced.

Struggling against a dark tangle of slashing limbs, Chase couldn't even draw breath to scream. There was no way to escape. At least death didn't hurt—his body just felt numb.

Like a shot from a cannon, something slammed into the Zinnjerha, tearing them away from Chase. It was too dark, things moved too quickly to see who his rescuer was. Strong arms swept him up in a tight hug, and they took off through the grass.

They burst onto the lawn of the Kaplan compound, crashing through the front door a second later. Long hair swept across Chase's face as his rescuer turned and kicked the door shut behind them. A series of thuds landed against the outside.

Chase stared in bewilderment as Mina set him on the foyer floor. With swift, determined movements she tore off his shirt and scanned him from head to toe. Her expression slowly changed to puzzlement. Her face and arms were covered in deep cuts, but there was something strange about them. Why wasn't there any blood?

More thuds rained against the door, joined by skittering noises on the roof.

"Defense, perimeter breach!" Mina shouted, jumping to her feet.

A deep, loud hum filled the air, with a resonance that sounded like it was coming from the bottom of the house. Wincing, Chase clapped his hands over his ears as it grew to a deafening pitch. When it finally wound back down again, all the other noises from outside had stopped as well.

Parker stood in the hallway, pale and wide-eyed. "What on Taras happened?"

Chase gaped up at him from the floor, too dazed to do anything but stare. The whole event had lasted less than a minute, but reality spun around him as if he were sitting in the eye of a tornado.

Mina cracked the door open and looked outside. "The teleport failed."

"What?" A sharp note of fear came into Parker's voice.

"It placed him outside the compound. I had to temporarily shut down the dome so I could run out and get him."

"But the Zinnjerha—"

Mina closed the door and nodded curtly. "They were out." She rubbed one of her slashed arms. "This is all ruined." With a loud rip, she tore the skin right from her forearm and tossed it to the floor.

Chase shouted in horror and pedaled his feet to push himself away from the flap of skin.

"Good lords, relax!" Parker barked. "She's an android. A robot. Are you really that dumb?"

The harsh words stung, but any embarrassment Chase might have felt was eclipsed by the sight of Mina's arm. Instead of muscle and bone, what lay underneath was a gleaming metal limb. She wasn't human. Finally, a few things were starting to make sense.

He looked up at Mina's pretty face, now disfigured by the savage gashes on her cheeks and forehead. "Your skin . . ."

"It's just bio-molding," she said with a dismissive flick. "I can fix it." She crouched down in front of Chase and examined him with a frown. "You were as good as dead out there, and yet you don't have a single scratch."

"Are you kidding me?" Parker stepped closer to look at Chase.

"Parker, go to your room," said Mina, but he ignored her and she made no move to make him leave.

Chase looked at his arms and frowned. She was right—there wasn't a mark anywhere on him. But there was no way those creatures hadn't cut him up. He'd felt their sharp claws slashing at his arms when he tried to fend them off. "I don't understand . . . ," he mumbled.

"You must be the luckiest kid alive, Chase." Parker laughed and held out a hand. Chase returned the grin shakily as he let Parker pull him to his feet.

A cold metal hand closed on his arm. Chase turned to Mina, his mouth open in surprise. He could tell by her grip that the gesture wasn't meant to comfort. "I'm sorry," she said. "I'm going to have to lock you in your room."

"What? Why? Dr. Silvestri said I wasn't a threat."

"No," snapped Parker. "Come on, Mina. This is ridiculous."

"It's not personal, Chase. But both the teleport malfunction and your unharmed condition are unexplained anomalies. Your actions continue to create too many red-flag factors, and I can't identify you as anything but a threat."

"But what happened wasn't my fault! Dr. Silvestri told you to protect me."

Mina nodded. "I am. But my primary directive is to protect Parker, and the only way for me to perform both of these tasks is to separate you and lock you in your room."

Her hand tightened on his arm, and Chase knew there was no use in arguing further with her programmed logic. He dropped his head and nodded. As Mina led him down the hall to his room with Parker's angry protests behind them, he couldn't help but feel like a guilty prisoner. *But I didn't do anything wrong!* cried a voice in the back of his mind.

After the *snick* of the lock confirmed that he wasn't going anywhere, Chase sat on his bed. He examined his left arm, whole and unblemished. It was strange—he really had felt a sting when those blades of grass sliced into his arms as he fell, and when the Zinnjerha were slashing at him. He told himself he must have imagined it. Parker was right, he had some kind of wild luck. Except for the whole amnesia thing, of course.

He lay back and stared at the ceiling for some time, reliving the attack over and over. Eventually the adrenaline began to wear off, and only weariness remained. He closed his eyes, visualizing the grass forest again, but this time his drowsy mind filled the forest with blank faces hiding between the blades. Sleep came like a tidal wave, crashing over and pulling him under.

✳　　✳　　✳

Chase awoke with a jump. His windowless room was pitch-dark, but he sensed he wasn't alone.

"Sorry, that was me," came Parker's whispered voice. "Hold on."

The overhead light flicked on and Chase winced, squinting in the brightness. "What are you doing here? I'm supposed to be locked in. I'm a threat to you."

Parker snorted. "Right. You're so threatening. Come on, get up. I've come to spring you from prison."

"Are you crazy? Mina's not going to let me go anywhere."

"True. But Mina's not here." Parker waggled his eyebrows. "She had to make a run to some warehouse on the other side of the planet, something to do with fixing her bio-molding."

"Isn't she supposed to be here protecting you?"

"Yeah, but Asa's got her running his affairs on this planet too, so she leaves all the time. If anything were to happen, she'd be able to find me anyway—I've got an ID microchip kind of like the one Dr. Silvestri found in you. Only mine's got a tracker so that she can find me anywhere." Parker made a wry face. "Lucky me, I'll never be able to get rid of her."

Watching Parker's goofy expression, Chase considered whether to tell him what he'd learned, how similar their microchips actually were. The eye contact lasted a moment too long, and Parker frowned.

"What?"

Chase redirected his gaze to the floor. A cautious part of him wasn't ready to share this information yet. "Nothing." He took a deep breath and realized that he felt pretty well rested. How long had he slept? "What time is it?"

Parker sighed. "It's leaving-the-house time. Are you coming with me, or did I just spend ten minutes breaking the code on your lock for nothing?"

"Go where?"

"We can go to Rother City. It's the only real city on Trucon. We'll grab some breakfast and look around. Maybe we can find something that'll jog your memory."

"Won't Mina just find you and bring us back?"

"She always does."

"And then I'll get in trouble."

Parker made a face. "She's an android. How much trouble do you think you can get into?"

"Uh, for starters she can lock me back in this room."

"Which she will," said Parker with a shrug. "But this is your one chance to escape for a little while and do some searching of your own. Do you really want to stay locked in here for the next week?"

It was a simple enough decision. Mina and Dr. Silvestri weren't going anywhere—he'd still have the chance to learn what his connection to Asa Kaplan was when the time came. Besides, Mina wouldn't even be able to contact Asa for at least another day, and this would give Chase a chance to ask Parker what he knew about his mysterious guardian. He was willing to live with a little scolding for the possibility of unlocking even a tiny portion of his memory.

Chase threw off the covers and jumped out of bed. "Wait. Are we going to have to teleport?"

"Never. I've got a much better plan. Now put on something besides those dumb pajamas and meet me in the hall."

Digging up some jeans and a clean shirt from a closet Parker pointed out, Chase dressed quickly, a small smile on his face. He couldn't believe that Parker had reached out to help him. At last he'd realized that Chase needed something more than virtual piloting games.

Parker was waiting for him in the foyer, and Chase followed him downstairs, where at the end of the hall they came to a bright, cavernous chamber at least three times the size of the living room. In the middle of the chamber, a long silver rectangle of a machine rested on squat metal legs. A row of nozzles lined each side of the craft, and the end facing them was made up almost entirely of a wide, reflective window.

"Ever seen one of these babies?" Parker asked, smacking the shiny metal.

"Um . . ." Chase wasn't sure how to answer that. Of course not? Probably?

"It's a Pentagalactic Starjumper, elite class." Parker pulled a slim metal card from within his jacket with a triumphant flourish.

Chase took in every detail of the vehicle, from the outlines of different access panels that covered its long sides, to the small yellow sign marked Cargo Egress above a door near the back. Everything about the Starjumper felt completely foreign to him. "You're allowed to take it out?"

"He who hacks the drivekey has the right to pilot." Parker pushed the card into a slot on the side of the vehicle, and an adjacent door popped free with a hiss and slid open.

"Do you know how?"

In response, Parker rolled his eyes before jumping up into the vehicle.

By the time Chase climbed inside, Parker was already in the pilot's seat. His fingers flew over a glowing console screen under the window, scrolling through lists and moving different information windows across the screen. The door slid closed.

"Door is closed," a neutral voice confirmed.

"Ugh," muttered Parker. "Why does she always leave the operational voice on?"

"Accessing CFC. CFC online," said the voice.

"CFC?" asked Chase.

"Coordinated Flight Channels," said Parker as he typed on the console. "It's the planet's central navigating system. You type in where you want to go, and the CFC slots you into the traffic streams and takes you there." He flicked through a few windows before leaning back in his seat, and looked over, his eyes dancing. "Are you ready? Lords, this is awesome. I've been wanting to do this for ages."

"Plotting course," said the neutral voice. "Preparing to exit defense dome."

Chase squinted as a bright shaft of light hit his eyes. Sunlight streamed in from a gap as the ceiling rolled away, slowly expanding until all they could see was the pale yellow of an early morning sky. Without Parker touching anything, the vehicle rose up, gliding out of the chamber and above the gray structures of the compound. Beyond it, the grass forest spread out in green waves. A single Zinnjerha leapt out and ricocheted off the defense dome. As they flew farther away, the vegetation tapered off into a rocky desert that stretched on as far as he could see.

Chase squinted at the horizon, wondering when the city would come into view, when the cruiser accelerated upward, pulling away from the terrain. He gripped the edge of the console and held his breath. It was still better than teleporting.

"Extraplanetary launch point in thirty seconds," said the console voice.

"Launch point?" A spike of adrenaline shot through Chase as he looked at the jumble of information on the console. "Where are we going? I thought you said we were going to the city?"

Parker's mouth curled up in a sly grin. "It's . . . a city."

"In five, four, three, two . . ."

With a sharp turn, the Starjumper rocketed straight up away from the ground. Through half-closed eyes, Chase could see only ochre-hued sky in front of them. His stomach flattened against his spine.

"I'm gonna be sick," he groaned.

"No way!" said Parker. "This is the best part." He looked down at the console. "About twenty more seconds until we leave the macrosphere."

"What?"

"Just watch."

Chase tried to lean forward, but the force of their flight pushed him back into his seat.

"Initializing gravity generator," the neutral voice informed them. A moment later, although they were still flying straight up, the gravity inside the vehicle shifted to the floor. Chase lifted his arm, amazed—it felt no different from when they'd been sitting inside the vehicle at Parker's home. Outside the windows, the sky darkened quickly into black space.

"Awesome," breathed Parker. "We've got about fifteen minutes to go, so you can chill out for a while."

"Fifteen minutes until what?" Chase asked. It irritated him that Parker had lied about their destination, but this was nothing compared with the anxiety that had begun to gnaw at his stomach. He had no idea how far from Trucon they were going—or if Mina could follow Parker's microchip this far, in case something happened. "Where are you taking me?"

Parker leaned back in his seat and smiled, saying nothing.

# CHAPTER FIVE

Chase glared out the front window as they traveled toward Parker's secret destination. Outside their cruiser, the dark expanse of space wasn't really dark at all. Peppered with millions of the tiny white speckles of distant stars and streaked with pale smears of far-off galaxies, it made him realize how incredibly tiny he was, and underscored how lost he felt.

"You're a jerk, you know that? Tell me where you're taking me."

For a split second, a hurt expression crossed Parker's face. Annoyance quickly replaced it. "Would you relax? I just want to go somewhere without her looking over my shoulder the whole time."

"You mean Mina?"

"Stupid machine," said Parker, stabbing at the console with one finger. "She runs my entire stupid life."

"So you thought it'd be a good idea to kidnap me?"

"I'm not kidnapping you. Calm down. I told you, we're on a mission to figure out who you are."

"Right, because that's what you were thinking when you lied to me about where we were going. Are you at least going to tell me now?"

Parker hesitated. "Mircona."

Chase shook his head. "What's that?"

"Mircona, the moon. Trucon's moon."

"The moon? What are we going to do there?"

"I don't know, have some fun. It's a cool place."

"*Have some fun?* So this wasn't about helping me at all."

Parker rolled his eyes in annoyance. "What's wrong with having a little fun? We can still ask questions, look for things you might recognize."

"Did you forget about the blaster wound on the back of my head? I need to figure out who did that to me, not go on a vacation!" Chase pointed at the console. "This was a terrible idea. Take me back."

A frown creased Parker's forehead. "Look, I promise nothing bad is going to happen. We'll go to Mircona for thirty minutes, and if that doesn't bring back any memories, then we'll go back to Trucon and try something else."

Chase drummed his fingers against the console and looked away. It wasn't like he could make Parker do anything—he'd given up that option as soon as he'd stepped into a space cruiser that he knew neither how nor where to pilot. There was basically no choice but to go with Parker and hope that something on the moon would spark a memory.

And anyway, Parker was probably right—nothing would happen. They'd be back at the compound before anyone knew they were gone.

"Fine," he muttered. "Thirty minutes."

"It'll be fun. Look, there it is." Looming ahead was the curve of a colossal tan sphere. As they zoomed closer to the sandy surface, a sprawling cluster of buildings came into view in the distance, their drab and featureless exteriors bleached out in the harsh sunlight.

"It doesn't look like much fun," said Chase.

"The atmosphere on Mircona's too thin to go outside. Everything's indoors, but it's supposed to be this really cool past-era resort." Parker leaned over the console again, scrolling through screens.

"You've never been?"

"Not yet," said Parker with a small smile. "I'm going to put us in an autodocking facility. We can take a transway into the city, check it out, and swing back. Sound good?"

"Whatever." A patchwork of enormous, windowless structures in various sizes stretched out below them, all connected by ridged metal tunnels. Different logos were painted on the roofs of the buildings. Chase squinted to read the print on one: Mirconan Leisure Endeavors. As the city scrolled by, Chase grew curious to see what was inside the buildings, but he didn't say anything. If Parker knew he was having fun, they'd probably never leave.

They dropped toward the surface, flying just above the vast cityscape. Traffic was sparse, and only a few other vehicles whizzed by in the distance. The Starjumper plunged lower and slowed as they neared the closest building. Chase caught a glimpse of a doorway expanding in the wall, but as they pulled up to it, the vehicle swung around automatically. The bleak landscape of Mircona filled their window, and looming in the distance, the gigantic orb of Trucon, sandy-brown with patches of dark vegetation. The Starjumper backed gently into the structure.

"Disengaging CFC," said the neutral voice. "Equalizing pressure, please do not exit." The outer wall slid shut before them, cutting off their view and enclosing them in the snug metal box of the docking compartment. Chase waited in his seat while Parker shut down the console.

"Ready?" Parker tucked the drivekey into his pocket and stood, a nervous grin on his face.

They exited through a door at the back of their docking compartment, where Parker entered a code on a small screen to lock the Starjumper inside. He led Chase down a long tunnel until it intersected a hallway with a high, arched ceiling.

"After you," said Parker.

Chase took one step forward into the hallway. Immediately his feet swept out from under him, and he fell on his back with a shout. Parker laughed as he receded in the distance, while the floor somehow carried Chase farther away.

"What is this?" Chase shouted angrily, trying to get to his feet.

Parker leapt onto the moving walkway and jogged over to help him up. "That was hilarious."

"Jerk," said Chase, rubbing his hip where he had landed.

"It was just a guess, but I figured you'd probably never used a transway."

"I can't even tell that it's moving," said Chase, looking down at the stationary floor as his feet traveled forward.

"It's a current moving through a layer of adamantine," explained Parker. "See the blue lights along the wall? That's how you know it's a transway. Don't step over the line in the middle—that side's moving the other direction." He grinned. "Come on."

They set off at a brisk pace down the long hallway, passing a few standing passengers who paid them no attention. There was a wide opening at the end of the tunnel, and this time Parker gave a warning when the transway was about to end. They stepped off as they exited the tunnel and stopped for their first real look at Mircona.

Although there obviously had to be a ceiling somewhere, the interior of the building had been created to make it appear as though they were standing in the middle of an open park under a wide blue sky. A few ragged clouds drifted past on a gentle wind. In the distance they could see trees and benches, and a couple picnicking on a hill.

"This is amazing," breathed Parker.

"Clear out, you're blocking the way!" screeched a high voice, and both boys jumped and moved aside to make way for an angry old woman who huffed past them. Chase glanced back at the transway tunnel. From the park side, it was camouflaged as an arched entrance to a small brick building.

"Come on," said Parker. The boys started down a paved path that led across the park and toward a large stone building. When they entered, they found themselves in another transway.

"Aren't we going to get lost?" asked Chase as they moved down the tunnel.

"Absolutely not. Step right. This is going to split."

Chase tried to commit their path to memory so that he could find his way back, but the transway split several times, and soon he was utterly disoriented. When they finally reached the end of the last tunnel, they stepped out into a quaint street lined with small eateries and storefronts. There were no vehicles here, only people who bustled along under the slanting sunlight, haggling with street vendors and filling the tables of small cafés.

As they walked, Chase looked around at the shops and the street vendors' wares on display. He tried to open himself up to the surroundings, to loosen his mind so that there was a place for an image or a sound, *anything*, to fit. He was watching a woman in a long dress scooping amber crystals into a paper cone, and nearly crashed into Parker's back because he didn't see that he had stopped. Parker was looking down at a display of random, tarnished junk laid out on a dirty blanket. A sallow man sat cross-legged behind his merchandise.

"Want something special for yourself?" the man asked, waving his hands over the blanket. "Take a closer look, son."

Parker crouched down to examine the items, picking up several different things—a flat metal box, a triangular badge of some sort, and an instrument that looked distantly related to a harmonica.

"How much for this?" he asked, pointing to a slim knife in a green sheath.

The man jutted out his lower lip. "That's genuine Falasian craftsmanship, sharp enough to shave an atom off an apple. Can't give that one away for a song."

"Try me," said Parker. He leaned over the blanket and

picked up the sheathed knife, waving it in the man's face. "My daddy's given me extra spending money today."

Chase watched over Parker's shoulder as the two haggled over a price. Negotiations were brief, and soon Parker reached into his jacket pocket and counted out a number of thin plastic chips. The man bared his ragged teeth in a leer as he took the currency. "Have a good day, boys."

Parker walked away smiling. "How much did you pay for that?" Chase asked him.

"Too much," he replied cryptically. After they had walked a little farther up the street, he added, "But not as much as I would have paid for this." He held out his hand and flicked his wrist, and something fell from inside his sleeve and into his palm. It was the badge that he had examined on the blanket, a dull silver triangle decorated with three horizontal stripes.

"You stole it?" Chase looked back to see if the junk merchant was coming after them, but there were so many people on the street, the man was already long gone from view. "Are you trying to get us in trouble?"

"Whatever. It was probably stolen to begin with. And he would have charged a lot more than I paid for the knife if he'd seen that this was what I was interested in." He tucked the badge and dagger back into his jacket. "I mean, don't get too excited. It could just be the access badge to a gasket factory. It'll be fun trying to decode it when we get home."

Ahead of them, the flow of pedestrians curved out in a wide arc, and everyone seemed to be keeping their heads down.

"What's that?" Chase asked, just as he saw what people were avoiding. Standing against a wall were two men in dark gray uniforms with elliptical badges. They monitored the activity on the street with flat eyes.

"Federal Fleet soldiers," muttered Parker, joining the stream of people. "Just keep your distance."

Chase couldn't help but glance over as they passed the soldiers. A tiny ripple of anxiety crawled under his skin, but only because of the way the other pedestrians were acting. The soldiers didn't fit anywhere in his mind either.

When they'd put a decent distance between themselves and the soldiers, Parker stopped and looked around. "Alright. I think I've seen enough of this."

"Let's head back," said Chase. The moon was fascinating, but nothing was triggering any memories. If they left soon, maybe there would still be time to go to the city on Trucon.

"Cool your jets. First let's go sit down somewhere." Parker cut through the crowd to an eatery with a narrow door and greasy windows. The inside was dark and smoky and filled with quiet men hunched over their drinks. Parker found a table near the windows, where he took out his stolen badge and began to fiddle with it.

Chase looked around to see if anyone was watching them. "Shouldn't you be hiding that?"

"Relax." Parker frowned, turning it over. "It's just a piece of junk."

A broad, tired-looking waitress slouched up to their table. "What'll it be?" she asked.

"My young friend here will have a Nevna fizz, and I'll have a pint of your best Lyolian ale," said Parker. The waitress arched an eyebrow, muttering something under her breath as she walked away.

Parker set the badge on the table and leaned back in his chair. "So, anything coming back to you yet?"

Chase shook his head. "I'll have to wait and see what else Dr. Silvestri can find out." He paused, examining his hands. Now was the time to start asking questions. "So, what exactly does Asa do?"

"I told you, he owns a tech corporation. That's all I know. Why?" Parker frowned.

"What's he like?"

Parker looked out the window. "Actually, I've never met him."

"What?" Parker had already told him that Asa didn't live in the compound, but wouldn't he at least want to see his ward, to check in on how he was doing? "But he's your guardian."

"He funds my existence and makes the rules, but I don't

know anything about him—where he lives, what he does, what he looks like. I know he's got a lot of money, but that's it."

"So you grew up with . . . ?"

"Just Mina, yes. I was raised by a robot." Parker said this like it was funny, but there was an underlying bitterness. "Dr. Silvestri only comes by every once in a while."

Chase considered what this must have been like, and wondered whether he'd grown up in similar circumstances. "Why did you tell me you lived alone?"

"Because she's not alive."

Chase opened his mouth to argue, but at that moment the waitress reappeared and set two glasses of foamy red liquid on the table. She turned and began to walk away.

"Hey!" Parker shouted. "What is this?"

She stopped and turned, placing her hands on her hips. "Two Nevnas."

"I didn't order this. Bring me a Lyolian ale!" Parker commanded. A deep flush was rising in his face.

"You can order Lyolian ale when you're of age to order Lyolian ale. Until then, you get a Nevna."

"This is ridiculous!" Parker rose to his feet, puffing out his chest indignantly. "Do you have any idea who I am?"

"Sure, you're the kid who's about to get thrown out of my pub," she snapped.

"I'm sorry, is he giving you trouble?" said a polite and

familiar voice on the right. Chase looked over with surprise. Mina stood beside him, a calm smile on her face.

Parker roared in frustration and swept both glasses to the floor with a crash. Red liquid spread out on the floor and ran under the waitress's feet.

"Parker!" Mina stepped forward, placing herself between Parker and the waitress. "Please take this with our apologies," she said, extending a handful of chips.

"Get him out of here," said the waitress, shoving the money into an apron pocket.

Mina seized Parker by the arm and dragged him out into the street. Chase rushed after them, feeling every pair of eyes in the pub follow him. Parker tried to jerk his arm away from her, but she kept her grip on his wrist.

"Let me go, let me go, let me go," he hissed through gritted teeth.

"Bravo, Parker." She released his arm. "This was your best escape yet. All the way to Mircona—very nice! I knew you'd figure out how to hack the cruiser eventually."

"Stupid robot!" he spat, rubbing his wrist. "I can't even get five minutes without you breathing down my neck!"

Mina smiled at him and turned to Chase, who stood off to the side, embarrassed by the scene. "Dr. Silvestri's been trying to contact you," she informed him. "I'll take you to see him, and then I'm going to place you in a different facility.

After this incident it's apparent you need to be in solitary confinement."

Chase glared at Parker, who kept his eyes trained on the ground. This was all his fault—he'd wanted to take Chase on his stupid joyride, and now it was Chase who was going to pay for it. He lunged forward, shoving Parker in the chest. "Idiot!"

"Hey!" cried Parker, although he still avoided making eye contact.

"You stupid, selfish jerk!" Chase shouted.

"Alright, let's—" Mina stopped abruptly and her eyes widened the tiniest bit. She turned her back on both boys. "Can I help you?"

The two soldiers in dark gray materialized out of the crowd, wearing matching grim expressions.

"ID check, ma'am," said one of the men. The other looked past her and examined both boys, staring intently at their faces.

"We don't need any problems here, officer, just a disagreement between friends. I've got the situation under control," Mina said.

"I'm afraid we're going to need to see your papers," the man insisted.

"The Fleet doesn't need to get involved in this," said Mina. "We'll be—"

"Do you know a Dr. David Silvestri?" the other officer interrupted.

Mina cocked her head. "What?"

What took place next went so fast, it seemed like it all happened at once. The man on the left began to reach for his sidearm. Mina leapt forward, grabbing one of the soldiers around his waist and swinging him into his partner. Chase barely dodged getting hit as the soldiers collided and tumbled to the ground.

Mina seized one of the men by the collar and swung her leg across the other's chest, pinning them both to the ground. The crowd around them rippled as people turned to stare.

"Mina?" Parker stood at the edge of the fight, eyes wide with shock.

She looked up at them, her long hair hanging in her face. "Both of you, get out of here!" she yelled. "Run!"

# CHAPTER SIX

Parker grabbed Chase by the arm and pushed him into motion. They took off up the street, weaving through the crowd and shoving aside the people who got in their way. Angry shouts followed them as they ran.

"There!" Parker dashed through a brick doorway into a dark tunnel, yelling a warning to the people ahead of them. They ran so fast on the transway there wasn't time to check the signs for directions. When the path began to split, Chase followed Parker blindly.

They emerged from the tunnels minutes later into a forest thick with tall, straight trees. Chase took a deep breath of humid air and glanced up at the dappled green canopy. "Wait! This isn't where we came from."

"Keep moving," panted Parker. Chase jogged after him down a path that twisted through the trees to a small creek. They ran along the water for several minutes, until finally

Parker slowed to a walk. Only the sound of rushing water and their hard breathing filled the air.

Chase looked back over his shoulder. "Are we clear?"

"I don't know. Maybe. That was crazy!" He gave Chase a friendly slap on the back, but Chase pushed his arm away. "Come on, we got away. Lighten up, will you?"

"Is this all funny to you?"

"Well, it's kind of funny—" Parker began to say.

Chase rounded on him, pushing him against a tree. "What is wrong with you?"

"I'm sorry," Parker said, flinching back against the tree trunk. "You're right, I'm a jerk, okay?"

"Yes, you are! This is all your fault. I never should have left the house."

Parker narrowed his eyes. "Oh, whatever. Maybe I switched up the destination on you, but you were more than happy to leave when I offered you the chance."

He was right. Chase had been so eager to get away and figure out some answers himself, he'd blown off the idea of consequences. Now instead of memories, he'd found more problems. He dropped his hands and let Parker go. "What's going to happen to Mina?"

Parker didn't look Chase in the eyes as he brushed bits of bark from his shirt. "She'll be fine. She can take care of herself."

"How do you know they didn't arrest her? Why were they asking her about Dr. Silvestri?"

"I don't know. Don't worry, everything's fine."

"Everything is *not* fine!" Chase grabbed a small branch and ripped it off the tree, throwing it at the ground. "Nothing is fine! I still don't know anything about myself!"

Parker stared at the torn branch for a moment, and he spoke in a cautious tone. "Aren't you afraid that maybe what happened to you is so horrible, once you find out, you'll wish you never knew?"

Chase froze. Of course he'd thought something like that, a possibility he shoved in some dark corner of his mind, but he'd never let himself believe it could be true. "Just leave me alone," he said, pushing Parker aside to speed ahead.

Bchind him, Parker muttered something.

"What did you say?" Chase asked.

"I said I forgot that badge on the table when Mina dragged us out of the pub."

"Well, you stole it anyway. Serves you right."

Parker didn't respond, and Chase stomped ahead on the path, fuming. They'd nearly been arrested, and Parker cared more about the stupid badge than about what was happening to Mina. After a few more minutes, they reached a point where the creek ran into a concrete tunnel on a sheer slope and the path curved up over a hill. Parker jogged up beside Chase as they climbed.

"We're home free," Parker said when they reached the top. Before them lay a wide park, and far on the other side was the small brick building where they had exited the first transway. Only a few more minutes and they'd be safely in the cruiser and on their way back home. Chase felt a strong urge to run the whole way to the cruiser, but restrained himself to avoid attracting attention.

"See, I told you everything would be fine," Parker said.

Chase turned to tell him that he could take his fine and shove it, but before he could get a word out, Parker dashed away. Maybe he thought Chase was going to take a swing at him. Chase shook his head, scoffing, and from the other side of the field, a flash of movement caught his eye.

The two soldiers raced toward them, blasters drawn. Without a second thought, Chase took off after Parker, sprinting toward the entrance of the transway. The relief he felt when Mina emerged from the tunnel in front of them evaporated as a flash of bright light exploded on the ground.

"They're shooting at us?" Parker shouted in surprise.

Even Mina looked confused. Summoning an extra burst of speed, the boys caught up to her and raced inside the transway.

"Is this because I hacked the cruiser?" asked Parker as they dodged around a young couple.

"This isn't about the cruiser," said Mina. "This is bad."

"Is it about me?" gasped Chase, but his question was drowned out by shouting that echoed behind them as the soldiers entered the tunnel.

Parker led the way toward a side passage, and they ran into the narrow corridor toward their docking compartment. When they reached the door, Mina stood in back to shield them while Parker fumbled with the lock screen. The door slid open, and Chase dashed inside.

"Get in, Parker!" Mina ordered.

Parker stayed in the hall, fingers flying over the screen. "I'm making sure they can't get through."

"Don't bother, just get in the—"

Chase turned around as another explosion of light filled the corridor. The beam hit Mina directly in the chest. Without making a noise, she flew violently against the door frame and crumpled to the floor. "Mina!" Chase ran to her side.

Parker stepped over her body and ran to the cruiser. "Clear her out of the door!"

Chase grabbed Mina by the feet and pulled, but it felt like he was trying to pull the cruiser, or possibly a small house. Was she made of solid lead? Straining every muscle in his back, he dragged her slender frame into the docking compartment.

The door barely slid closed in time. A second later someone pounded on it from the outside, and a burst of explosions erupted as the soldiers tried to blast their way through.

"Get in!" shouted Parker, once he had situated himself in the front seat of the cruiser.

Chase paused to get a better grip on Mina's feet. "Help me!"

"Just leave her!"

"What? No!" Chase yelled over the loud shooting from outside. "We can't!"

"She'll be fine!" Parker tore his attention from the piloting console and looked back through the door, his eyes blazing. "She'll find me again. She always finds me. Get in!"

"No!" Chase ran around to Mina's shoulders and hoisted her up. The door rattled behind him as the blasts continued. With a roar, he pulled her around and heaved her up into the cruiser.

"Unable to access CFC network," said the neutral voice of the cruiser.

"Why isn't this working? I can't access the pathways!" Parker pounded his fists against the console.

Chase climbed over Mina and into his seat. "They're almost in!"

"Close the door, open the gate," Parker mumbled to

himself, his trembling fingers carrying out the commands manually. As the gate rolled back to reveal the horizon of Mircona, a steering yoke and throttle levers emerged from a panel on the dashboard.

A final explosion and a loud clatter told them that the men had finally blown off the door of the docking compartment. Seconds later another blast shook the entire cruiser.

"Go! Go! Go!" screamed Chase.

Parker seized the controls and yanked hard. The cruiser shot out of the gate, ricocheting off the edge of the portal with a crash. They hurtled over the enclosed city, but there was much more air traffic than there had been when they arrived. Dozens of other vehicles careened wildly through the sky, following no particular path or trajectory.

"I think they're all offline!" said Parker. He jerked their Star-jumper out of the way of the oncoming vehicles. "Is the entire CFC system down? I've never seen anything like . . ."

They both gasped as another cruiser shot up from below, narrowly missing their vehicle. A shock wave traveled through the thin atmosphere and sent them rocking backward. The pilot of the other cruiser reacted with a sharp turn and clipped the tail of a second vehicle whizzing by, sending it into a spin.

"Get us away from here!" said Chase, clutching onto the console.

With a white-knuckled grip on the controls, Parker yanked them upward and jerked the vehicle around. They sped toward the outer limits of the enclosed city, where congestion was thinner. Finally they passed the last buildings and cruised for a minute over the rocky brown surface of the moon. Only a few other vehicles traveled within view.

"Can we please contact Dr. Silvestri now?" asked Chase.

"Yes." Keeping one hand on the yoke, Parker scrolled through a number of screens on the console, tapping in information. A silvery panel at the top of the console lit up, and after a minute, Dr. Silvestri's face appeared.

"Parker, where have you been?" he barked. He looked exhausted and sweaty, and sounded out of breath. His glasses were missing. "Where's Chase?"

"He's right here," said Parker. Chase tried to lean in toward the doctor's face.

"I'm sorry, I can't find my glasses right now," mumbled Dr. Silvestri. "Listen, Chase—something's happened. I think I made a mistake. I contacted a former colleague about that DNA sample I'd taken from you, and within five minutes my entire system was locked. Fleet transport vehicles are pulling up outside the lab right now. I'm sorry, Chase, I had to destroy your microchip."

There was a loud crash in the background, and Dr. Silvestri jumped. "I have to go. Parker, can you find Mina?"

"She's here with us, but—" said Parker.

"Have her get in contact with Asa—he'll know what to do next." He glanced over his shoulder as more crashes rang out. "I have to go."

Parker waved his hand at the screen. "Wait, Doc, it's not that easy. We just got chased by a bunch of Fleet soldiers, and they were firing at us and, well, Mina's actually out of commission right now."

"What?" The horrified look on Dr. Silvestri's face sent tendrils of dread through Chase's stomach. "They must have been following Mina already. Look, whatever you do, *don't go home*. Don't go to any authorities—and *do not* go to the Fleet, not under any circumstances. Oh, Parker, I was afraid this would happen to us someday. Listen to me, you have to find Asa. Look for him at—"

An extremely loud roar drowned out the rest of his sentence, and a woman's screams filled the background. "Anna!" shouted Dr. Silvestri, turning. He rose from his seat, and the screen went blank.

The boys sat in shocked silence. The cabin gradually darkened as they cruised away from sunlight into the dark side of the moon. Lights from the console illuminated their faces.

"What on Taras is going on?" Parker turned and looked at Chase. "Who *are* you?"

The scream still echoed in Chase's mind. "Are they going to be okay?"

"The doc and his wife?" Parker shook his head. "I have no idea."

Chase stared at the console. "It's all because of me. Maybe I should turn myself in to the authorities."

"Are you stupid? Dr. Silvestri just told you not to."

"But they were looking for me, weren't they? Why is the Fleet looking for me?"

"You don't know for sure if they were looking for you. The doc sounded like he's been expecting something like this to happen for a long time. He might have been doing illegal stuff in his lab."

Chase gave him a skeptical look. "You think that's why they were shooting at us?"

Parker opened his mouth to speak, but no answer came out, and instead he shrugged.

"So how are you supposed to get in touch with Asa?"

"Yeah, so, there's a problem with that. I don't have the first clue how to find him. Mina's the only one who's ever been able to contact him."

"Why?" For being Parker's guardian, it sure seemed like the guy made a huge effort to ensure Parker had as little to do with him as possible.

"To keep me safe? To keep himself safe? I don't know if

you'd noticed, Chase, but the guy's kind of obsessed with safety. That much I know about him." Parker looked down at the console and made a few adjustments to their path as they soared over the dark terrain. "This is so stupid."

"What are we going to do?" asked Chase.

"We can't go home. I guess we find a place to hide out on Trucon for a while, and I'll take Mina into Rother City and try to get her fixed."

Chase looked out at the moon and watched it roll away underneath them as they cruised onward. Why would the Fleet be after him—who was he? He might never know, now that the chip had been destroyed. He rested his head on his hand, wishing he could rewind back to the morning, when the only thing he had to worry about was how soon Mina could contact Asa Kaplan.

They were nearing the sunlit side of the small moon again, and the cabin slowly began to lighten. Chase leaned forward and gazed at the stars all around them when a soft beep sounded from the console. He looked down. "What was that?"

Parker frowned and slid a few frames across the screen. "A distress signal?" He took the yoke and steered by watching their beacon move across a map on the console.

Chase watched out the window. "Look!"

A mass of something hovered far in the distance above

the moon's surface, and as they neared, the shape became clearer: a wrecked spacecraft, its sleek black frame twisted. Lights flickered on its underbelly.

Parker cursed. "It's a Khatra! What happened?" He steered down toward the ruined vehicle.

"Careful!" said Chase. A small, dark object had appeared on their right. Parker swerved hard to the left, and a pair of boots flashed by the window.

"Sweet ladies of Taras," Parker said. "I think that was a person!"

"What?" As Parker swung the Starjumper around, Chase realized that he could see the outline of four limbs floating motionless. "Is he dead?"

"I don't know. Probably. Looks like he's wearing a protective suit; I think you can survive for a couple of hours in one of those. The crash probably killed him already." Parker stared out the window, shaking his head.

Chase glanced at Parker. "You're not going to leave him out here, are you?"

"Oh. Of course not." Parker began typing at the console. "I'll try to scoop him up in the cargo hold." He moved the Starjumper alongside the still figure and pulled just past him. Twisting the steering yoke, he gently swung the vehicle a full 360 degrees. "I think I got him. Let me close the hold and put us in autocruise."

Chase followed him through the door in the back of the cabin, stepping over Mina into the bunkroom. The cargo-hold hatch had a red light beside it, and when it turned green, Parker pulled the cover open and started down a ladder. By the time Chase's feet touched the floor in the bare, brightly lit room, Parker was already leaning over the suited figure splayed out in the corner.

Parker fiddled with the man's face mask until he finally found the clasps that made it spring loose. Gripping the sides of the helmet, he pulled it away to reveal a young man with dark hair and very high, sharp cheekbones. Before Chase could ask Parker if he was dead, the man groaned.

"He's alive!" Chase tapped the man's face a few times, but he didn't open his eyes. "His skin's really cold."

"I bet he was out there for a while," said Parker. "But he's Lyolian. What on Taras was he doing in a Khatra?"

Chase stared at the man's sharp features, trying to remember what he'd heard about Lyolia when they were watching the newsfeed. "What do you mean?"

"That Khatra's a Fleet fighter," said Parker. "Lyolians aren't allowed in the—"

A tremendous *WHOOSH!* interrupted him, and a shock wave rocked their cruiser, sending them both sprawling across the cargo-bay floor. Parker scrambled for the ladder and rushed to the operating console. "What was that?" Chase shouted, staggering behind him into the cabin.

What they saw through the front windshield was so horrific, it took them both several seconds to comprehend.

They had drifted around the moon far enough that the complete sphere of Trucon was visible. But the planet looked nothing like the peaceful, sandy orb they'd seen before. Now waves of red and orange and black spread out across the surface in great whorls.

It looked like the entire planet was on fire.

# CHAPTER SEVEN

Chase stared out the cruiser's front window, mesmerized by the slow swirl of fire that blanketed Trucon's surface, and struggled to put together what was happening. Not half an hour ago, the planet had looked fine. How could it have been consumed so quickly? A sickening realization came to him: This couldn't possibly be a natural disaster. It must have been a deliberate attack. And behind that realization, a tiny question bubbled up: Was this somehow related to him?

He finally managed to spit out two words. "What happened?"

White with shock, Parker whispered a reply without turning away from the window. "We're dead."

At first Chase didn't know what Parker was talking about. Out here they were safe, separated from the inferno by many miles of space. Then he saw the wave of movement as thousands and thousands of vehicles, large and small, fled from the planet. As they came closer, the space between Trucon and its moon grew thick with traffic, each ship forging its own frantic path. There was a sudden burst of orange as two ships got too close and crashed into each other. Vehicles were headed in every direction possible, but many appeared to be headed for the moon, and only minutes away.

"Parker—they're coming our way," Chase said. "We need to move."

Parker said nothing, still staring at the devastation that had been his home.

"We need to move, Parker," Chase repeated. The first vehicles in the onslaught were getting close, and a few of the fastest fighters and cruisers zipped past. "Parker!"

Parker blinked a few times and reached for the controls. "I . . . I don't know where to go," he murmured.

"Anywhere! Get us out of here!"

More vehicles rushed past them, all at safe distances, but thousands were following, like a giant moving wall. Trembling, Parker pulled up on the controls to steer away from the moon and out of the path of the oncoming traffic.

"Faster!" said Chase. More and more vehicles filled the space around them, and many of them appeared to be slowing down as they neared the moon's surface, adding to the congestion. The Starjumper surged desperately upward, but it was clear that they were not going to outrun the deluge of ships.

Suddenly they were surrounded by hundreds of vehicles, beside them, above them, oncoming, and none following a straight path. Parker swerved erratically to avoid them, but he had lost all confidence in his piloting and his reactions were slow. Chase clutched the arms of his seat, yelping at every near miss, bracing for impact.

Bursts of color flickered around them as more vehicles collided in the packed space. The cruiser darted through narrow openings between other ships, flipping and turning in a dizzying way. Parker was losing control. Chase squeezed his eyes shut in anticipation of a crash, but they hit a clear patch and zoomed forward, veering in a sharp arc down toward the moon's surface.

"Get us out of here!" Chase yelled.

"I can't!" Parker's voice was hysterical. "We've gotta try the breakaway!"

"The what?"

His face frozen in a rictus of terror, Parker flipped open a clear cover on the console. Underneath was a round lever. "Hold on!"

Then he yanked the lever.

The last thing that Chase was aware of was being thrown

violently backward out of his seat and, briefly, the feeling of his head crashing into the cabin ceiling.

✳    ✳    ✳

When Chase opened his eyes, he saw Parker's body lying crumpled beside him. "You okay?" His voice sounded brittle in the silent cabin.

Parker grunted and rolled over onto his back. "I feel like I got hit by a planet."

A glance out the front window told Chase that they were no longer part of the flood of traffic from Trucon. "What just happened?" he asked, pushing his palms to his temples.

"Breakaway."

"What?"

"I pulled the breakaway. The emergency escape. It hypercalculates and folds us over to a random coordinate."

"What?"

"Good lords, dummy. It moves the cruiser without us having to calculate where it's going. You pull it as a last resort." Parker climbed gingerly to his feet and returned to the piloting console. "We could be anywhere within a fifty-parsec range of Trucon. We're lucky it didn't put us in the middle of a star."

Chase crawled to Mina, who lay in a jumbled heap in the corner, and rolled her over. Her eyes remained closed. He leaned in toward her ear and murmured her name.

Parker glanced over his shoulder. "She's not going to wake up without some serious technical intervention. Why don't you check on the guy we picked up, make sure he's still alive?"

"Probably not after this," said Chase. He left Mina in the corner and went back down to the cargo hold, where the man in the space suit still lay flat on his back. He was breathing, but his skin was deathly pale and he didn't stir when Chase prodded his neck. Looking at his face, Chase realized that the man was much younger than he'd first thought—underneath a layer of scruffy facial hair, he looked about nineteen years old, maybe twenty at most.

Chase returned to the piloting cabin. "He's not waking up. What should we do with him?"

"I don't know," said Parker. "Let's worry about ourselves first."

Chase sat quietly beside him. The scene above Trucon replayed in his mind—the frantic flood of spaceships, the doomed planet in flames. "What happened back there?"

"I told you, the breakaway. How hard did you hit your head?"

"No, before that."

Parker was quiet for a minute. "Something pretty awful."

"Do you think it was an attack?"

Parker shrugged and shook his head.

"What about your home? What about Dr. Silvestri?"

"Stop." Parker's face was pale and glazed with sweat. "I don't want to talk about it. We need to focus on the immediate problem."

Looking at the complex piloting console, Chase knew he wouldn't be able to help Parker with the cruiser. Piloting was definitely not in his semantic memory. "So how do we do this?"

"I've just got to find our coordinates, and map a route to, uh . . ." Parker trailed off, and the cabin fell silent.

There was nothing to see out the front window except never-ending, star-speckled space. Chase closed his eyes and tried to absorb everything that had happened in the course of only a few hours. He'd just been getting used to the idea of being on Trucon, and now the entire planet was gone, along with Parker's home, and probably Dr. Silvestri as well. Mina was basically useless, and Chase was pretty sure she wouldn't have had time to contact Asa before everything happened. Not that Asa could find them now anyway.

Panic rose up in his throat. If they couldn't reach Asa, he wouldn't be able to ask questions about his microchip. He'd never be able to find his identity. Feeling his panic edge toward hysteria, he stopped himself. *First things first.* Before they could do anything, they had to find their way to another planet. Then get Mina fixed. And then he could get back to work figuring out his identity.

"Are you sleeping?" Chase's eyes snapped open to see Parker glaring at him. "So you're not going to help? I have to figure out how to get us out of this mess by myself, is that right?"

"What am I supposed to do?" said Chase. "Can't you just punch in the CFC destination or whatever?"

Parker hunched over the screens and shook his head. "Out here in deep space everything works differently. Different communication system, different piloting system. And I can't figure out these stupid mapping programs—do I calculate in the rate that the universe is moving when I plot a route, or is that already figured into the equation?" He banged his fist against the console in frustration.

Chase didn't have the slightest clue how to answer these questions, but he racked his brain for an idea. "Um . . . maybe if we wait for the guy down there to wake up? He must be able to pilot."

"And what if he's in a coma and isn't going to wake up?" countered Parker. "He might have suffered too much exposure by the time we found him. And even if he's fine, we can't trust him. He's not a Fleet soldier. I bet he stole that Khatra."

"What do you mean?"

"Like I was telling you before, he's a Lyolian. A Khatra's a Fleet vehicle. He can't be from the Fleet, because even though they call it the *Federal* Fleet, it's pretty much run by Earth and only Earthans are allowed to be soldiers. He's probably a smuggler."

So not only were they stranded and homeless, but they were probably ferrying a criminal around in the cargo hold. Things just kept getting better. "How do you know he's Lyolian?" Chase asked.

"Because he looks like one!" Parker exploded. He began rapidly typing information onto one of the screens. "I'm just going to plot a small fold to test it out. I'll try to move us over to the next star system." Parker's finger hovered over a button on the screen. "Better buckle in."

"Don't, Parker." Chase tried to move his finger away from the button. "Let's wait one more—"

"Don't tell me what to do," Parker snapped, and pressed his finger against the screen.

Chase was slightly more prepared this time, and so he fully experienced the fold. There was a strong jolt, and he felt as if his head were being sucked backward and his body being compressed. A bright flash filled his vision. He blinked a few times, feeling almost like he had blacked out for a moment. Strange, dark shapes filled their front window, but before Chase could figure out what they were, their ship shook with a loud *bang!* Something had hit the side of their cruiser. It hit again. *Bang!*

"It's some kind of debris field!" Parker grabbed the manual controls and spun the cruiser around.

"Oh, this is much better than where we were!" shouted Chase. "Look out!"

A massive rock appeared right in front of them, and Parker pulled up hard on the yoke. Something else struck the roof of the cruiser with a painfully loud crunch. He fought with the controls, wheeling the ship back in the other direction. A long metallic squeal rang out, echoing throughout the vehicle as their port side dragged along another giant cosmic boulder.

"Oh lords," Parker choked out. "I think...did we puncture...?"

A zipping noise sounded behind them as the door to the bunkroom opened. Chase whirled around in his seat. The young man staggered through the doorway in his space suit, his sunken eyes roving wildly.

"Are you trying to kill us?" he shouted. "Move aside!"

"Hey! What are you doing?" yelled Parker as the man shoved him away from the controls and squeezed into the seat in his bulky suit. "This is my cruiser. You can't just take it over."

Whoever the guy was, he proved that he knew his way

around a piloting console by quickly slowing the cruiser to a stop. They hovered motionless among the particles while he slid his fingers across the screen and opened up a map on the console. On the screen, hundreds of white dots surrounded the pulsing beacon of their cruiser. The field of debris around them was thick, and so large that it went all the way to the edges of the map.

"We're in the middle of an accretion disk. How did we get here?" the man asked in a strange, lilting accent. He opened up another screen, full of numbers.

"I had to pull the breakaway to get us away from Trucon," said Parker. "It put us here."

The man opened up a few more screens and studied them for a minute, and then he sighed loudly. "You're lying. There've been two folds."

"Oh, well, I think the ship took a double-jump, must've been—" Parker faltered.

"Don't lie to me. What happened?" The man glared at him, his dark eyes blazing feverishly against the unhealthy pallor of his skin.

Parker stared at him, lost for words. The man lurched to his feet and grabbed Parker by the collar. "Tell me the truth!"

"We tried to plot a route," Chase blurted out.

The man turned his glare on Chase for a moment, his lip curling. "Idiots! Do you know how much energy a single fold uses up in a granny cruiser like this? We'll be lucky if we last another day!" Shaking his head and muttering in another language, he began to unfasten his space suit.

Chase looked back at the console, trying and failing to see how much energy the cruiser had left. "Do you know where we are?"

"Not yet." As he undid the latches on his sleeves, the man glanced around the cabin. His eyes rested on Mina for a moment, but he didn't say anything.

"Who are you?" asked Parker, squaring his shoulders and brushing a few sweaty strands of hair out of his face. "Did you know we saved your life?"

The man pulled off the top half of his suit. "My name is Maurus."

"And you're from Lyolia."

"That's right."

"We found you floating next to a wrecked Khatra over Mircona. What happened?" asked Parker.

Maurus stepped out of the bottom half of his suit and tossed it on the cabin floor beside Mina. Underneath he wore a trim black jumpsuit. "That's none of your business," he said, and returned to the pilot's seat.

"You're not from the Fleet. Did you steal the Khatra?" Parker asked.

Maurus ignored him.

"Did you see what happened to Trucon?" asked Chase. "Do you know what caused it?"

"Will you both shut up?" Maurus ran a hand through his hair and shook his head. "I can't do this if you're babbling in my ear the whole time."

Parker scowled and watched over Maurus's shoulder with his lips pressed together. Chase tried to watch as well, but the blur of screens, numbers, and maps made no sense to him. He looked back at the vast field of rubble crowding around them, the massive, dark shapes outlined by the light from some distant star.

"Clear out," said Parker, nudging Chase from his seat.

Chase hastily buckled himself into one of the seats on the back wall as Maurus announced the next fold. With the same brain-sucking feeling, they left the debris field and reappeared in an area of blank, empty space.

"Do you know where we are now?" Chase ventured.

Maurus didn't answer.

"Do you know—" Parker began to repeat.

"Still working on that," snapped Maurus. They sat in tense silence as they waited for Maurus to complete his calculations. "We're within a five-parsec range of Senica."

"Alright, let's go there," said Parker.

Maurus pondered the screen for a few more moments. "No. There's an emergency signal being broadcast. They're telling all survivors from Trucon to go to Qesaris. The Federation is setting up refugee camps there in the capital."

"Do we have enough power to make it that far?" Parker asked.

"I can squeeze it out of her."

"No." Parker stood up straighter and crossed his arms. "This is my cruiser, and that means you're under my command. Go to Senica first and replenish the core."

Maurus made one last entry on the console and turned in his seat, regarding Parker with a cool stare. "Your command, is that right?" Behind him, all the screens went black. "I'm not flying into any planetary zone until I know how two Earthan boys ended up piloting a vehicle unattended, with a blitzed android in the cabin. Did you hijack it?"

"No. It's my cruiser," began Parker.

Maurus arched his eyebrows. "I don't believe you. What are your names?" He turned around to face Chase.

"He's Parker and I'm—"

"That's my little brother, Corbin," interrupted Parker loudly. "Parker and Corbin Mason." Chase tried not to look surprised and plastered a fake smile on his face.

Maurus seemed not to have noticed, as he had turned his attention to Mina, who was still slumped against the back wall. "You're runaways then, aren't you?" he said. "You blasted your nanny and took off for a joyride in the family cruiser."

"We didn't blast her," said Parker. "But she's ours."

"And covered with blast marks? Who was shooting at you?"

Parker narrowed his eyes. "How did you end up stranded in mid-space beside a wrecked Khatra?"

For a moment the cabin fell silent as Maurus and Parker stared each other down. In a low, deliberate tone, Maurus said, "I'm not stopping on Senica. I can get us to Qesaris. Refugee camps are easier to slip through unnoticed, which apparently would be best for us all."

"Are you sure we can make it?" asked Chase.

"I'm sure."

Parker's face twitched. "Alright. Thank you for presenting our options." He spoke stiffly, like he was still in control. "I agree with your suggestion. You can plot a course to Qesaris."

Maurus gave him a dangerous look before turning back to the console. "Keep that up and see where it gets you."

Motioning for Chase to follow him, Parker led the way into the bunkroom and allowed the door to slide closed behind them. "Start looking for rope or anything we can use to tie with."

"Why?" Chase watched as Parker pulled a bundle of cable from a cabinet and tied a practice knot with it, testing the strength. "What are you going to do with that?"

"This guy could be anything—smuggler, slave trader, assassin. If he tries something, we have to be ready to defend ourselves."

"Defend ourselves? With what? A piece of cable and your amazing wit?"

Parker gave him a dirty look. "With this." From his pocket, he withdrew the knife he'd bought from the junk merchant, still in its green sheath.

"Are you crazy? You don't have a chance against him. Put it away!"

"You won't be saying that when he puts you in shackles and tries to sell you into the slave trade."

"Or maybe he'll just take us to Qesaris like he said, and we'll be that much closer to getting Mina fixed."

Parker shook his head. "Maybe he will. But if he tries anything on us, even if he just tries to steal our cruiser once we land"—he made a slashing motion with the sheathed knife—"he'll have this to deal with first."

# CHAPTER EIGHT

With a bad feeling growing in his gut, Chase watched Parker stash the knife up his sleeve and place the cable on the floor just inside the doorway. He rose to his feet. "Ready? Play it cool for now."

Chase tried one last time to stop him. "Think about it. If you try to use that blade against Maurus, you'll end up with it jammed against your own throat. And if he really is a criminal, he won't think twice about using it on you. Don't be stupid." Maurus wasn't exactly muscle-bound, but he looked tough and definitely strong enough to overpower a pale houseplant like Parker.

"Just let me handle everything, you wimp." Parker touched the entry pad, and the door slid open.

Maurus sat facing them, his arms crossed.

Quickly Parker tucked his arm behind his back. "What?"

"Second Lieutenant, Expeditionary Squad." Maurus's voice was calm, but his eyes glittered fiercely.

"Huh? I don't know what you're—" Parker began.

"I wasn't planning to give you any information beyond my name. But before you go trying to start a mutiny, I thought I'd better tell you that you'll be attacking an officer from the Intergalactic Federal Fleet."

"I don't know what you're talking about," mumbled Parker.

"There's an intercom," said Maurus. "To the bunkroom. I heard everything you said."

Chase wanted to sink into the floor and vanish. An intercom? How could Parker be so dense?

"You're Lyolian. You can't be in the Fleet," said Parker, his cheeks blooming scarlet.

Maurus opened his jacket and pulled off an elliptical silver badge, holding it out like a shield. "It's real. You want to check?"

Parker glanced at the badge and returned his gaze to the floor. "What ship do you serve on?"

"The *IFF Kuyddestor*."

"And . . . who's your commanding officer?"

"Captain Lionel Lennard." Maurus's dark, severe eyes bored into them. "What, is that it for the interrogation? Come forward." Both boys stepped through the doorway, and the door slid shut behind them. "There, I've locked it. We're all going to stay up here in the pilot's cabin for now. Hand over the knife. Handle first."

Parker shook the weapon from his sleeve, avoiding Maurus's eyes, and passed it over. Glowering, he sank into one of the seats on the back wall.

"Corbin, come take a seat up here." Maurus made a few entries on the console and then turned to Chase, studying his face for a minute. "Is this your cruiser?"

From the corner of his vision, Chase could see Parker's gray eyes blazing in his direction. He bit his lip.

Maurus waited a moment and shrugged. "You're lucky. I'd turn you in myself, but because of the situation with Trucon, I'll need to report for duty right away."

"Do you know what happened back there?" asked Chase. "Was it an attack?"

"Nothing's certain yet. The whole galaxy's in an uproar." He turned back to the console. "We've got a few hours ahead of us until we get to Qesaris. I'll monitor the emergency band for more information."

If Maurus really was from the Fleet, he didn't seem to recognize Chase, so that was a good sign. Maybe it was just because Parker had given a fake name for him. Chase closed his eyes briefly in gratitude for Parker's one good move and turned to give him a nod of encouragement, but Parker kept his eyes glued to the floor and wouldn't look up.

Chase gazed back out the front window of the cruiser, barely aware of the movement as they hurtled onward through space. He wasn't able to say whether the past few hours were some of the worst of his life so far, but they were certainly some of the hardest he had spent in the short time he could remember. The seat was too uncomfortable to sleep in, and in his exhaustion he stared off into space, his weary brain returning to the same questions. *Who am I? What happened to me?*

Why had Dr. Silvestri's lab been raided? And why had those soldiers tried to shoot them on Mircona? Was someone trying to have him killed? His hands clenched on the armrests. No, maybe someone important was trying to find him. All sorts of possibilities bloomed in his mind, and he imagined several different fantastic scenarios before his thoughts crashed back down again with the recollection that nothing was the same as it had been before Trucon burned.

His thoughts cycled back and forth like this for the next few hours, until the stress twisted his stomach into a grizzled knot. He looked over at Maurus for the first time since they had stopped talking, and gasped.

Maurus looked like he'd gone berserk. He stared at the

console with wild eyes, his cheeks flushed. His lips moved as if he were in the middle of a heated debate.

"What's wrong?" Chase's first thought was that it must have been about him. Maybe the Fleet had reached Maurus with news about his young passengers. Panicking, Chase leaned toward the console. What he saw there was a line of streaming words, and an ID photo of someone with dark eyes and sharp cheekbones.

Maurus slapped the console, and the image vanished. A coordinate map filled the screen. "What? Everything's fine." His eyes were still wide and glazed over.

Chase blinked, still processing the flash of an image he'd seen. "Was that photo of you?"

"No," he said too quickly.

"Are we running out of energy?" Chase asked.

Maurus shook his head and touched something on the console. "No, we're good. Almost there." His face twitched.

Chase glanced over his shoulder at Parker, who slept in his seat, his face mashed up against the wall. "You looked like . . . I thought something bad had happened."

"No, everything's fine," Maurus said brusquely. "We'll be able to fold over to Qesaris shortly—we need to close in on this gas giant first." Maurus gestured toward the window. "We're starting to come up on it now."

After a moment Chase spotted the tiny yellow-orange

speck, far, far away. He realized how fast they were moving as it grew steadily in size, and within half an hour the details of the colossal globe began to come into view. A mesmerizing pattern of brown and white swirls and faint streaks of green decorated its orange surface. Soon the planet filled their entire window and it was all they could see. It was bigger than anything Chase thought could possibly exist, and it was beautiful.

"We're going to use its gravitational pull to assist our fold, aren't we?" asked Parker, who had awoken and leaned forward in his seat.

Maurus grunted. "Prepare for fold," he said a minute later. He steered the cruiser to the right, so that a small sliver of black space appeared at the top of the window. Chase continued to watch the planet, transfixed. "And four, three, two . . ."

Again Chase experienced the strange full-body compression of the fold, and it was as though he'd blinked his eyes and the glorious gas giant vanished. In its place was a different planet, much smaller and visible only as an iridescent sliver as they came up on it from the darkened side. What they could see gave off a bluish-gray cast.

"Qesaris," announced Maurus, hunching back over the console. "I'll see where we should enter to reach the refugee stations."

"Just get on the planet's flight channels," said Parker from the back of the cabin. When Maurus didn't respond, he continued. "I'm sure it's been marked as a local CFC coordinate, just enter it in and the cruiser will take care of the rest." There was a pause. "Hello, are you listening?"

"The CFC is for housewives, autobuses, and children who don't know a thing about piloting," said Maurus, without looking up from the console.

There was silence from the back of the cabin, and Chase didn't dare to turn around to see what kind of death stare Parker was delivering to the back of Maurus's head. After a minute, Maurus took the yoke and began steering them toward the blue planet. Ships of all sizes dotted the space around the planet's atmosphere.

"Plenty of Fleet ships up here," said Parker. "You have to report for duty on one of these?"

"Yes." Maurus veered around a giant cluster of vehicles, muttering to himself, and suddenly turned the cruiser and zoomed down through the crowded space, weaving easily between vehicles to approach the planet's atmosphere.

He tapped a screen on the console. "Vector 217, refugee PSJ-E class requesting slot assignment." There was a brief pause, and then a disembodied voice came crackling from the console.

"This is 217, you are assigned entry number 1498. Please maintain orbital trajectory until your number is broadcast."

Maurus huffed and tapped the screen again. "217, PSJ-E class requesting immediate slot assignment."

"Cruiser, there is a line going halfway around the planet," snapped the voice. "Wait your turn like everyone else."

Maurus rolled his eyes and drummed his fingers on the controls. "217, I have a medical emergency on board. Request immediate landing privileges in the capital."

There was a long break, and finally the voice responded, sounding tight and irritated. "Entry assignment in transmission."

Chase looked over at Maurus. "You could have just told them you needed to report for duty," he said.

Maurus ignored him and veered the cruiser down toward the planet's surface. It took Chase a moment to figure out what looked strange about Qesaris as they drew closer—the entire landscape was gray, covered in buildings and construction. There were slivers of blue water, but no green vegetation anywhere to be seen.

In the midst of all the structures, they flew over a monstrous hole in the ground, big enough to fit fifty cruisers end to end across the diameter. It was black and bottomless, rimmed in glowing blue lights. Before Chase had the chance to ask what it was, Maurus steered them straight down and plunged the ship toward the gaping tunnel. Chase leaned back in his seat, gripping the armrests. As they moved closer, he could see other vehicles flying in and out of the chasm.

Maurus looked over at Chase's rapt gaze and frowned. "It's a portshaft," he said. "Once we're docked, get away from this cruiser as quickly as possible. I'm sure there's plenty of police on hand and you don't want to be linked to a stolen vehicle."

"Not stolen," muttered Parker in the back.

"Do you think we'll be able to get Mina fixed in the refugee camp?" Chase asked.

"The android?" Maurus paused a moment. "I can help you get it repaired. I know a good electrostruct."

Chase looked back at Parker, who rolled his eyes and shrugged. He was probably sulking over the fact that Chase was right and Maurus was actually helping them. "Sure, thanks."

Maurus looked back at him again, but said nothing.

When they passed below the surface and entered into the wide chasm, Chase was at first captivated by what he saw around them—the interior of the giant shaft was lined with circular platforms that jutted out from the wall, and thousands of vehicles were docked in orderly rows on each level. Beside him, Maurus jumped from his seat and charged into the bunkroom with his discarded space suit. Chase yelped when he realized there was no one piloting the cruiser.

"Don't worry, it'll dock itself," said Parker, getting up from his seat. "He's finally doing what I told him to." His face was calm and determined as he slid into the pilot's seat. "I should lock him in the back and leave him there for the police to find," he said as he touched the console.

"Don't, Parker." Chase grabbed his wrist. "He's going to help us."

"What are you doing there?" asked Maurus behind them. He had emerged from the bunkroom with a slim silver case in his hand.

"What's that?" asked Parker. "Did you take that from my cruiser?"

"It's nothing," said Maurus, tucking the case into his jumpsuit. "It's mine."

The Starjumper was slowing its descent and began to swing backward onto one of the docking platforms. Once it settled on the firm surface, Maurus opened the exit door and swung out onto the platform. He reached inside to hoist Mina out of the vehicle, grunting with effort as he lifted her and turned away.

"Wait!" Chase scrambled out of the vehicle after him.

Maurus quickly crossed the platform toward the back wall of the shaft, where there was a series of sliding metal doors. He carried Mina in both arms, her face pressed into his chest and her long brown hair trailing out over his arm.

"Where are you going?" Chase called after him.

"Hold up!" shouted Parker, climbing out of the cruiser.

Maurus turned back to Chase, freeing one hand to fish something from his pocket. "Here," he said, holding out Parker's knife in its green sheath. "You should carry this."

Chase took it, confused, and slid it into his pocket. "But we're coming with you."

Maurus opened his mouth to speak, but was interrupted by a small hovercraft that zipped onto the platform. A medic in white uniform leapt down from the controls and approached the group.

"Sir, I understand you have a medical emergency here," said the medic.

"My wife," said Maurus loudly, stepping toward the back of the platform as he spoke. "Prone to seizures. She'll be fine. I can take her to the hospital myself. Would you please help my two young friends over there? We rescued them from a disabled ship. Both their parents have perished in the disaster and they're very distraught."

As the medic turned his attention on Parker and Chase, Maurus stepped through a set of metal doors at the back of the platform with Mina in his arms. The doors slid closed behind him and he was gone, leaving the two gaping boys behind.

# CHAPTER NINE

"Wait, stop!" Chase stared at the metal doors that slid closed behind Maurus and Mina. What had just happened?

Parker bolted past and pounded the console beside the doors. He turned as Chase jogged up behind him. "Why did you let him go?"

"*I* let him go?"

"You stood there and watched him take her!"

"Then go after him!" Chase said, waving his hand at the doors.

"That's an airshute, you idiot." Parker rapped on the console again. "By the time these doors open, he'll be long gone on the surface."

The medic stood next to his hovercraft. "Hey, boys, come on," he called. "I can take you from here."

Parker pushed Chase out of the way and marched toward

the hovercraft. "Take us to the surface. We can still catch his trail if we hurry."

The medic shook his head. "I'll take you to the refugee station so you can get registered. That man can take care of his wife's problems on his own."

"Are you a moron? That wasn't his wife, he just stole my android! We need to go after him, right now."

The medic's expression hardened. "You'll have to report it at the refugee station. Now get on board."

Parker crossed his arms and scowled at the medic. At the edge of the platform, a gray-uniformed Fleet soldier stepped down off the hovercraft. "Are these boys giving you trouble?" he asked.

Chase took a step backward. Maurus might not have recognized him, but Dr. Silvestri's last words echoed in his mind nonetheless: *Do not go to the Fleet*. He exchanged a quick glance with Parker, and without a word they spun around and ran.

"Hey!" shouted the medic. "Get back here!"

Leading the way, Chase sprinted toward the vehicles docked along the circular platform. He dodged around a long, narrow airship, right into a hanging metal flap that the owner must have forgotten to close. Stumbling a step, he grunted in surprise, but was already past it, his face tingling where he must have grazed it.

A second later, he heard a thud and a cry behind him. He looked back, still running, and skidded to a stop. Parker lay flat on the platform, his hands clutched to his face. A streak of blood painted his forehead right at his hairline, where he'd opened up a wide gash.

Chase looked back at the metal flap, touching his own forehead. How had he managed to miss it? He looked at his hand, but there was no blood.

"Aughhhh," Parker groaned.

Chase started back to his side. "Are you okay?"

"Oh, that's just great," said the medic, who'd jogged up beside them. "Why do you dumb kids always have to run? That laceration's too big for steamgel. You're going to need a lasobind." He pulled a bandage from his satchel and pressed it on Parker's forehead, helping him to his feet. "Come on, kid. You've earned yourself a trip to the medical center."

Chase kept his head tipped down and didn't look the soldier in the eyes as they boarded the hovercraft. A practical side of him insisted it was silly to constantly think he might be recognized, but the memory of the soldiers who'd chased them on Mircona was still too fresh in his mind to take any risks. He crouched in the back of the vehicle as they flew into the deep shaft and zipped past rows of docked vehicles, cool air rushing through the open hovercraft.

Parker glared at him with one eye, pressing the soaked

bandage to his head. "Thanks for warning me there was something in the way."

Chase gave Parker a pat on the shoulder. "Sorry about that. I guess I was running too fast." Inside, he fidgeted, wondering how long it would be until they could get away from this soldier and look for Maurus and Mina.

"Hey, am I going to have a scar?" Parker asked, raising his voice.

The medic turned from the front, where he sat beside the Fleet soldier. "No, but you might have a concussion. You'll have to get a scan."

The hovercraft emerged from the portshaft into muted daylight. Chase wasn't sure how many hours had passed since they'd left Trucon, but based on how exhausted and hungry he felt, it was at least the middle of the night for him. Here on Qesaris, it looked like early morning. They flew into an endless forest of gray buildings and headed around an enormous, circular structure with grand arched entryways. Throngs of people milled in and out of the building, and even from where they flew, Chase saw expressions of shock, grief, anger, resignation—an overall atmosphere of misery and loss. He tried to look for Maurus, but instead his gaze was caught by a sobbing woman clutching the arm of the grim-faced man beside her, while a few feet away an older man with a white beard screamed at the sky. Soldiers in gray uniforms milled through the crowds around them.

They soared away from the stadium and down a street buzzing with sky traffic, darting between vehicles as they sped ahead. Tall skyscrapers hemmed them in on either side, disappearing into a smoggy haze above. After a few turns and one very long stretch, they pulled up outside a monstrous building. Its exterior was several shades darker than most other buildings, and covered almost the entire block, looming over the street. Half the windows were covered in metal bars.

The medic jumped off the hovercraft and led them inside the dark building into a lobby packed with confused, angry people. He looked around, shaking his head. "What a mess. Just, uh, get in line here, and someone will come take care of you."

"Get in *line*?" asked Parker. "I could die of a concussion before I get helped."

The medic rolled his eyes. "You'll be fine." He turned and left, abandoning them in the middle of the chaos.

A group of soldiers entered the lobby and began weaving through the crowd. Chase lowered his head and tried to casually block his face with his hand. "We need to get out of here," he said under his breath.

"What, you think I'm okay to go?" Parker said loudly, lifting the bandage to reveal the oozing gash on his forehead. "Does it look good to you?"

Chase winced. "Alright, yeah. You need to get that looked at."

"They're probably only going to make me check in, but if they ask you, don't try to give your real name this time—you're still Corbin Mason, and I'm your brother."

"Shouldn't you change your name too?"

"You're right. I'll be Livingston Mason."

"Livingston?"

"You have a better one?"

"I could think of a thousand."

Parker rolled his eyes. In front of them a tall blond boy turned around and gazed at them with watery, bloodshot eyes. "Where were you?"

"Huh?" said Parker.

"When it happened, I was on an autobus, heading home from school," the boy continued in a shaky voice. "The driver yanked the bus offtrack and headed skyward . . . I don't know where my . . . my . . ." His eyes filled with tears.

"Oh. Well, we were on Mircona," said Parker awkwardly. "Didn't even realize what was going on until the whole planet looked like a bonfire. Wild, right?"

The boy stared at Parker for a moment. "Freak," he mumbled, turning away.

"What is wrong with you?" hissed Chase.

"What?"

Chase shook his head and looked away, embarrassed. On one side of the room, a makeshift registration area had been set up. Chase squinted at the men sitting behind the tables, taking people's information. They weren't human—even he could see that—their movements were stilted, and they had smooth, peach-colored skin and glassy eyes that never blinked.

"Are those androids?"

"Ding ding ding, genius," said Parker. "Lords, I'm starting to feel dizzy."

An older female officer in a tan uniform cut her way across the room, shouting orders at the soldiers. "Get a system in place! This is not hacking it, private," she barked. She stopped in front of Parker. "What have you got under there?" she asked, nodding at his bandage. When he showed her, she pulled an instrument from her belt.

Chase dropped his head, hiding his face. From the corner of his eye he watched the woman's round, rosy face, with a clipped blond-gray bob and bright blue eyes, making her look like the world's oldest baby doll, dressed in military gear. She held Parker's chin with one hand and pointed the device at his forehead with the other.

"Ow, that stings!" said Parker.

"Of course it does," she said. "Where's your family?"

"Dead."

The officer bit her lip and didn't speak as she finished mending the gash on Parker's forehead. When she was done, she gave it a wipe and examined her work.

A soldier appeared on her right. "Colonel Dornan, vector command wants you in a telecon right away."

The woman nodded, focusing all her attention on Parker as she pulled out another device and held it in front of each of his eyes. "We should see about sending some of the orphans over to recruiting," she said quietly to the soldier.

"Kinda young, isn't he?" he asked.

Chase glanced up to see her reaction. Recruiting? Did she mean for the Fleet?

Colonel Dornan shrugged. "Okay, you're all set," she said to Parker. "Wait here and someone will take you back to refugee registration." She turned to the soldier, and as they walked away, Chase heard her complain that they should be processing everyone this quickly.

He looked at Parker. "Can we go now?"

"After you."

It was easy to slip out of the chaotic medical center and onto the street. Hovercraft traffic zipped by in orderly lines overhead, but on the ground only a few wheeled vehicles rolled past. Chase sped down the street, trying to put as much distance as possible between himself and the medical center. "Which way?" he asked, stopping on a corner.

"I think we're okay now." Parker placed his hand against a building. "Woo, dizzy. Let's sit down somewhere. There." He pointed down the street to a doorway with a magenta sign hanging over it that read Captain Orion's.

Inside was a bustling, brightly lit café, filled with the comforting smells of fresh baking and hot grease. They squeezed their way through the tightly packed room and took seats at a small table near the back. The walls of the café were covered in video screens, each one blaring an advertisement for something called ReNuvaGel, accompanied by images of a nondescript woman's wrinkle-free face. Parker tapped on the illuminated tabletop and began scrolling through a list of pictures.

Chase laid his head down to rest his cheek on the cold, smooth surface. His head whirled as the remaining shreds of panic dissipated. They were safe. For now. "What did that officer mean about recruiting you for the Fleet?" he asked.

Parker shrugged. "Another warm body to serve the Federation. They're always pulling shady stuff like that. Yes! They have scrappies here! I hope you're hungry." His fingers flew excitedly over the tabletop. "What's wrong with you?"

Chase took a deep breath. He couldn't remember the last time he'd eaten and he was starving, but that wasn't his first concern. "What are we going to do now? There's no way to contact Asa without Mina, right?"

"Right. We just need to find her."

"Okay," Chase said sarcastically. "No problem."

"You're forgetting something, dummy."

"What?"

"Maurus told us what ship he serves on. The *Kai Desser* or something. We just have to find it and then we'll be able to find him."

Chase snorted. Parker had a magical way of making things sound easier than they really were.

"Hey, sit up. Food's here."

"Already?" Chase lifted his head off the table as Parker took drinks and paper packets from a tray hovering beside them. Chase unwrapped one of the packets and found something that looked like a dense orange sponge. He poked it cautiously.

"It's called a scrappy—soy-chitlin-riboflavin patty," said Parker. He broke his own patty into quarters and folded each piece meticulously in half before cramming it in his mouth.

Chase tentatively took a bite. The texture was strange— melty smooth on the outside, unexpectedly crunchy on the inside, with a rich, almost cheesy flavor. In three bites he devoured the whole thing. He washed it all down with a huge gulp of the fizzy red drink, wincing a little at its sweet-sour taste, like raspberries soaked in vinegar, and reached for another scrappy.

Parker swallowed and grinned. "Good, right?"

Nodding vigorously, Chase took a huge bite.

"One time last year, I snuck out and went into Rother City to a Captain Orion's and bought like a hundred scrappies, and brought them back and hid them in my closet."

"Ew. Did they get all nasty?"

Parker's face lit up. "No! That's the crazy part—they stayed exactly the same! I was eating them for a month."

Chase laughed. "That's gross."

"I know. They're probably really bad for you."

"Did Mina get mad?"

Parker gave him a devilish grin. "She never found out. Her central processor almost caught fire trying to figure out how I skipped every meal for two weeks and never lost any weight." He frowned at the scrappy in his hand. "Actually, this is the first time I've eaten one since. For a while, I couldn't even think about them without getting sick."

Chase took a long pull on his red drink. The flavor had become strangely appealing. "Why didn't you just have your autokitchen make them for you?"

Parker made a face, shaking his head. "Synthesized food seems like a great idea. You store the basic molecules of food—proteins, fats, sodium, the like—and the machine reorganizes them in a million different ways. But after years of eating nothing but synth, you realize that everything has this same underlying bland taste like, I don't know, petroleum jelly."

"That breakfast we had at your house was pretty good," argued Chase.

"It's not inedible, but you can't compare that synth croissant with a real, freshly baked croissant, can you?"

Chase mentally reached for the comparison, but there was no memory of a freshly baked anything. Did that mean he'd never had one? Maybe he'd eaten a thousand croissants in his lifetime—or maybe he'd eaten nothing but animal feed from an aluminum chute. His grin faded, and he looked down at the table. "I don't know," he said.

For a moment Parker was silent. The chatter of the café rose up around them. "Sorry."

Chase shrugged. When he raised his eyes to meet Parker's sober gaze, he felt self-conscious, but there was no trace of pity in Parker's expression. For a moment Chase got the feeling that Parker really saw him, really understood how he felt. Then Parker picked up the rest of his scrappy and shoved the entire thing in his mouth at once, making his cheeks bulge out like twin balloons.

"Now finish your unidentified indestructible food product," he warbled around the mouthful. "Who knows when we'll eat this well again."

With a wan smile, Chase reached for his third scrappy when he noticed that the noise of the café had started to die down. The wall of screens had switched to a video feed showing a blond female newscaster standing like a perky sail in a sea of distraught refugees, and everyone was watching. Her voice echoed at them from all directions.

"With aid primarily provided by the Federal Fleet, refugee centers on Qesaris are processing most of the survivors of the Trucon disaster. If you're just tuning in, this is Parri Dietz reporting on the event of the millennium, a devastating and unprecedented attack on the Federal colony Trucon. With stolen military technology, the attacker used nuclear thermo-detonators in the oxygen plants of Rother City to scorch the atmosphere . . ."

Her image was replaced by a view of Trucon from Mircona, looking peacefully blue and sandy. Everyone in the café watched in horror as a black smudge appeared on the globe, expanding and blossoming with red and orange as it moved out over the entire planet. Just as it was about to eclipse the last bit of blue ocean, the newscaster's image reappeared.

"One moment, Boris, I'm getting an update here," she said. "Early reports indicated the involvement of the Lyolian resistance group, Karsha Ven, and now we do have a photo. The suspected mastermind of the Trucon disaster is a Lyolian pilot serving in the Federal Fleet, a Lieutenant Elmans—I'm sorry, I'm not even going to try to pronounce this one—Lieutenant E. Maurus."

The screen changed before Chase's brain caught up, and he gasped when he saw the image that flashed across the screen: Maurus in his military gray, wearing a severe expression, his dark eyes arrogant and fierce.

"Lords!" yelled Parker. He slammed his half-eaten scrappy on the table.

"That's right, a Lyolian in the Federal Fleet—part of an experimental officer interchange program," the newscaster continued. "Lieutenant Maurus has been serving as a pilot on the *IFF Kuyddestor*. Although we haven't received a copy of the image yet, he was photographed on Trucon shortly before the disaster, meeting with members of the Karsha Ven rebel group, where he allegedly provided them with the stolen thermodetonators.

"Although the Karsha Ven have not yet claimed responsibility for the attack, security analysts have been expecting some form of anti-Federation assault for the election of the new Lyolian president. Lieutenant Maurus is suspected to have died in the ensuing disaster. We'll have more on this story as it unfolds, Boris."

Chase opened and closed his mouth several times, trying

to find words for all the thoughts tumbling through his head. "But he's not dead."

"No, genius, he's not." Parker slammed his drink on the table. "Because we saved his life. We saved the life of the biggest mass murderer in history. Why did they let a Lyolian in the Fleet to begin with?"

"They said it was an experimental program—" Chase began.

"That's stupid! It's like if I 'experimentally' invited a Zinnjerha into my house to see if it'd make a nice pet."

"There's a slight difference between Maurus and a Zinnjerha."

"Right, because at least I know what a Zinnjerha's intentions are from the start. Lyolians are physically the most similar to Earthans, but they're all sneaks and liars. Their planet's been in a messed-up civil war forever and the Karsha Ven are just . . . they're monsters. They've killed tons of innocent people. I don't even know what their goal is, other than making trouble for the Federation."

Parker's railing on about the Karsha Ven wasn't getting them any closer to finding Mina. Chase took a sip of his drink to clear the tight feeling in his throat and rubbed his forehead. "I guess we're not going to find Maurus on his ship then, are we?"

Parker loosed a torrent of profanity. "He may think he's gotten away with Mina, but when she wakes up, she'll break his neck." He crumpled up a wrapper and threw it at the table. "She'll come back to me."

Chase looked back at the screens. Out of the corner of his eye, he noticed a tiny movement, but before he could focus on it, a sudden coldness spread in his lap. Parker's glass lay tipped over on the table, its fizzy red contents spilling everywhere. Chase leapt to his feet, wiping the liquid off his pants. "Thanks a lot!"

"I didn't touch it," said Parker, using the tray to push the puddle of red drink onto the floor.

"Yeah, sure."

"Whatever. Go ahead, blame me. Washrooms are over there, klutz."

Shaking his head, Chase skirted through the tables and slipped into a small room in the back, closing the door behind him. He tried to prop his knee against a sink, but something dug into his thigh and he pulled Parker's knife from his pocket, placing it on the only available space, a shelf above the sink.

He had just splashed a handful of water onto his pants when something dropped down from above and crashed into him, knocking to the floor with a surprised shout.

Someone small—a girl—was on top of him, her tiny hands

grabbing at his throat as he tried to twist out from under her. A hard, cold edge pressed against his neck.

"Stop!" she demanded in a high, thin voice. "Unless you want this to end right now."

Chase froze. The girl, no older than ten, was perched on his chest, her skinny bare knees digging into his ribs. She wore a light blue smock—a hospital gown?—and her pale hair stuck out in a spiky halo. Violet half-moon bruises were slashed under her wide, unstable eyes.

She was holding Parker's knife to his throat.

"What are you doing?" Adrenaline snapped through his body.

She leaned forward, examining his face with a scowl. "What are you?"

"What?"

"I saw you standing next to Dornan. She didn't see your face, but I did. You're a perfect copy. Who made you?" She pressed down harder on the knife.

"I don't know what you're talking about!" he choked, pushing his cheek against the washroom floor and away from the blade's edge.

"Of course you wouldn't, not if they made you to be perfect," she spat. "But that doesn't make you innocent. I won't be tricked into thinking you're something you're not!" The words poured out of her in a hysterical jumble. "Something you never could be! I won't let them do this! They wrecked everything! They ruined us! I won't let them use—violate my—my—"

With a savage cry she slashed the blade across his throat and plunged it into the side of his neck. Chase jerked back against the floor, and his body began to tremble. He locked eyes with the girl. She stared back, her face a mask of horrified shock.

He rolled his eyes over to look at the hilt of the knife, pressed against his skin. His neck felt numb. The girl followed his eyes, and suddenly recoiled, pulling the knife out with a start. It clattered to the floor, and she slid off his chest.

Heart pounding, Chase cupped his hands around his neck, trying to stop the blood that would be pouring out, taking his life with it. But he felt no wetness, and when he tentatively probed his skin, it was warm and whole, all his blood contained within the furiously throbbing veins.

The girl's pale eyebrows bunched together in a bewildered expression. "What are you?"

He looked up at her, dazed. "I don't know. I woke up a week ago at someone's home with no memory of anything before that. They told me my name is Chase. Do you know who I am?"

Her mouth dropped open. "If . . ."

"If what?"

She shook her head. "No. This is a trap. You can't be Chase!"

"Why not?"

She shook her head again.

"Why not?" he repeated impatiently.

"Because he's dead!"

It felt like someone had knocked all the wind out of his lungs. "What?"

"Chase is dead." She looked away, her voice breaking on the words. "I saw it happen."

The room spun and compressed, narrowing in to one tiny little point on the girl's face. He couldn't speak—every thought process had short-circuited. She glanced over her shoulder and looked back at him. Her eyes were turbulent, full of a wild mix of fear and hope and anger.

"Someone's coming. If you have any of Chase's memories, then you have to know the safe place. Please remember it, they told us so many times. Go there! Tell them I'm alive and that I'm being held by the one who led the end. Tell them to come and get me!" Her face crumpled, and for a moment she looked like nothing more than a frightened little girl.

"Tell who?" Chase grabbed her narrow shoulders. "Asa Kaplan?"

"Who? No . . ." She paused, and her eyes seemed to lose focus. "Guide the star!"

And then she vanished.

Chase stared in shock at the empty space where the girl had been. His hands hung in midair, holding nothing. "Come back!"

The washroom door opened and Parker's head poked inside. "Hey, are you taking a bath in here or something?" He frowned down at Chase sitting on the floor. "I'm not going to ask what you're doing down there. Get up. We need to go."

"What? Parker, I just—"

"Shut up, I don't care. Let's go."

Chase froze. "Is something wrong? Did they find us?"

Parker's mouth twisted up in a crooked smile. "No. But I know where we can find Maurus."

# CHAPTER TEN

Chase's mind spun as Parker led him back through the café. Nothing the girl had said made sense. *Perfect copy. Can't be Chase. He's dead.* Her wild eyes were burned into his mind. She'd known who he was—or at least, she knew another Chase who she believed was dead. But she was wrong about that. Wasn't she?

They stepped out onto the street, and Chase finally found his voice. "Parker. There was a girl. In the bathroom."

"Um, what?" Parker cut him a sideways glance before starting down the sidewalk. "You were alone in the bathroom, Chase."

"No, I wasn't. She vanished right before you opened the door."

"Uh-huh."

Chase rushed around Parker and stood in front of him, blocking his way. "I'm serious! She tried to stab me with your knife, but it didn't work, and then she said I was a perfect copy, and that Chase was dead."

"Dead," repeated Parker. He squinted at Chase, inspecting him. "And the knife 'didn't work.' Buddy, did you fall and hit your head in there? Because this sounds crazy."

"I'm *not* crazy! She even said 'guide the star.'" Surely that would convince Parker she was real.

Parker gazed down the street for a moment, looking thoughtful. "Maybe you're having a weird reaction to the food." He stepped around Chase and started walking again. "Now which way is the Shank?"

Chase grabbed at Parker's sleeve, yanking it with such force it nearly tore at the shoulder. "Will you listen to me?" he shouted. "It happened! She was really there, and then she just disappeared. I'm not making it up!"

Parker looked down at Chase's hand. "Okay," he said slowly. "I believe you." His expression said otherwise.

Chase released Parker's shirt. "Whatever. You're not listening to me. Someone *recognized* me. Someone who knows who I am." *Or was.* A knot had formed in his chest.

Parker squeezed his eyes shut for several seconds and snapped them back open. "Alright. I'm sorry. I get that this could be huge. But whatever happened to you back there is not going to help us get Mina back, and we don't have much time left. Once Maurus splits from this planet, he'll disappear forever. While you were in the bathroom, you missed the breaking news flash. The Fleet's already discovered that Maurus is alive and made it here to Qesaris."

Parker's chatter flowed past Chase's ears, not sinking in. If only he'd had enough time to ask the girl what "guide the star" meant.

"Hey!" said Parker. "Did you hear me? The Fleet found out where Maurus went."

"Yeah. What?" Chase forced himself to absorb what Parker was saying. Maurus. Mina. Girl or no girl, they still needed to find Asa Kaplan. "How do they know he's here?"

"Because there's surveillance footage of him heading into the Shank with a 'mysterious bundle' over his shoulder."

"Heading into the what?"

"The Shank. It's some sort of district—I'm guessing fairly nearby."

"So how does that mean—" Chase began to ask, but a sudden roar drowned him out.

A fleet of hoverbikes, at least thirty or forty, zoomed over-head, with gray-uniformed soldiers atop. Every person on the street stopped to stare as they roared past and vanished around a corner.

"What was that?" Chase asked.

"That would be the Fleet, heading to the Shank to look for our friend, the saboteur." Parker headed down the street in the same direction the bikes had gone. "We just have to follow them and we'll find him."

Chase grabbed his shoulder. "Wait. If they're looking for Maurus, that place is going to be crawling with Fleet soldiers. This isn't a good plan."

"It's the only plan!" said Parker, jerking his shoulder away. "We know this is where he took Mina—how else are we supposed to find her?"

"We'll get caught!"

"We'll be careful."

Chase rolled his eyes. When was Parker ever careful? "How do you expect to find Mina?"

Parker didn't answer. He stopped a woman in a blue dress who was walking in the opposite direction and asked her, "Is this the right way to the Shank?"

The woman made a face and hurried away.

"Rude," muttered Parker.

"Do you even have a plan for how to look for her?" Chase asked. They knew Mina was in a particular district, but what was that? A few streets? A few blocks? A quarter of the planet?

"Mina's a very sophisticated android," said Parker. "You saw those andies at the registration, right? Plastic skin, glass eyes, brainpower of a calculator? Most of them are like that."

"So?"

"Head down." Parker stuck out his arm to stop Chase. A

moment later, another flock of hoverbikes rushed past, turning left in the distance. "Mina's very special," he continued. "I don't know why Maurus took her to this district—maybe to fix her, maybe to sell her. Either way, someone there is going to have heard about her. We just have to ask around."

Chase waited for the rest of Parker's plan, but he seemed to have said everything he was going to say. *"Ask around? That's the best you've got?"*

Parker ignored him, cupping his hands to his mouth as he shouted to a man across the street. "Hey, mister, is this the way to the Shank?" He pointed down a street that led to their left.

The man squinted at them and shook his head. "You boys trying to get yourselves killed? Stay outta the Shank!"

Uneasiness crept into Chase's stomach. "What is this place we're heading into, Parker?"

Parker grimaced. "My guess is that it's a gray sector."

"What's a gray sector?"

"You'll see. Hey, check that guy out."

It was easy to see who Parker was talking about. The people walking on the street around them looked fairly normal to Chase, but one extremely tall man in a wide-brimmed hat stood out, weaving through the crowd with his collar turned up and his hands in his pockets.

"What about him?"

"He doesn't belong here—Epsilons aren't supposed to be in an area like this. Let's follow him. I bet he'll lead us to the Shank."

"Epsilons?"

"Epsilon-level species, one grade down from Alphas, like us."

"Why aren't they supposed to be here?"

"Because this is a blue sector—Alpha only. Don't you see the blue lights on the street corners?"

The more Parker explained, the less sense it made, so Chase stopped asking questions. The man turned onto a narrow side street, and they followed him for several blocks, when suddenly he ducked into a narrow space between the buildings, an alley so dark that it looked like they were stepping into nighttime. Chase's pulse quickened as they followed the man into the black corridor, but after a few meters it widened into a dirty street.

The people on these back streets were a world apart from those they had left behind. From the corner of his eye Chase caught glimpses of strange features—a pair of pointed, hairy ears, a shimmer of translucent skin. The man they were following stopped to join a group clustered outside a doorway, and the boys kept walking. A few steps away, a figure wrapped in a dirty blanket lay huddled on the ground.

"What is this place?" Chase whispered. A hulking creature

with a wide, vicious mouth burst through a door beside them. Chase jumped away with a gasp.

"Calm down," muttered Parker.

They squeezed through a narrow alley and came out into a small, busy plaza ringed with vendor stalls. A strange variety of people did business here—some looked almost human, but others were too tall, too wide, their features placed wrongly on their faces.

"This is a gray sector," Parker finally said. "There are no restrictions on which species can come here."

"Why would there be restrictions?" asked Chase.

Parker pressed his lips together. "Because not everybody gets along very well." He headed for a stall in the back corner of the plaza. A small, battered yellow sign that read Mama T: Lyolli Nodel hung from the top of the stall, and beneath it was an open counter with a few stools.

"More food?" asked Chase, frowning. Parker shook his head.

A squat little woman worked at a stovetop behind the counter. Her round face was dominated by a long, pointy nose that stretched down toward her equally long, pointy chin, and Chase wondered if it was the dim lighting of her stall that made her skin appear to be such a strange, dusky green-gold hue. As she cooked, a long, bronze limb unfolded from behind her shoulders and reached up to take another pot down from its hook on the ceiling.

Chase stopped and took a step backward.

"What's wrong?" asked Parker, following his gaze to the multitasking cook. He looked back at Chase and shook his head with a sigh.

Chase could not take his eyes off the strange woman as another long, bony limb extended from her back to keep stirring the pot. With human-like arms at the front of her body, the woman began chopping a pile of nubby black vegetables.

Parker leaned over the counter. "Excuse me, I have a question."

The woman stayed bent over her chopping and ignored him. She wore a loose sort of pants, but instead of human-type legs, her saggy, bulbous midsection rested on a pair of folded haunches.

"Just one question," Parker repeated.

"No food, no answer," the woman snapped.

Parker sighed and sat on one of the stools.

"We'll take two of whatever you've got," said Chase. He didn't expect a food-stall cook to know much, but at least it was a start. "Can you tell us if you've heard anything about a very special android that's shown up in your district today? A broken android?"

Parker looked at Chase in disgust and rolled his eyes. "Way to be subtle."

The woman still didn't look up, and Chase racked his brain for something that would catch her attention. "She was brought here by the guy that's on the news, the Fleet soldier who helped the Karsha Ven destroy Trucon."

Parker jumped off his stool and punched Chase in the arm, hard. "How stupid are you? We need to get out of here now."

With a juicy slap, two packages landed in front of the boys, thick rolls wrapped in brown paper already blooming with grease spots. "Pay now!" screeched the woman behind the counter.

Parker tossed a handful of currency chips on the counter and pulled Chase away, leaving the greasy packages behind.

"What?" asked Chase.

"Don't you ever mention Maurus or the Karsha Ven again in this district, not unless you want to get killed."

"But people must know he's here!" In fact, Chase realized, it was more likely that people would be able to answer questions about Maurus than about Mina.

"That doesn't mean—"

"Excuse me, boys?" A strange man with bone-white skin and an oddly flat face had walked up behind them. "I couldn't help overhearing your questions at the noodle bar."

"It was nothing," said Parker quickly. "My friend's an idiot."

"Of course, nothing, I understand," said the man with a

gracious nod. "I just, you know, may have heard a thing or two about a very special android. If, you know..." He coughed and lowered his beady eyes, set so far apart they were almost on the sides of his head.

Parker paused and reached into his pocket. "This is all I've got." He opened his palm to show four plastic chips.

The man stared at the money and sniffed. "Well. I guess it's a good day to be charitable." He swept up the chips with one smooth gesture. How many fingers were there on his hand? "There's word going around that a certain, um, gentleman has been trying to sell a high-ticket item on the black market."

"Did someone buy her?" asked Chase. Parker jabbed him in the side with an elbow.

"That part isn't known," said the pale man, looking over his shoulder. "But word is that the item in question is broken and will need to be fixed. You'll probably learn more if you check with a local electrostruct."

"Where's the best electrostruct in the district?" asked Parker.

The man paused and coughed gently. He looked back and forth at each boy.

"I don't have any more money!" Parker said, patting his pockets.

The man shrugged. "And I don't have any more answers." He turned and walked away.

"Great, thank you!" Parker called after him. "Thanks a lot!"

"So all we have to do now is ask around until we find—" began Chase.

"If you open your mouth here again, I swear to God I will strangle you. You can't just say anything to anyone. Not here in the gray sector."

"What is it with the gray sector?" Chase asked. "I don't get it."

Parker pulled him back against a wall, looking around. "This is an alien ghetto," he said softly. "You have to know which species you can talk to, and which ones would rather tear your limbs off. You clearly don't."

"But I've never seen any of these things before," said Chase, gesturing at a pair of creatures with bullet-shaped, aquamarine heads who chatted at a table, their webbed feet swinging from tall chairs.

"Never steal puckered grapes. Does that ring a bell?" Parker asked.

"What in the world are you talking about?"

"Never. Steal. Puckered. Grapes," repeated Parker. "N-S-P-G. The planets in the Epsilon grade."

Chase shook his head.

"Namat, Sharto, Pranatine, Gox. The woman back there in the noodle booth, she's from Sharto. The Shartese are easy to bargain with, because they're parasites. Namatans are creepy-looking, but they're harmless, so they don't really matter. And if you see a Goxar, stay far, far away."

Chase looked around the plaza, confused. Which was a Namatan? Which was a Goxar? "What was the guy who just spoke to us?"

"Wow," muttered Parker, shaking his head. "Of course you don't know the Alphas. That guy was Ambessitari. Every. Living. Animal. Feels. Kingly—those are the Alpha civs. Earth, Lyolia, Ambessitar, Falas, Kekilly. None of this sounds familiar?"

Chase shook his head. He barely recognized a couple of the names spilling out of Parker's mouth and knew he wouldn't remember the others.

Parker sighed. "You're hopeless. Let's go look for an electrostruct. But keep your mouth shut. I'll do the talking."

A commotion started down the street, and Parker froze. As the shouts quickly drew closer, a group of gray-uniformed soldiers burst into the plaza, shouting orders and pointing their weapons. Half of the people lay obediently on the ground, but the Shartese woman behind the noodle bar started to scream, a high-pitched keening that made Chase clap his hands over his ears. A soldier raised his weapon. There was a flash of red, and the woman collapsed, her screams cut short. The rest of the plaza broke into complete pandemonium, creating an excellent distraction.

"Go!" snapped Parker. They bolted into an alley, but they

only ran a short distance before he grabbed Chase by the arm and switched to a quick walk. "Slower. Head down. Don't attract too much attention."

Chase matched Parker's pace on legs stiff with panic. The soldiers were everywhere, searching businesses, ransacking homes. The motley residents of the Shank stood in small clusters, watching the soldiers with expressions of anger and fear.

How many different kinds of alien species were there? Parker seemed to know every type, while he felt like he'd fallen into some kind of freakish nightmare. A pair of women with identical maroon hair walked past, clutching each other's hands. One glanced at Chase and her large eyes flashed silver. Feeling chilly, he pulled his jacket closer around him.

They walked farther into the Shank until they made it to an area the soldiers hadn't reached yet. Outside one of the buildings, a tall, broad creature with a tapered snout and an extremely wide mouth stood guard. A roar of shouting and cheers poured out of the open doorway behind him, but the creature remained perfectly still.

They couldn't keep walking aimlessly forever, not with the soldiers so close by. Chase turned before Parker could stop him and approached the tall creature. "Sorry, can you help us find an electrostruct?"

The creature glared down at him with beady eyes and grunted.

"I'm sorry, my friend is new around here," said Parker, running up beside Chase. "And we don't speak Horga. Sorry to bother you." He started to walk away, but the creature grunted again and pointed down the street.

"I'm sorry," said Chase, who hadn't moved. "I don't know what you mean." The creature glared at him for a moment and then crossed its arms and resumed its vacant gaze.

"Did I not tell you to keep your mouth shut?" said Parker, pulling him away.

"He didn't seem so bad," said Chase. "And he told us to go this way."

"Oh yeah, clearly he understood what we were talking about," scoffed Parker. "Clearly he knows exactly what . . ." He paused, looking up, and mumbled, "an electrostruct is."

A jagged blue lightning-bolt symbol was painted on the sign above the shop before them. "Is this it?" asked Chase.

Without answering, Parker walked into the shop. The room was long and brightly lit, lined with benches covered in tools and devices. Shards of plastic chips and metal wires covered the floor. There was no one in sight.

"Hello? Anyone here? I'm looking for the best electrostruct in town," Parker called as he picked his way across the shop floor. "I don't suppose anyone would know where I could find him?"

A broad figure wearing a heavy protective mask and gloves rose from behind one of the benches at the back of the room. "I do, in fact," the person said in a muffled voice, and pulled off the mask to reveal the same sort of icy white, flattened face as the man from the plaza—but this one appeared to be a woman. An Ambessitari, Chase reminded himself, an Alpha, like him. She grinned at the boys with small, stubby teeth that ended in dull points. "I'm the only electrostruct in town."

"You're the only electrostruct in the entire Shank?" Parker asked.

She shrugged. "The only one worth knowing. What are you boys doing in this part of town?"

Chase started to open his mouth, but Parker gave him a warning look and he stopped himself. The woman seemed friendly, but he didn't want to say the wrong thing.

"I'm looking for something," Parker said slowly. "Something nice."

The electrostruct took off her gloves and set them on the workbench. "That's rather vague. Care to specify?"

"It used to belong to me, but someone took it. I'm hoping you can help me find it." Parker paused, making his way over to her bench.

She narrowed her wide-set eyes. "I don't know anything about any stolen goods. You boys should probably leave."

"I think you might, actually. It's a *very* special thing, and it's broken."

The electrostruct looked past the boys at the alley outside her shop. "You boys need to leave my shop right now, or I will pull out a blaster and shoot you dead. You're in over your heads, Earthies. Do yourselves a favor and get out of the Shank."

"Happily, once I get my an—"

A scuffling noise sounded behind them. Chase looked back at the shop door as three Ambessitari men entered, each one larger, filthier, and more unfriendly looking than the last. They filled the front of the shop with their bulky frames, blocking the exit.

"Parker!" Chase said.

Parker whipped around and froze.

The largest of the three men squinted at the boys with one beady eye, a mass of gnarled tissue where the other should have been. "What's this? Earthies in the Shank? You boys part of this Fleet interference?"

"We've got nothing to do with that," blurted Chase, squeezing his sweaty palms against his legs. These men looked like exactly the kind of creatures who would tear his limbs off.

"These boys were just on their way out of here," said the

electrostruct. "They were asking for directions. What did you come here for, Gorma?"

"The Rezer needs to see you immediately," growled the one-eyed man. He added something else in a choppy, harsh-sounding language.

"Understood. I'll be right there," the electrostruct said in a tight voice. Under her breath, she muttered, "You boys get out of the Shank. Get back to where you belong."

Chase grabbed Parker's arm and took a step toward the front door, where the thugs stood and waited. "Thanks so much for your help," Parker chirped, too brightly, as he twisted around to the electrostruct. "I don't suppose you have a back exit?"

"Don't be so hasty, boys," rumbled Gorma. Eyeing them with frightful interest, he grinned, revealing his small teeth, which, unlike the woman's, were filed to sharp points. "Wouldn't you like to meet the Rezer?"

"The what?" asked Chase.

"Uh, sorry, we really have to be going," said Parker, pulling Chase back toward the workbench.

"The Rezer," said Gorma, a sly expression unfolding across his wide face. "Rezer Bennin. He's our leader—why, here in the Shank, he's everyone's leader. I think he'd very much like to meet you." He took a step closer, his companions flanking him. "We can give you a hand with those directions, and maybe you can help us resolve some of the . . . misunderstandings . . . stirred up by today's Fleet intrusion."

Chase shook his head. "I don't think we—"

"Don't do this, Gorma," said the electrostruct sharply. "You're just bringing more trouble on the Shank."

The one-eyed man's smile vanished, and he shot her an ugly glare. "You will not tell me what to do. These boys are coming with us." His hand slid to the blaster at his waist. "Now."

# CHAPTER ELEVEN

Sweat trickled down the back of Chase's neck as he stumbled through the narrow alley alongside Parker. The three men behind them didn't speak, but their presence—and the presence of their blaster guns—made Chase's back tingle. He repressed a strong urge to bolt, certain that the one eyed man would not hesitate to fire on him if given the opportunity.

With a bag of equipment slung across her back, the electrostruct led the way at the front of the group. As their path through the winding alleys of the Shank narrowed and darkened, Chase struggled to keep his legs moving forward. He pretended to trip and nudged Parker's arm.

Parker barely glanced at him, shaking his head. "Just keep moving," he whispered.

"Quiet up there," barked Gorma.

The electrostruct turned down a slanted side street that

opened into a small, dilapidated courtyard filled with a milling crowd of shifty-eyed Ambessitari men. They hunched together on pieces of broken foundation and lurked under the overhanging roof. In one corner of the courtyard, a group of them clustered around a squealing commotion on the ground. Most of the men paid no notice as the small group passed through and headed up a set of stairs into a ramshackle building.

When they entered the doorway, a slender woman with cascades of dark maroon hair stepped out of the shadows. "The Rezer is waiting for you," she said in a smooth, harmonious voice. She looked from the electrostruct to the boys and tipped her head to the side, her silver eyes flashing with curiosity.

They entered a long chamber decorated with thick carpets and gilt-edged wall panels inlaid with pearl, an unexpected contrast to the rough exterior of the building. Chase glanced back at Parker, who looked as intrigued as he felt. Gorma threw open a set of wrought-metal doors and stepped into a short entryway, putting his arm out to stop the others from entering behind him.

"Rezer Bennin, may we enter?" he asked.

A loud sigh echoed from inside, and a voice rang out in a cold tone that automatically conveyed a subtle threat of pain. "Did you bring the electrostruct?"

"Yes, sir." Gorma bowed his head and swept his hand across his forehead before grabbing the electrostruct from the group and pulling her into the doorway.

She stepped forward and made the same subservient gesture. "At your service."

"Come in."

Prodded by the two men on either side of them, Chase and Parker followed the electrostruct through the entryway. The first thing Chase saw when he crossed the threshold was a man standing in the middle of a richly decorated chamber, wearing a long, dark coat with huge embellishments on the shoulders. He was a beady-eyed Ambessitari like his minions, and his wide face looked as hard and cold as marble, making Chase feel anything but hopeful. This Rezer Bennin didn't look up to see who had entered, as he seemed to be staring at something on the side of the room. When Chase turned, he saw what it was.

Maurus sat hunched on a gilt bench against the wall, with Mina lying askew at his feet.

Hearing Parker suck in his breath, Chase grabbed his arm and dug his fingers in, willing him to keep his big mouth shut. Starting a fight surrounded by these dangerous men seemed enormously foolish, and just like something Parker would do. Maurus stared at the floor, one hand raking through his hair. He looked up after they had all entered, and immediately his gaze zeroed in on the two boys. His dark eyes widened.

Rezer Bennin spoke, still fixating on Mina. "The Lyolian wishes to sell me this damaged android. You must tell me if it can be repaired and at what cost."

The electrostruct ducked her head and hurried across the room, slinging her bag on the floor beside the android. With no gentleness, she grabbed Mina's shoulder and laid her flat, examining the blackened scar on the bio-molding of her chest and yanking her head to the side to pry open a panel on her neck.

Maurus wrapped his fingers around the edge of the bench and inched forward, his gaze jumping back and forth between Bennin and the boys. "Are these your friends, Rezer Bennin? I thought we'd agreed on a private transaction. What are they doing here?"

"You can't do this." The words were out of Chase's mouth before he could stop them. He pressed his lips together, cursing himself for doing what he'd expected from Parker.

Bennin looked for the first time at the two boys, and an expression of surprised disgust crossed his face in a way that would have been comical, had it not been so terrifying. "I have no idea," he said slowly. "Gorma, would you like to explain why there are two Earthan boys in our midst?"

Before the one-eyed man could answer, Parker exploded,

"We're here for him, the murdering thief!" He lunged at Maurus, but Bennin reached out and snatched Parker by the throat, wrapping his wide hand all the way around his neck. He stared at Parker as if he were a talking chicken and turned back to his henchman.

"It's, uh, we found them at the electrostruct's shop," stammered Gorma. "I thought maybe we could use them to barter back some of the items the Fleet confiscated."

Parker wheezed and scrabbled at Bennin's hand as the Rezer pulled him closer. "Barter them? Like livestock? Your stupidity confounds me, Gorma. How likely do you think the Fleet is to show us leniency if we tell them we're holding two Earthan boys as hostages?" He released Parker, who stumbled backward into Chase, gasping. "What were they doing at the electrostruct's?"

"I . . . I don't know, sir," Gorma stammered. The electrostruct cast a cautious glance back at the boys, but kept her mouth closed.

Bennin stared at his henchman for a long time, until Gorma lowered his head uncomfortably. On the other side of the room, a sequence of beeps rang out from a piece of equipment the electrostruct held over Mina. Bennin stalked across the gilded chamber, his long coat swinging at his ankles, and stood over her. "And?" he barked. "Can it be fixed?"

The electrostruct startled slightly and turned her head.

"Yes, sir. It's an easy fix, shouldn't take me more than fifteen minutes."

Bennin gazed at his new possession, his eyes glittering with greedy pleasure. "Very well." Without even looking in Maurus's direction, he said, "I'll give you twenty thousand for her, Lieutenant, and no more."

Maurus's mouth tightened. "I'll need that immediately."

"I'll bet you will." Bennin waved his hand, and one of his men left the room. "I don't know how you came across an android this fine, and I don't particularly care to know. I don't do business with strangers very often. Woe to you if this turns out to be some sort of a trick."

"It's no trick," said Maurus, his eyes flashing dangerously at Chase and Parker. "I won her, fair and square." Anger surged through Chase as Maurus spoke, as smooth and straightforward as if he were telling the truth.

Bennin had settled his stare on the two boys. The indifferent coldness in his black eyes sent a shot of fear through Chase. "Now what to do with these Earth rats. We can't just let them go—they'll run straight to the Fleet with news of this transaction."

"No, we won't—promise!" blurted Parker.

Bennin ignored him. "If my new particle disperser had arrived, I could try it out on them, but . . . no. I don't want them hanging around here that long." He turned back to

Gorma. "Take them over to the port. There's a Goxar slave trader docked there—just sell them off and get rid of them. Do not keep the profits for yourself, Gorma. You are not being rewarded for terrible judgment."

Gorma nodded and jabbed his blaster into Chase's arm. Chase didn't move. Mina was right there, right in front of them—they'd gotten too close to just give up. But what could they do, surrounded by all these men and their weapons? Maurus's dark eyes burned into him, and the expression on his face lay somewhere between a snarl and a triumphant leer. Chase tried to direct the sheer energy of his fury at Maurus, wishing he could blast the arrogance right off his face.

"You won't get—" Parker's outburst was cut short as Gorma slammed the butt of his blaster gun into his ribs. He doubled over with a gasp. Gorma raised the weapon again, and Chase grabbed Parker's arm and dragged him hobbling out of the room, where they were hustled back through the courtyard and into an alley.

"You know, you don't have to take us to the port," said Parker with a nervous laugh. "You can just let us go."

In response, Gorma fired a blast at the ground. Parker jumped aside with a shout as a shower of dirt sprayed against his legs.

"If it weren't for the money, I'd just kill you right here," the one-eyed henchman growled. "Now move!"

✳  ✳  ✳

They descended into the port, a deep pit in the middle of the Shank, by taking one of the open lifts that ran along the craggy walls. Ships shot up and down in the middle of the vast space, miraculously not hitting one another or the towering metal poles that circled the basin. An assortment of vehicles filled the floor of the port, surrounded by a stream of constant activity.

Men ran among the vehicles, wheeling containers and carrying equipment. The din of the mechanics working on parked machines was deafening. What stood out most of all, however, was the cluster of gray-uniformed Fleet soldiers standing near a building in the middle of the port, and the wide berth that everyone else was giving them.

"Hey!" Gorma shouted at a pointy-faced creature who buckled under the weight of a metal crate on its back. "What's going on over there?"

Without looking over, the creature responded in a high-pitched, oddly fluid voice. "Soldiers inspecting every vehicle. No departure without inspection."

Gorma muttered something ugly and herded the boys forward. Chase looked around frantically, trying to see a way to slip into the crowd without getting shot. Nothing good would happen if Gorma sold them to a slave trader—a *Goxar*

— 150 —

slave trader. Wasn't it the Goxar that Parker had claimed were a species to avoid? Beside him, Parker furrowed his eyebrows and watched their captor warily.

They wound their way through the maze of vehicles and stopped in front of a long, dark freighter covered in angled spikes. A metal gangway extended down from the open entrance. Gorma pounded his blaster gun against the side of the ship.

"Traders! Got a bargain for you. Two Earthan boys, five thousand for the pair."

A shadowy shape appeared inside the recesses of the entrance. Chase couldn't make out anything but a pair of eerie yellow eyes.

"Five thousand!" Gorma repeated, shoving Chase toward the dark figure. Chase tried to push back against his hand. The yellow eyes didn't blink.

From the corner of his vision, Chase saw movement and sensed something very large approaching out of the chaos of the port behind him and Gorma. The man that towered over him a second later was monstrous, at least a foot taller than Gorma, with impossibly wide shoulders and long, rangy limbs. Tawny hair fell to his shoulders in straggly knots, and a chaotic design of tattoos covered the sleek, almost feline angles of his face. A moment later, the smell hit—a rank, musky odor so overpowering Chase could practically taste it.

"Bennin?" the tattooed man barked in a coarse voice.

Gorma scowled up at him, his hand sliding down to the trigger of his blaster. "Excuse me?"

"You work for a Rezer, name of Bennin?"

Gorma's eyes narrowed. "Who wants to know?"

Chase looked back at the entrance to the freighter. The yellow Goxar eyes had vanished. He stepped back beside Parker.

For a second the tattooed man glared down at Chase. His dark irises were ringed in electric blue, wild against the inky patterns circling his eyes. He inhaled deeply, lifting his chin in a way that looked like he was smelling both Chase and Parker. Then he turned back to Gorma. "I seek the Lyolian who had business with your Rezer Bennin."

"Along with everyone else in the galaxy," said Gorma. "I know nothing."

"You lie. Everyone in the Shank knows that the Lyolian is hiding within the Ambessitari syndicate."

"Who are you working for, tracker?"

The tattooed man grabbed his shirt. "That is not your concern. Where is the Lyolian?"

Gorma's eyes flickered to the hand on his chest. "Take your paw off me, you stinking Kekilly dog." He tipped his head downward to indicate the blaster gun he'd pointed at the tattooed man's rib cage. The man's lips curled back, and a low growl rattled in his chest.

Gorma had all but forgotten the two boys standing beside him. Chase took another step backward, and before he even had the chance to glance over, Parker yanked his arm hard and took off running. Chase dashed after him, his mind a blur of panic screaming, *Run run run run.*

Behind them, Gorma shouted, and a beam of blue light flashed to their right. Parker dashed past the side of a wide ship. Chase was just behind when the blue light erupted all around him. A cold feeling spread through his chest, and he staggered a few steps as though he had been shoved.

"Parker?" he wheezed.

Parker looked back at him and almost crashed into a man wheeling a piece of equipment. "Go!" he screamed, sprinting away. Chase stumbled after him, rubbing his chest. The cold feeling passed after a few ragged breaths.

With Gorma still yelling somewhere behind them, Chase caught up with Parker and zigzagged around vehicles and scrap heaps. They turned and found themselves in a loading zone where stacks of metal crates and containers created a towering maze. As they ran between them, Chase wondered if there was a way they could climb up on them and hide.

Movement flashed by in gaps between the stacks to their

left—someone was running in the next row. Gorma's shouts still sounded somewhere behind them. Had the tattooed man joined the pursuit? Or had more of Bennin's henchmen arrived?

Chase grabbed Parker's sleeve and pulled him into a narrow space between containers on their right. They edged their way through to the next row.

"There!" Chase pointed. The tall stacks around them made it hard to see, but they could tell that this row led straight to a lift that was readying to rise off the ground. If they ran hard enough, they could jump onto the lift and make it out of the port. Chase threw himself into a sprint and had just taken his first few paces, when a figure stepped out into the middle of the row, bringing them both to a skidding halt.

It was Maurus. And he was holding a blaster gun.

Chase took a step backward. Was Maurus helping Gorma now too? Parker cursed and wheeled around to run back the other way.

"Stop!" A flash of blue exploded at their feet, and Parker fell to the ground, screaming and clutching his ankle. Chase froze and raised his hands.

Maurus flung open the door of a container. "Get in."

"I can't walk," cried Parker.

Maurus leveled the blaster at Parker's face. "Get. In."

Silently Chase helped Parker to his feet. Parker limped

over and pulled himself inside the container, which was barely two shoulder-widths across.

Maurus pulled a communicator from his belt. "It's container 249XU5," he said into the mouthpiece and paused, listening. "Yes, you'll get the money!"

Chase stopped in front of the container. "You can't do this to us. We saved your life."

Maurus responded by pressing the nozzle of his blaster against Chase's chest. His eyes blazed. Chase hoisted himself inside the container, shaking with anger, and squeezed beside Parker.

Behind them, the door clanged shut, and they were engulfed in darkness.

# CHAPTER TWELVE

The sound of frantic breathing echoed off the walls of the tiny container. In total blackness, Chase placed his hands against the door and ran his fingers along the edges, but there was no way to open it from the inside. Maurus had boxed them up like a gift for Gorma and the Goxar slave traders.

Parker groaned behind him, and there was a metallic *thung* as he hit the wall with a frustrated grunt.

"Parker, are you okay?"

"Yeah. I'm fine."

"Your foot—"

"I'm *fine*. Switch places with me, let me try the door."

Parker had just squeezed past when something struck the outside of the container with a deafening *clang*. With a squeal of metal, the container rocked wildly from side to side, throwing Chase into Parker. Someone was moving them.

"Let us out! Help!" Parker hammered at the wall as they rocked and swayed, but between the thickness of the container and the unbroken racket of the port, Chase guessed no one would hear them. He braced his arms against the walls, trying not to slide as the container continued to rock. After one last scream of scraping metal from underneath, as though they were being dragged across a floor, there was silence. He tipped his head back against the wall, his ears ringing.

A light, skittery sound danced over the top of the container, like claws being dragged over its surface. Chase stared into the darkness.

"Parker, what's a Goxar?" he whispered.

"They're Epsilon grade." Parker's voice trembled. The scraping sound meandered down the wall, behind their heads.

Chase's voice dropped lower. "But, what are they?"

"They're the most dangerous species in the galaxy. They don't live like normal people, with rules and stuff. They're crazy. And they have these super-poisonous spikes on their backs that they can tear off and throw."

"Are they going to kill us?"

"Probably. Eventually."

The skittery sound went away. Some muffled footsteps followed, and soon it was silent again. The air inside the container was getting moist and stuffy. Sweat dripped down Chase's face and pooled on his back. "We're going to suffocate before they let us out."

Parker shifted his weight beside Chase. "We've got to be able to open this." A second later the container reverberated around them as he slammed his body against the door. "Ow!"

"Let's try together." Chase reached out and found Parker's shoulders, rotating him. "Here, turn sideways. In one, two, three . . . go!"

Chase rammed his shoulder against the container door, and the jolt traveled through his body in a prickling rush as he tumbled out onto a grate floor. He sucked in a breath of clean air, about to whoop with joy, and stopped. The door of the container was still closed. He stared for a moment, confused. Frantic pounding sounded from inside.

"Chase! Where'd you go?" came Parker's muffled cry.

Stunned, Chase mutely twisted the container's exterior deadbolt and wrenched it clear. Parker pushed the door open and crawled out, staring at him. "What was that?"

"What do you mean?" asked Chase, looking around the

dim room. Stacks of long containers on the metal grate floor created narrow walkways in what had to be the cargo hold of a ship. He avoided Parker's eyes, but his mind asked the same question: *What just happened?*

"What do I mean? Chase, you got outside without opening the door! How on Taras did you do that?"

Chase ignored the question, walking toward a ladder on the wall that led to a ceiling hatch. "Let's get out of here."

"Let's get—what the heck? What aren't you telling me?"

Chase whirled around. "Nothing! Nothing! I don't know anything!" It was exactly as Parker had said—he'd passed right through a locked door. The strange incidents were starting to add up, and a question was forming at the back of Chase's mind, but he squashed it into a deep, dark corner. "I must have fallen through a weak spot or something."

"On a solid metal door? Are you joking?"

"Just let it go! We need to get out of here." Chase turned back to the ladder.

"If you can walk through doors, a whole lot of things are going to start making sense about you. What are you?"

"Shut up!" shouted Chase. He started up the rungs of the ladder, the combination of shock and defensive anger generating an electric energy that coursed under his skin. At the top of the ladder he opened a circular hatch, poking his head out into a narrow metal hallway. There was no one in sight. He pulled himself up into the hallway, and Parker joined him a second later.

"How do you think we get out of here?" Chase asked in a whisper.

Parker eyed him warily. "I don't know. Why don't you try jumping through another door?"

Chase ignored the comment, slipping down the hall. It terminated in a circular room with four closed doors and a set of metal stairs leading up. Without a word, Chase went straight for the stairs.

The stairs ended in the control cabin of the ship, fortunately empty. A curved window stretched over the consoles at the front of the cabin, with a view of the next parked vehicle in the port.

Chase turned to leave and bumped into Parker. "This isn't the way out," Chase said, grabbing Parker's arm to pull him back down the stairs. "What are you doing? We've got to go." But instead of leaving, Parker stepped forward and looked at the controls.

This ship was nothing like the Starjumper. The front consoles were covered in splats of dried food and pieces of yellowed tape, and above them hung a mess of cables and levers that dangled around a wide and well-cushioned captain's seat. The whole place had an unpleasantly stale, yeasty smell.

Parker touched the console, muttering to himself. "Hold on. I don't think this is . . ."

"Are you stupid? Let's get out of here!" Chase dragged him one step away from the console. A noisy clattering rang out in the hall below.

Parker's head snapped around. "Hide!" He pushed Chase toward the back of the cabin, where a row of low storage cabinets lined the wall. Parker yanked open two cabinet doors and climbed inside one, indicating that Chase should do the same beside him. Wedging himself among a jumble of hoses and cables, Chase hooked his fingers around the lip of the door to yank it shut. "Idiot!" he said under his breath. Now they were trapped in the control cabin—not much better than being trapped in the cargo room.

Once his eyes had adjusted to the darkness, Chase realized that the cabinet's metal door was perforated with thousands of tiny ventilation holes, giving him a hazy but decent view of the control cabin. A dark bulk passed before the storage area, blocking Chase's view. When he could see again, there was a very fat man sitting in the captain's seat. He said something in a high-pitched, whiny voice, and was answered with a yelp by someone that Chase couldn't see. Chase squinted at the captain, his heart racing. So, this was a Goxar.

The fat captain leaned back and strummed his fingers on the armrest of his seat. After a few minutes, someone else climbed the stairs into the control deck. Heavy boots stomped across the floor.

"I'm glad you decided to keep your mouth shut during the inspection," came Maurus's lilting accent. "If everything is ready, we should leave now."

Chase's eyes widened. What was Maurus doing on the slave ship? Was it not enough that he'd overseen their sale—he was catching a ride with their captors as well?

"Yes, everything fine," whined the fat man in a sulky voice. "Inspection fine." He barked something unintelligible, and a small creature skittered around out of view.

"If you're going to keep a deck hog as your only crew, you should at least keep it in a decent condition. This one looks pathetic," said Maurus. "Your ship stinks too."

"You want to take other ship?" cried the fat man.

"You want to give me back the money?"

The captain muttered to himself, interjecting an occasional incomprehensible screech. A hum vibrated through the floor as the ship powered up, and the fat man leaned forward over the consoles. Two long limbs unfolded from his back and reached up to grab at the cables dangling around his chair.

Chase gave a small gasp. These were limbs like he'd seen on the woman at the food stall—Shartese, Parker had called her. Maurus hadn't sold them to the Goxar after all. So where was he taking them?

As the ship began to lift off the ground, Maurus walked around the cabin and sat down. The small creature that Chase couldn't quite make out waddled past, and the next thing he heard was Maurus's boot skidding across the floor.

"Keep that thing away from me!" Maurus growled. "It's disgusting."

"You strap in?"

Maurus reached for the bands on his seat, and the captain reached up and pulled a long lever over his head. The engine surged, and Chase fell back inside the cabinet, pressed by the gravitational force. At nearly the exact same moment, there was a loud *BOOM*, and the entire ship shuddered violently.

"Stop! Stop!" cried Maurus. "What on Taras was that?"

The vehicle spun wildly, and a sound of tearing metal splintered the air as alarms blared from the console. Chase clutched at the walls of the cabinet, his head slamming into the cables. A robotic voice announced something about structural breach.

Chase closed his eyes and braced for impact. He had enough time to wonder whether he would feel it when they crashed or die instantly. But the spinning slowed, and they resumed a wavering course. He peered out of the cabinet.

The captain hunched over the control panels, while his back limbs wove and danced among the cables and levers.

"What was that? You told me your ship was safe!" Maurus

joined him at the console, grabbing one of his limbs. "Did your stupid Lakito leave the docking struts attached?"

A crackling voice came from the front of the cabin. "STS-40, return to port immediately,"

"Port auth, everything A-OK here," said the captain loudly. "Ship under control."

"STS-40, your trajectory is erratic and you appear to have a stowaway aboard. Please return to port for further inspection."

Maurus touched something on the console. "We need to fold out of here," he said in a low voice. "What's the damage? Can the ship handle it?"

The captain made a disgusted noise and pushed Maurus's hand away. "No stowaways, port, we clear inspection. Vehicle A-OK."

There was a pause, and a new, harder voice crackled from the console. "STS-40, this is Fleet command. Return to port now or we will be forced to take offensive action."

Maurus put his hand back on the console. "You'll face the death penalty for harboring me. If the structure is sound, you need to make the fold now."

The captain looked at the console. "Structure fine, but ship still in atmosphere."

"We're high enough that there won't be any repercussions on the surface. Do it, now."

"Your funeral, Maurus," muttered the captain. A moment later, Chase felt the air around him contract and warp as they made a fold through space. Then there was stillness, punctuated only by the sound of the captain tapping on his consoles.

Maurus collapsed into his seat. "What's the damage report? Did someone fire on us?"

The captain began to mutter something when the sound of footsteps clanging up the stairs cut him off. He whirled his immense bulk around in his chair.

Maurus leapt to his feet, pulling out his blaster as a figure stepped onto the control deck. "What are you doing here?" he cried.

Chase squinted through the vent, pressing his fingertips against the door. He couldn't make out the new arrival.

"Don't open the door to the rear storage room," came Mina's placid voice. "I had to breach the hull to get in, but the door's sealed, so it's contained for now. Just watch for resistance when we're in atmosphere."

Chase melted against the cables and hoses and closed his eyes in thanks. Finally, their first piece of luck since they'd left Parker's home on Trucon. He tried to climb out of the cabinet, when he realized that, just like in the container, there was no way to open the door from inside.

"That was you?" Maurus cried. "You tore a hole in the side of the spaceship? Were you trying to kill us?"

"You wreck my ship, stupid girl?" screeched the captain. "You sneak aboard? I throw you into space!"

"It was the only way I could board. You were already starting your ascent when I arrived at the port, so I jumped off the sidewall and caught you midair. I made as clean an entry as I could—I'll fix it for you when we land again."

Maurus groaned. "So you're the stowaway that ground control meant. How did you even know—"

"Who is this, Maurus?" the captain demanded.

"This is the android I told you about," said Maurus.

"You said you sell android!"

"I did." Maurus turned to Mina. "What have you done? How did you find me?"

"I wasn't yours to sell, so the sale was technically invalid. When the electrostruct reanimated me, I left."

"You just . . . left?"

"They put up a small fight. I may have broken someone's arm."

"And you followed me here?" asked Maurus.

"Actually, I was following him," said Mina. She turned and pointed at the storage cabinets. Chase felt a prickling flush rise in his face.

"What?"

"Come out," Mina called.

There was a pause, and then Parker's muffled voice sounded from the next cabinet. "We can't, we're locked in."

"What on Hesta's seven suns?" shouted Maurus.

Mina marched across the cabin and yanked open both cabinet doors. Parker tumbled out and jumped to his feet. Chase crept out of the cabinet, looking around at the other occupants of the cabin. The captain stared at his new passengers with disgust. A small, piggish creature with greasy pink skin and perky, brown-crusted ears huddled at his side.

"How did you get out of the cargo hold?" Maurus asked, shoving his hand through his hair.

"You mean out of the container where you left us to suffocate?" Parker stormed across the cabin. "Right after you locked us up to be sold to slave traders?"

"Sold to—I was trying to get you out of there!" Maurus looked like he wanted to throttle Parker. "I locked you in the container to get you past inspection, and then I told Vo which one to grab before hiding myself on his ship."

"Where are you taking us?" Chase asked.

"This ship's going to Lyolia."

"What? Why are you taking us there?" shouted Parker.

"*I'm* going there—you're just along for the ride! Would you rather have gone with the Goxar? I hear it's a fine life aboard their slave ships, the week or two that you'd have left!"

"So you're escaping to your homeworld now, you coward?" asked Parker.

With a shout of rage, Maurus took a swing at him, clipping him in the chin. Before Parker could strike his own blow, Mina grabbed each of them by the elbow and squeezed hard enough to make them both gasp.

Maurus tugged in vain at Mina's iron grip. His arrogant eyes and fierce scowl suddenly seemed less vicious. Had he really admitted to saving them?

Vo sat back in his chair as he watched the scene, and now smacked his fleshy lips and narrowed his eyes. "I understand you, Maurus. You most-wanted man in the universe, so you kidnap two Earthan boys to take with you back to your homeworld. Boys make good collateral, maybe? You owe me extra now for more passenger."

Of course. Maurus hadn't saved them out of the goodness of his heart. He'd taken them along as a sort of human shield. The Fleet wouldn't attack if they knew he had children on board.

Vo leaned forward, jowls wobbling eagerly, and reached out with one of his long bronze limbs to take Maurus by the chin. "But you stupid too," he sang. "You greedy. You sell android to most dangerous man on Qesaris for big money, and then have her return to you. Now you have Rezer Bennin's money *and* Rezer Bennin's android. You must have real death wish!" A smug smile spread across his face, and he rubbed his overhanging belly with his humanoid arms. The pig-like creature jumped up and down in excitement.

Maurus gritted his teeth, still yanking against Mina's grip. "I didn't plan it like that. None of this was supposed to happen!"

"Maybe I take you back to Rezer Bennin, see if you can sell android a second time, pay for extra passengers?"

A beep sounded from the console. Still chuckling, Vo glanced at the screens. The folds of his fat face drew together in a sudden frown, and without another word he turned to the controls.

"What is it?" asked Maurus. The alarm in his voice sent a shiver down Chase's back.

"Someone hailing us," Vo muttered. "Not good, not good."

"Who is it?" Mina released Maurus and Parker and joined Vo at the consoles.

"Someone's followed us. Get us out of here," Maurus hissed.

The center panel of the windshield shimmered and became a screen showing the grizzled face of a gray-haired man with pitted cheeks. Maurus threw himself against the side of the cabin, his eyes locked on the screen. Out of instinct, Chase did the same. He didn't know who the man was, but he knew the fact that he was contacting them was bad.

"Salutations, this is Captain Lionel Lennard, commander of the *IFF Kuyddestor*," said the man on the screen in an oily drawl. "Prepare to surrender your vessel."

# CHAPTER THIRTEEN

"We are circling you from a distance of two parsecs, and we have the entire nuclear capacity of our starship aimed directly at your vessel. If you do not surrender immediately, you and everyone on board your ship will be destroyed." Captain Lennard's cold eyes pierced the screen, and although Chase knew he was outside the frame of view, he still felt like the Fleet captain was staring directly at him.

Vo raised his arms from the console, his fat chin trembling. "I not do nothing. Just commerce vessel."

"The entire Federal Fleet knows that you are harboring the galaxy's most-wanted fugitive. More ships will arrive in just a few minutes. Hand over Lieutenant Maurus now, and I'll make sure you live."

While Lennard spoke, Maurus dropped to his knees and crawled up to the control console. He stayed just out of sight as he squeezed in front of Vo and started entering information on the screens.

Parker leaned toward Chase and whispered, "We have to turn him in." Chase frowned and shook his head. He wanted nothing to do with the Fleet to begin with, but something in his gut told him they needed to stay far away from Captain Lennard.

Vo did an admirable job of keeping his face impassive as he kicked at Maurus in front of him. "I know not what you talk about, Captain. Only myself and Lakito deckhand on board."

Captain Lennard shrugged. "If that's how you choose to play it, then prepare to meet your maker. In five, four, three, two—"

Parker took a step toward the screen, and Chase grabbed a handful of his shirt.

"Okay, okay!" Vo screeched. "Surrender!"

Maurus leapt up and yanked down on one of the levers surrounding the captain's chair. With a savage twist, the air collapsed around Chase, but this wasn't like any other fold he'd experienced. Just as the compressed feeling started to fade, it amped up again, over and over in waves. There was a tumbling sensation, as if he were falling down a spiraling hole. Bright colors and black abysses flashed through his vision, and he was paralyzed, unable to grab his whirling head or reach out for help.

When it finally stopped, everyone was sprawled on the floor except for Vo, who gripped the cables around him with every limb available. Chase rolled onto his side, pressing his hands against his pounding temples.

"Never touch my controls again!" Vo barked. "I kill you!"

"What was that?" moaned Parker.

Maurus was already on his feet. "Kathadaxus maneuver. That'll buy us five minutes, tops. We need to turn off the trackers and fold once more so he can't follow us."

"Impossible," said Vo. "With no trackers we fold into solid object. Everybody die!"

"We have to take the risk, just this once. The odds of catastrophic fold are infinitesimal."

"Odds of catastrophic death high! Deal over, Maurus. Take back your money. I turn you in."

"It's too late for that, Vo. What do you think, they're just going to let you go after this? I saw what you're carrying in the cargo hold—they're not going to let an annirad missile smuggler just slip through their hands."

Vo's eyes rolled wildly in his head. "Stupid human!" he raged. "You ruin me!" Heaving and slobbering a little at the corners of his mouth, Vo glanced around the cabin. "Have to leave now! I eject you into space!"

"Vo, you're outnumbered," said Maurus. "And if you try

to touch any of us, there's a very powerful android here who will stop you dead in your tracks."

"I'm here to protect the boys, not you," said Mina flatly.

Maurus glanced at Mina with a small frown. "We're running out of time. Turn off your trackers, make the fold."

Vo muttered to himself in a high, angry voice and turned back to his console. He folded his humanoid arms. "No."

"Well then—" Maurus reached toward his belt and pulled out a handblaster. "I'll take out your trackers with this."

Vo turned in his seat and stared at Maurus with his mouth slightly ajar, an expression of astounded fury crinkling his delicate pointy nose. "You dare . . ." He turned his beady gaze on Chase, who stood just behind Maurus.

Suddenly two of his long back limbs shot out and snatched both Chase and Parker by the necks, dragging them across the cabin. Chase wrenched free with a terrible burning, tingling sensation, but beside him Parker screamed as the pincer-like device on the end of Vo's limb clamped down on his shoulder.

"Let him go!" shouted Maurus. Another of Vo's long limbs came up from behind and cracked him in the elbow, sending his handblaster skidding across the cabin floor. Vo's pig-like crewman darted forward to grab the weapon, but Mina kicked the creature aside as she grabbed the limb attached to Parker's shoulder. There was a cracking sound, and with an ear-piercing shriek Vo released his hold.

Chase dove across the floor and grabbed the handblaster. On his knees, he whirled around, pointing the surprisingly light weapon at the ship's captain. Maurus took a step toward him.

"Very good, Corbin, now just give the weapon back to me," he said softly. He reached out to take it.

Panicking, Chase pointed the blaster at him.

"No!" Maurus shouted.

Vo's long limb was already traveling through the air toward the weapon. Chase swung the weapon back at him, his heart pounding. Vo froze in place.

Maurus raised his hands. "You don't have to give the blaster to me. But you have to take out the trackers, or Captain Lennard will catch up with us and we'll all die. Just blast that comm box." He pointed at a metal box on the corner of the console.

"Don't listen to Maurus, he's lying!" shouted Parker. "He wrecked Trucon, he destroyed my home! Shoot him!"

"Kill him," barked Vo. "He die, trouble gone."

Maurus's dark, intense eyes locked on to Chase, holding his gaze. "Whatever you think I am doesn't matter. Just think of yourself. I know Captain Lennard, and he is a vicious, brutal man. Even if I agree to go easily, he'll kill everyone on this ship just to cover his tracks."

Chase gripped the weapon tightly, paralyzed by the decision. If Maurus really was responsible for the destruction of Trucon, he was probably lying now to save his own skin. Based on the other things he'd done—stealing Mina, leaving Chase and Parker stranded—it was entirely probable that he was just trying to trick Chase into letting him escape.

But he'd also saved them from being sold into slavery, and probably saved their lives. If he was telling the truth about Captain Lennard and Chase ignored him, it would be a fatal mistake.

"Just shoot him!" screamed Parker. "He's only trying to save himself!"

"Think of your friends! Save their lives!" yelled Maurus. "Do it now, you're almost out of time!"

Even if Captain Lennard let them live, they would end up in the hands of the Fleet. It was better to travel with the devil they knew than the devil they didn't.

Chase raised the weapon and pulled the trigger. The comm box exploded into black, twisted metal.

Vo screeched.

"You jerk!" Parker stormed across the room and tried to take a swing at Chase's face. Dodging him, Chase tripped backward, the blaster falling from his hand with a clatter.

The little pig-like creature darted forward to grab the weapon and scuttled back behind Vo's seat.

"Fold!" called Maurus from the console, where he had already shoved Vo out of the way. The warping air caught Chase by surprise, and he fell to his knees as the ship jumped through space.

Parker slid down the wall beside him. "I hate you. You're as much a traitor as he is."

Chase didn't answer. He was already second-guessing his choice. By choosing to travel with the most-wanted man in the universe and run from the Fleet, had he made them criminals now too?

"We're safe," said Maurus. "Vo, start a course for Lyolia." Vo bared his teeth and hissed, cradling the limb Mina had squeezed. "Do it. And tell your deck hog to give me back my sidearm as well."

Raising his humanoid limbs in indignation, Vo barked an order, and the blaster slid out from under his seat. Maurus picked up the weapon and examined it. "He's removed the munitions chamber. This is useless!" Vo ignored him, and Maurus holstered the weapon with a frown and returned to his seat near the console.

Parker glared at the back of Maurus's head. "You're just going to sit there like everything's fine, aren't you?" he asked. "We all know what you did. You killed thousands of

people—you ruined an entire *world*. For what, Lyolian poli-
tics? For the stupid Karsha Ven?"

Maurus whipped around. "You believe everything you
see on the news, do you?" He shook his head. "Do you think
I'd bother helping two stupid Earthan boys if I'd just killed
thousands? I'm not a traitor. I serve the Fleet."

"Oh really?" countered Parker. "Because I'm pretty sure
that was the Fleet who just tried to kill you. If you're so innocent, why are you running away to your homeworld
instead of staying to defend yourself?"

A shadow crossed Maurus's face. "I'm protecting myself,"
he muttered, turning back to watch Vo's movements at the
console.

Again Chase wondered if he had made the wrong choice
by helping Maurus escape the Fleet. He looked up at Mina.
"Can you contact Asa now?"

She shook her head. "Not since you shot the trackers.
That box held the entire communication system for the ship,
so you've left us unable to contact anyone."

Chase's heart sank. "I did?" He could feel Parker's angry
eyes boring into the side of his head.

"No communications, even if emergency happen," added
Vo over his shoulder. "Better hope ship not break down."

"I'm sure there's a distress beacon in your escape shuttle
that we can activate, if need be," said Maurus. Vo made a

rude noise and turned back to the console. "You can communicate with your people as soon as we reach Lyolia, Corbin."

"We'll figure it out," said Mina. "And his name is Chase."

"What?" Maurus glanced back, frowning.

"His name isn't Corbin."

Maurus stared at Chase for a moment. "Whatever. Take them down to the bunkroom and keep them out of my way."

"I should probably stay up here and help you navigate," Mina said. "With the trackers down, the ship will be more vulnerable."

Maurus shook his head. "We'll be fine. Vo's not going to leave the control deck because he's afraid we'll lock him in his cabin, so I'll stay here to make sure he takes us to the right place."

Mina stepped beside Parker, who was still sitting on the floor. "Come on, let's go downstairs," she told him. Chase thought Parker might fight to stay on the control deck, but he jumped to his feet and charged straight to the exit.

Chase followed him down to the back of the ship, past the cargo room they'd escaped from. At the end of the hall was a cluttered bunkroom that smelled like sour old sweat. Six bunks lined one wall, and a rickety table and chairs stood opposite them. The back of the bunkroom was filled with stacked boxes that Parker immediately began to search through.

Chase pulled out a chair and sat, putting his head in his hands. He spoke at the floor. "I'm sorry. I didn't have any better choice. And he did save us from getting sold to those slave traders."

"It's great, yay, we're saved," muttered Parker. "We're traveling with a mass murderer who's wanted by every government in the galaxy, and thanks to you, we have no way to contact anyone if we need help. I feel safe, don't you?"

"That's not fair," said Chase. "We don't know if he had anything to do with Trucon."

Parker looked up at him with narrowed eyes. "You're right. I don't know. Actually, I don't know much of anything right now. I don't know where I'm going, or where Asa is. I don't know who decided it would be a good idea to set my homeworld on fire. And I sure as shooting stars don't know what you are."

The distrustful look on Parker's face sent a cold feeling into the pit of Chase's stomach. "I told you, I don't know how I got out of the container. Do you really think I'd lie about that?"

"I don't know what I think anymore." Parker slid one stack of boxes out of the way and started on the next row. "All I've got is my gut, and my gut tells me that you are not normal, and that Lyolians are huge liars who can never be trusted."

He slammed the box he was holding onto the floor. "I can't believe you sided with him!"

"Dr. Silvestri told us not to go to the Fleet under any circumstances."

"I don't think Dr. Silvestri expected any of this to happen, do you?" Parker shouted. He threw a box lid against the wall, making Chase flinch. "Helping Maurus escape was the stupidest thing you could have done!"

Mina walked through the bunkroom door. "Calm down, Parker."

"And you!" Parker shouted at her. "You're supposed to protect me. Why are you going along with this? You could have taken them both down before they had a chance! We could take over the ship and go wherever we want."

Mina shook her head. "It's Vo's ship, and we'll go where he takes us. Unless your life is directly threatened, mutiny is a crime with very severe punishments." She took a seat at the table. "You'd better settle in. It's going to take at least two weeks to get to Lyolia. With the trackers gone, it's too unsafe to make any more folds."

"Stupid machine!" Parker cursed in frustration, kicking a box. He turned back to Chase. "This is all your fault. If anything bad happens, it's on you."

Too beaten down by doubt to challenge Parker, Chase lowered his head again and nodded.

# CHAPTER FOURTEEN

Chase had been walking in pointless circles around the lower deck of the ship for half an hour, trying to ignore the growling in his stomach. After four very long days aboard Vo's ship, he regretted his decision to travel with Maurus more than ever. The ship was boring, it stank, and occasionally a worrying rattle echoed from deep within the walls. But worse yet was the constant, gnawing hunger. As a smuggler, Vo usually hopped from planet to planet, trading and resupplying at each stop. After Chase destroyed the trackers, it didn't take long to realize there wasn't enough food stocked on the ship for a two-week voyage with five hungry mouths— not including Mina, who functioned on bimonthly doses of lithium oil.

He returned to his cabin, restless. Parker was lying in the lower bunk, flipping through a stack of brochures he'd found in one of the boxes.

"Hey, you want to play a card game?" Chase asked, hoping to distract himself from daydreams about a closet full of delicious scrappies.

Parker glanced up and shook his head. Although he didn't seem angry anymore, his behavior had shifted. He was quiet and moody, and on several occasions, Chase caught Parker watching him with that same guarded expression he'd worn after Chase's unexplained escape from the cargo container. Mostly Parker kept to himself, reading whatever he could get his hands on or studying the contents of the engine room.

Chase crossed the room and looked at a couple of the brochures Parker had tossed on the floor, but he couldn't read the language they were written in. "I'm starving," he muttered.

Parker cocked an eye at him. "Good luck getting something to eat."

In his role as jack-of-all-trades, Vo's tiny deckhand, a creature called a Lakito who answered to the name Ferkel, also served as the ship's cook. The disgusting little thing ruled over the ship's low food reserves with an iron fist, doling out skimpy meals at irregular intervals. Both Chase and Parker were quick to complain about what Parker called "orphanage gruel," but Mina refused to interfere after she determined that Ferkel's watery betaprotein stews met the minimum caloric requirement for teenage boys.

Hearing a noise outside the bunkroom, Chase looked down the hall and caught a glimpse of Ferkel scrambling up the stairs to the control deck. He'd left the door to the mess room wide-open. Seeing the one chance he might have for days, Chase dashed from the bunkroom to the small kitchen. Yanking open cabinets, he was disheartened to see that the first three were already empty. Two skinny boxes sat in the fourth cabinet, with names he didn't recognize: Mapoflakes and Qorn Qrisps. He reached for the shiny red Mapoflakes box.

"Not that one." Parker stood behind him, his eyes glittering with hunger. "Grab the Qrisps."

With a guilty thrill, Chase ran back to the bunkroom, the Qrisps tucked under his arm. As he closed the door behind them, Parker grabbed the box from him and tore it open, showering a heap of crumbly golden triangles on the table. "Dinnertime," he said with a grin.

Chase grinned back, as happy to see a glimmer of the old Parker as he was about the delightfully greasy pile of snacks in front of them. His stomach roared with approval as they shoveled the crackers in their mouths by the double-handful, chewing as fast as possible.

An outraged squeal from down the hall announced that their theft had been noticed. A second later Ferkel charged into the room, scrambling onto a chair and diving across the table. Crackers flew everywhere.

"We're hungry!" bellowed Chase, snatching up loose crackers.

"Hey! Give those back!" Parker tried to push Ferkel away, and the little creature took a swipe at him, leaving a long scratch down Parker's forearm. "What the—ouch!"

"What's going on in here?" Maurus stood in the doorway, haggard and sunken-eyed. Seeing Parker's arm, he grabbed Ferkel by the nape of the neck and lifted him off the table. "Do I need to lock you in a closet?"

Kicking wildly, Ferkel answered with a stream of indignant squeals. Although it sounded like gibberish to Chase, Maurus must have understood at least some of it, because he waved his hand dismissively.

"No, we aren't going to run out of food. One box of crackers won't make a difference, and don't say otherwise because I've seen the secret stash of junk Vo's hiding upstairs." He set Ferkel back on the floor, where the creature flared his frilled nostrils and hacked a wad of brown spit at his boots. Maurus swung his foot, more a warning than an attempt to actually kick Ferkel, but the Lakito had already scampered from the room. "And bring me a pot of hot caff," Maurus shouted after him.

With a cautious glance at the boys, Maurus sank into a chair and absently stuffed a few crackers in his mouth. "Have a seat," he said, gesturing at the other chairs. His eyes were bloodshot, and his hair hung loose and stringy around his face. Chase took the seat across from him, scraping up another handful of crackers as he did. After a moment's hesitation, Parker joined them.

"How bad did he get you?" Maurus asked, indicating the fiery scratches on Parker's arm.

Parker wiped his hand over the marks. "It's nothing."

"You both doing okay down here? Other than the food?"

Chase shrugged. "Just kinda bored." Parker swept most of the remaining crackers into a pile on his side of the table, his expression daring Maurus to say something about it.

Maurus rubbed his eyes for a long time and ran his hand through his hair. "I wish we could drop you off somewhere, but it's just not..." He trailed off and took a deep breath. "You'll be well taken care of when we get to my people. They'll help you on your way."

Maurus looked Chase in the eyes as he said this, his expression weary but earnest. Chase felt a strong urge to share their whole story with him—how he'd shown up on Parker's lawn, how they'd been chased by the Fleet, even the part about the identical microchips that Parker didn't know about. But that seemed like a good way of making sure that Parker would never speak to him again, so he just nodded acknowledgment.

Ferkel waddled back into the bunkroom holding a metal carafe that was nearly half his size. He hoisted it onto the table and left, returning a few moments later to slam a mug and a bowl of sugar alongside it. Maurus poured a stream of dark, steaming liquid into the mug.

"At least it looks like we might be able to trim a day off our original schedule." He scooped generously from the sugar bowl and gave his drink a quick stir. "I've been running some upgrade processes on the ship's flight software."

Parker glanced at him and lowered his eyes back to his cracker pile. "There's a generator in the engine room that looks like it could use a software patch. Its cycles are running too high."

Maurus arched his eyebrows in surprise. "Really? That's good to know. I'll take a look at it."

"I can do it," muttered Parker.

Maurus hesitated. "Maybe we can look at it together." He added another two scoops of sugar to his drink.

"You already added sugar," Chase pointed out.

"I like things sweet." Maurus lifted the mug to his face and inhaled the drink's malty aroma.

Parker snorted. "Like all Lyolians."

Maurus shook his head and took a big gulp. His eyes

bugged out as he swallowed, and his face twisted in a horrible grimace. "Ahhhh!" he gagged, slamming the mug on the table. For a terrified heartbeat, Chase thought Ferkel had poisoned Maurus, but Maurus just leaned over the floor and spat. When he sat back up, he was making a disgusted face that lay somewhere between hideous and hilarious.

Maurus grabbed the half-full mug and jumped to his feet, running from the bunkroom as he shouted, "You'd better hide, little hog!" Ferkel's terrified squeals were muffled behind a closed door. "Open up! Open up and give me a bottle of water right now!"

Chase stared at Parker. "What just happened?"

Parker leaned across the table to dip his finger in the sugar bowl and pressed his fingertip to his tongue. A smile forced its way across his face, and he bit his lips together trying to stop it.

Chase tasted the sugar as well and winced at the unexpected flavor. "Ugh, it's salt!"

Maurus came back into the room, chugging from a rubber canteen. He paused to take a deep breath. "Oh, this's funny, is it?"

Chase glanced at the contorted expression on Parker's face, and when their eyes met, the boys burst out laughing. Maurus sank back into his chair. "I'm going to kill that little bugger." He pushed his hair off his face again and squeezed his temples, closing his eyes. He smiled a little and shook his head as their laughter rose and fell in giddy, uncontrollable bursts.

After several tries Chase managed to get his voice under control. "I'm sorry. You look really tired," he finally said.

Maurus nodded. "I am."

Calculating backward, Chase realized that Maurus probably hadn't slept since they'd picked him up over Mircona. Did being unconscious count as sleep? "Why don't you take a nap?"

Maurus shook his head. "Can't afford to. I have to keep an eye on Vo."

"Mina said she'd help you navigate." Chase glanced at Parker as he spoke, but Parker had leaned back in his chair and was staring into the distance, seeming deep in thought. If he could get Maurus to stay in the bunkroom and keep Parker from leaving it, he'd get a chance to talk with Mina in relative privacy.

Maurus gave Chase a doubtful look. "I don't think it's a good idea for me to leave the control deck for more than a hot caff..." He glanced at the mug and scowled. "A water break."

"Just sleep a couple hours. You look like you're about to drop dead."

Maurus glanced longingly at the empty bunks. "A couple

hours is pretty tempting. And, to be honest, I think I'm start-ing to hallucinate a bit." He stood up, rolling and cracking his neck. "I'll tell Mina I'm taking a break."

"I'll do that for you. Just go lie down."

Maurus glanced at him for a second and shrugged. "Thanks." He dropped heavily onto one of the lower bunks, and within two breaths he was asleep.

Chase stood, silently hoping that Parker wouldn't want to come with him to the control deck. "So, I'll go talk to Mina."

Parker glanced up and nodded but made no move to join him. Breathing a sigh of thanks, Chase left the bunkroom.

Mina was at the console piloting the ship by herself. Vo dozed beside her in his crusty captain's chair, his chin wet with saliva. Based on the chair's heavy padding and general disgustingness, Chase wondered if Vo ever left his seat even when he didn't have four stowaways aboard.

"How are you?" Mina asked.

"Okay. Maurus is taking a nap."

"I heard." Chase frowned at her, and she smiled. "My hearing sensors are very sensitive. It's a small ship."

Chase gazed out through the windshield at the light-streaked universe before them, slightly stunned as always at the unfathomable enormousness of it. "Do you think Asa's out there somewhere looking for Parker?"

Mina adjusted a slider on the control panel. "I'm not authorized to talk about Asa with you."

He stared at her. "Are you serious? Why not? Who is he?"

Mina didn't answer. It was true, Chase realized, that she'd only spoken of Asa to Dr. Silvestri or Parker, never directly to Chase. This put a kink in his plans. He racked his mind for ways to get information about Asa without directly asking about him.

"Who do you think made my microchip?"

"I never saw your microchip."

"But Dr. Silvestri said . . . ," he began, trailing off so she could finish the sentence. She didn't take the bait.

Chase had been thinking about Asa a lot in the past four days. Maybe Asa designed his microchip like Dr. Silvestri said, but there was no guarantee their connection went any further than that. At first Chase had suspected he was probably a ward of Asa's, like Parker, living in a different compound that had been attacked. But the little girl he'd seen didn't seem to know Asa, and she definitely knew Chase. Or at least she knew the Chase who she claimed was dead.

Chase looked down at his hands. The question driving him crazy ever since he'd seen the girl was whether he was actually a clone of some other, dead Chase. That would explain the lack of memory, but not the blaster wound or the microchip with the name Chase Garrety on it. The micro-chip that Asa Kaplan may or may not have made. All his questions just kept feeding back into one another, and think-ing about them too hard made him feel like he was caught in a maze.

In his encounter with the Zinnjerha on Trucon, he re-called how he'd been unharmed after the creatures had slashed at him with their razor-edged pincers. He'd felt his skin being cut—hadn't he? In retrospect, he was no longer sure. And when the girl attacked him in the bathroom on Qesaris, how had she managed to stab him without leaving a mark? She looked crazy. Maybe she was just an escaped mental patient who'd overheard his name from Parker.

But even if he wasn't sure about the attacks he'd sur-vived, Chase could not deny his escape from the metal con-tainer. He'd simply passed right through the door. That wasn't normal. He wasn't normal. But what was he?

Feigning interest in the control console, Chase glanced at Mina's still face. "Have you ever heard of people running through walls?"

"Running through walls? That's called phasing."

"So there are people who can do that?"

Mina shook her head. "No, it's just a hypothetical ability invented by Earthan storytellers."

"But maybe on another planet there are people who could?"

Mina was still for a moment. "Every species has its own unique abilities. The Falasians have the most advanced extrasensory skills—part of their communication is a form of telepathy. But phasing just doesn't exist. Why are you asking this?"

Chase barely heard her question as he tried to figure out how to express his next idea. "What about, um, man-made people? Could they do phasing?"

"You mean androids?" Mina smiled. "The physics involved in creating a phasing android would be nearly impossible. It would have to be capable of a very sophisticated kind of self-controlled teleportation. Humankind has mastered teleportation for transportation uses, but the only further development that's come from that invention is weapons research."

"Teleportation weapons?"

"Annihilation weapons. Teleportation breaks things up at a particulate level and puts them back together. Particle dispersers skip the second step."

Chase frowned, trying to visualize this. "What do you mean?"

"A particle disperser can vaporize things—people, buildings.

They're illegal." Mina paused. "These are strange questions, Chase. Is there a reason why you're asking them?"

"Just curious," he said quickly. He couldn't be a phasing android—he knew from his passage through the container that he wasn't controlling anything. As the days passed and the memory lost its sharp edges, he began to wonder whether that was actually what had happened.

Chase padded back through the metal hallway to the bunkroom. Maurus had passed out hard in one of the bunks, and Parker had also fallen asleep, another brochure lying half on his face. Chase climbed into his own bunk, which smelled musty and sour but was otherwise comfortable, and drifted off to an uneasy sleep.

✳ ✳ ✳

Out of nowhere, a terrible rumbling tore through the ship.

Chase sat up in his bed, adrenaline flooding his veins. The walls shuddered as if the ship were coming apart. The door to the bunkroom was open, and Maurus was already gone. Shouts echoed down from the control cabin. Parker was headed to the bunkroom door to look out by the time Chase had jumped down from his bunk.

Maurus ran down the hall at them, wild terror on his face. "Stay in there!" he shouted as he ran. "Shut the door and do not come out!" He grabbed the door and slammed it in their faces.

The ship still shook. "What's going on?" Chase grabbed the bed frame to hold himself upright. "Did the Fleet find us?"

Parker's face had gone pale.

Maurus's shouts came through the door. "We need to build a barricade! No, find something heavier!"

"We can help," said Parker, opening the door again. This time it was Mina who pushed them to the back of the room.

"Stay in here, stay away from the door," she ordered.

"But we can—" Parker began to say, but she had already slammed the door shut again.

They stood near the back of the bunkroom. Outside in the hall, footsteps pounded past their door along with the metallic scraping of something heavy being dragged. "Where did you put the munitions chamber?" Maurus yelled over Ferkel's panicked squeals.

Finally the ship stopped shaking, and for a moment there was silence.

Chase took a deep, shaky breath. In a whisper, he asked, "What's hap—"

An explosion rattled the walls, and Chase fell to one knee with a gasp. Another loud blast, and then another followed it. He tried to brace himself on the floor, and Parker kneeled beside him. Had the Fleet already found them?

Maurus's and Vo's shouts were barely audible over the explosions.

"Halt!" came Maurus's voice. "I am an officer of the Intergalactic Federal Fleet, and I have conscripted this vessel. You are trespassing illegally on IFF property!"

Chase looked at Parker and frowned. Why would Maurus say this if it was the Fleet that was trying to board?

A sound like a dozen saws being dragged over a metal edge echoed down the hallway.

"Oh lords," gasped Parker, his gray eyes huge.

"What was that?" The look on Parker's face frightened Chase more than the noises in the hall.

"Leave this vessel immediately!" yelled Maurus. "If you take one more step, I will be forced to fire!"

There was a pause, and then a jagged series of blasts reverberated through the ship. Chase held his hands over his head, pressing his forehead against the floor, as fear turned his stomach inside out. Someone was blowing up the ship. They were all going to get flung out into space to die.

When the blasts finally stopped, the ship was miraculously still intact. A steady hiss and a few isolated clatters sounded in the hallway. Where was Maurus's voice? Where was Mina?

A footstep sounded outside the bunkroom. The handle turned, and the door swung open.

The thick metal snout of a powerful-looking weapon appeared at the edge of the door frame, and the creature that cautiously appeared after it was unlike any Chase had seen before. A red-orange, scaly reptilian face peered at them with gleaming yellow eyes. Chase had seen eyes like these before, peering out of a dark ship in the Shank port.

This was a Goxar.

There was nowhere to hide, nowhere to run—they were trapped in the tiny bunkroom. Chase steeled himself to fight, but his body felt frozen with terror. The Goxar took a step toward them and waved its weapon, saying in a barely understandable growl, *"We take."*

Chase surprised himself by answering, "No."

The Goxar cocked its head like a dog, and took a few shuffling steps forward until it had his weapon pointed directly at Parker's head. *"We take,"* it repeated in a strange, rattling voice. Silent tears streamed down Parker's face.

Parker didn't move and neither did Chase, though more out of fear than defiance. The creature swung its weapon and cracked Parker in the back of the head. *"Go!"*

Chase staggered to his feet, feeling strangely out of body, and helped Parker up. This wasn't real, couldn't be—he was just having a vivid nightmare. He wasn't sure if his wobbly legs would carry him, but he managed to walk out to the hallway, where another Goxar manned the doorway of the storage room that Mina had sealed off after her unconventional entry. Blackened holes smoldered in the hallway walls, and sheets of metal were torn away like peeling wallpaper. Maurus and Mina were nowhere in sight.

The Goxar shoved its weapon into Parker's back, sending him stumbling forward into the storage room. The one at the door watched them with flat reptilian eyes. More of the scaly creatures carried freight boxes from Vo's ship through a ragged hole into a connecting portal into their ship.

Their captor motioned toward the portal, seeming to indicate that they should board his ship.

"No, no, please," said Parker, backing up against the wall. The creature shouted something incomprehensible and pointed its weapon at them.

A blur of motion streaked across the room, and their captor flew backward, landing on the floor with Mina hugging it in a headlock. The Goxar at the door raised its weapon and fired multiple blasts, hitting its accomplice while Mina crouched behind the limp body, using it as a shield.

The Goxar stopped shooting and grabbed both Chase and Parker by the wrists to pull them through the portal. With a sharp tingling sensation, Chase yanked his wrist right through its grasp and seized Parker's other arm, pulling him back. With its free hand, the Goxar lifted the weapon hanging from its shoulder and pointed it at Parker.

"Mina!" Parker screamed.

In a flash she was there, snatching away the Goxar's weapon. She turned it on the scaly creature, and it released Parker with a menacing hiss and backed into the portal to its ship.

Just as the portal was closing, the Goxar reached back over its shoulder and threw something at Parker. A glittering shape flew across the room. Without a thought, Chase leapt in its path, tensing up against expected pain that never came.

He looked down and laughed, giddy with relief. The Goxar had missed. The door to its ship sealed with a pneumatic hiss.

"Urgh," moaned Parker.

Chase turned and gasped. Sticking out of Parker's chest was a spike that the Goxar had pulled from its back. Parker stared at the red-and-black prong jutting from his skin, and looked up at Chase with a confused expression. He staggered back against the wall. "Oh lords," he mumbled.

"No, no!" Chase cried, running to his side. It was impossible—he was directly in front of Parker. The spike should have hit him. Mina caught Parker as he slid down the wall and lowered him gently to the floor. Foamy spittle bubbled from his lips. His eyes rolled back into his head, and he began to tremble.

"What's happening to him?" Chase asked.

"You have to get out of here," came a cracked voice from the outer hallway. Maurus stood just outside the cargo hold, clutching the door frame for support. Half his face was covered in blood. "They're breaking the airlock—we have to seal this room off. Come on!"

Mina gathered Parker into her arms and carried him past Maurus, who slammed the door shut after Chase had passed. The ship rocked around them and deafening metallic squeals filled the air. Mina kicked down a mattress that lay angled against the wall and laid Parker on it. He screamed and thrashed as she worked the thorny spike out of his skin and tore open his shirt to examine the wound.

"I don't know how it happened," Chase said. "I tried to block it."

Maurus placed a hand on his shoulder. "It's okay, Chase, you tried."

Mina glanced up at him briefly, and the look she gave him told him she'd seen what really happened. He dropped his gaze, feeling almost ashamed.

"Will he be okay?" Chase asked, gripping the edge of the mattress.

Mina shook her head. "It's Goxar poison—his blood has to

be cleaned. He'll die unless we can get him to a medical facility. How fast can we get to the next colony?"

"They tore up the energy core." Maurus leaned against the wall and slid to the floor. "We won't be able to get the engine functional for days—this ship's as good as dead." He put his hand on his forehead, leaving the next sentence unspoken: *And so is Parker.*

"Where is Vo?" Mina asked.

"That coward is hiding out on the control deck."

She climbed up the ladder, leaving Parker trembling on the mattress. With a groan of effort, Maurus stumbled to his feet and went after her.

Chase kneeled beside Parker. "I'm so sorry," he said. "I tried to block it."

Parker's eyes rolled around in their sockets, but he managed to look at Chase for a moment. Through agonized gasps, he uttered, "Why?" He closed his eyes as tremors racked his body.

The words *I don't know* hovered at Chase's lips, and stopped there. "Because you're my friend." Guilt swamped him like a tidal wave. What good was the ability to jump through doors and evade injury, if he couldn't protect anyone who mattered?

Parker stared at him a second longer and opened his mouth like he was going to answer, but his eyes fluttered closed. Shouting from the cabin room drew Chase's attention, and he climbed the stairs and crept into the control cabin.

Vo sat in the captain's chair facing Mina, who stood squared for a face-off.

"He needs to get to a medical facility in the next twenty-four hours," she said.

Vo laughed viciously. "Oh no, not going to happen. Ship ruined. And no comms." He glared at Maurus and Chase.

"But you have an escape shuttle," said Mina. "You'll give us that." She took a step toward his chair.

Vo reached into the folds of his baggy clothing and withdrew a short blaster rifle.

"Where was that weapon when we were fighting off the Goxar, you self-serving coward!" shouted Maurus. "You wouldn't even give me the munitions chamber for my own weapon. I confronted them with an empty chamber!"

Vo barely glanced at Maurus, brandishing his weapon at Mina. She stood very still, but Chase could see that her eyes were calculating the situation and her odds.

"Vo, please—put the weapon down," said Maurus. "Just let them take the shuttle."

"No. What if Vo need to escape?"

"A child's life is at stake," Maurus pleaded.

"Earthan child, who care? Millions of Earthan child in universe, one less not matter. Goxar already take Ferkel, probably eat him for dinner." Vo shrugged. "More where he came from."

"I can't control what this android will do to you if you don't let her leave your ship."

Vo looked at Mina and smacked his lips in thought. "How you pay me?"

"Pay you? For what? For the escape shuttle?" Maurus shook his head. "I can't pay you anything else, I've got nothing left. Mina?"

"Parker's guardian can pay you once we reach him," she said.

Vo swung his head from side to side. "No pay, no shuttle."

"I don't know what else we could give you," said Maurus. "Just let them take it, and I'll help you fix your ship so we can continue on our way."

Vo looked around the room. His greedy eyes rested on Chase, who for a moment feared that he was going to ask to keep him on his ship. Maurus seemed to think the same thing, and he took a step to block him. Vo smiled, and his eyes narrowed within the fleshy folds of his face.

"One thing," he purred. "You think you so secret, but I see. You carry silver case inside jacket. I see you peeking at it."

Maurus stared at Vo in horror. A memory flashed through Chase's mind, Maurus slipping a slim silver case into his jacket as he left the boys in the Starjumper.

Vo giggled nervously. "Yes, you not so secret. I trade you, shuttle for secret case. Yes?"

Maurus cursed and shook his head. "I can't," he said, to Chase's disbelief. What could be more important than Parker's life?

Vo's eyes glittered with the knowledge that he had hit on something important, and he lowered his weapon. "So small package for nice big shuttle, I give you good trade. Only choice."

Maurus brought his hands to his face and looked away. With his dark eyebrows knitted together, it reminded Chase of the crazed look he had seen on Maurus's face when he was piloting the Starjumper. "I can't," he repeated in an anguished voice. "Please. You have to give us another option."

Vo smiled, shaking his head.

Mina turned away from Vo, her shoulders slumped in defeat, and walked to the back of the cabin. Chase watched her from the corner of his eye as she crouched down to the floor, and realized only at the last second what she was doing when she stood with a piece of loose metal cabinetry in her hands. "Look out!" he shouted.

Maurus started to turn, and Mina swung the metal into the side of his head, knocking him flat on the ground.

Both Chase and Vo gaped as she stepped forward and

rolled Maurus's unconscious body over. She dug inside his jacket and extracted a slim silver case.

"Is this what you want?" she asked. "We're taking the shuttle."

Vo extended a long bronze limb to pluck the case from her hand, his fleshy lips curling up in satisfaction.

"We'll leave him here," she said, gesturing at Maurus. "You can take him to his destination."

"Oh no," said Vo, shaking his head with a sneer. "You take him with you. Not wanna be around when he wake up."

# CHAPTER FIFTEEN

Maurus awoke in a fury, spewing profanity. "You idiots!" he cried hoarsely. "What have you done?" He kicked out with his feet, nearly connecting with Chase's head.

"I'm sorry, but it was the only way to get the shuttle," said Mina. She had bound Maurus's hands and feet before placing him in the back of the tiny escape shuttle, a two-seater with just enough cargo space for a limp body. "Once you made it clear to Vo how important that case was, he wasn't going to accept anything else."

"And you couldn't have bashed his head in instead of mine?"

"That would have been mutiny, a crime with severe—"

Maurus pounded the back of the seat with his boots. "You've ruined me! When I get my hands free, I'm going to rip out your wiring."

Chase cringed at the outburst, but Mina said nothing, making some adjustments on the guidance console. Vo's shuttle was as well maintained as his ship: A jagged fissure ran across one of the consoles, and the cracked seats were patched with yellow stripes of sealing tape.

"I curse myself for ever trying to help you blasted Earthan trash," Maurus roared. "Useless boys! Not worth the oxygen you consume."

Parker lay sandwiched between Chase and Mina, drenched in sweat and alternating between violent tremors and utter slackness. Mina had bandaged the puncture wound on his chest with a piece of clean fabric, but he radiated a sickly heat as his body fought the poison in his bloodstream.

Mina slid a few markers on the console screen and leaned back in her seat. "We're going to be here awhile, so you may want to save some of your insults for later. This shuttle can't reach a speed much beyond a camber of two."

"That's because it's an antique," spat Maurus. "You'll never make it anywhere in time to save Parker. He was dead as soon as that spike hit him."

"Shut up," said Chase. He glanced over at Parker, whose dark hair was plastered to his face with sweat. His eyes were closed, and Chase hoped he was oblivious to the conversation.

"I've activated the distress beacon," said Mina. "We're not too far from a commerce route. It's only a matter of time before a ship sees it and picks us up."

Maurus snorted. "Fantastic. I'm sure the Fleet will be on top of us any moment now."

Chase's stomach plummeted.

"Not necessarily," said Mina. "There are plenty of trade ships out here that could pick up the signal. And if it's the Fleet that finds us, then I suppose you'll just have to face the consequences."

Maurus said nothing for a moment. "I'm a dead man as soon as I step on any Fleet ship," he finally muttered.

"That seems like something you should have been prepared for, given what you did on Trucon," said Mina.

Maurus stamped the back of the seat again. "I told you I had nothing to do with the attack!"

"Then tell us who did," said Chase.

"There's a traitor within the Fleet, but it's not me. I was sent on a solo mission to Trucon to investigate a report of nighttime slave traffickers outside of Rother City. Shortly after I arrived I was ambushed by four Fleet soldiers. They were the ones who set the thermodetonators. The silver case you just gave away? I took that from one of them. It contained the maps and access codes for the oxygen plants that were attacked, but more importantly, there were orders that probably could have been traced back to whoever gave them."

"That makes no sense. Why would the Fleet attack its own colony?" asked Mina.

"I don't know! Nothing makes sense anymore."

Chase's thoughts were still on the silver case. "If you had information about the attack before it happened, why didn't you try to stop it?"

"After I took the case, I was just trying to stay alive. I didn't actually look inside it until I was in your Starjumper, after everything had happened. It would have been too late anyway. They'd already sabotaged the plants before they came after me."

"How did you end up in that wrecked spacecraft?"

Maurus's voice began to lose its vigor, his anger deflating. "Because once I escaped from the soldiers, I was chased and shot down by a Keklly mercenary. He must have been hired as a backup in case the initial plan to kill me failed. And I would've been a goner if you and Parker hadn't found me."

Chase started to tell him how they'd found his wreckage over Mircona, but Maurus kept talking, the words pouring out of him like he couldn't stop now that he'd started. "When I woke up in the cargo hold of your cruiser, I thought maybe I'd been captured, and the first thing I did was go through that case, to see if I could find any clues about what was going on. So then when I learned what had happened on Trucon, I already knew who'd done it. I planned to take everything in the case straight to my captain, but while we were traveling to Qesaris, something else came across the newsfeed. I saw that I was being framed for the entire disaster."

Chase took a deep breath as understanding dawned on him. This was why Maurus had looked like he was losing his mind during their flight to Qesaris.

"My captain, aside from sending me on a completely bogus mission to Trucon, was the first person to publicly accuse me," Maurus continued. "So I know he's one of the traitors, but I don't know how many other people are involved. If I took the evidence to the wrong person, they'd just thank me for returning their property before shooting me in the heart. That's why I was trying to get back to my homeworld, where my people will keep me safe until I can clear my name."

Mina hunched over the console suddenly.

Chase leaned forward and looked at the puzzle of numbers and bars, but he couldn't decipher a thing. "What's happening? Did someone find us?"

"No. Something's wrong," she told him. "We're losing speed way too fast."

"What?" Maurus wriggled up to a seated position and

peered over her shoulder. "Why are the cambering shields at half power?"

"Because something's failing in the drive system," said Mina. "Look at the CF levels."

Maurus cursed under his breath. "Thank you, Vo. He's given us the most useless, poorly serviced escape shuttle in the galaxy." He looked on for a minute. "You've got to let me pilot."

"That would not be in Parker's best interest," said Mina.

Maurus made an exasperated noise. "I'm not going to run this marble hopper to Lyolia. It'd take a month and we'd all be dead long before we arrived. Untie me and I'll reconfigure the energy cycles. I can make sure we get to the next colony."

"Just tell me what to do," said Mina.

"Piloting isn't something you tell, it's something you feel. The way you're running the vehicle, we'll burn up all the energy before we get anywhere. And once the power's gone, we won't last half an hour out here."

"Please, Mina," Chase said. "Let's untie him. He's a good pilot."

"We can't trust him," said Mina.

"I'm not the villain you think I am," said Maurus.

Chase turned in his seat to get a look at Maurus's face. "You swear everything you're telling us is true?"

Maurus scowled. "Of course."

"Can you prove it?"

Maurus laughed bitterly. "I could until a few hours ago."

With a sinking feeling, Chase realized what Mina had done to Maurus by giving away his silver case. "Let him pilot," he told her. "It's not like he can do anything to hurt us."

Mina was silent, calculating. "Fine. I'll go in the back with Parker. But if you try anything . . . ," she warned.

Maurus wriggled around on the floor of the shuttle so that Chase could undo the bindings on his hands. With a little artful squeezing, he swapped places with Mina and helped her transfer Parker's limp body into the back. He glanced over at Chase before starting at the console. "I'm sorry about what I said about Parker. I'll do my best to get him help."

Chase said nothing and watched tensely as Maurus set to work, fingers sliding over the screens as he muttered to himself.

"How does it look?" Mina asked from the back.

"We're down to just under a camber of two, but I think I can hold it steady here."

"What's a camber?" asked Chase, more to distract himself than out of curiosity.

"It's a measure of bending." Maurus rubbed his arms and flexed his fingers. "The shuttle's engine bends space around us so that we can move through it at a speed faster than light. Most important invention in humanoid history." He glanced at Chase, and frowned. "I'm surprised you don't know this."

Feeling stupid, Chase leaned back in his seat and looked out the window. He didn't ask any more questions.

✳   ✳   ✳

The escape shuttle had been designed for emergencies rather than comfort, and after about eight hours trapped inside, Maurus and Chase were both shifting uncomfortably in the front seat. There was no noise from the back, where Mina kept watch over Parker.

"How's he doing?" Chase asked.

"Not well," said Mina. "No one's picked up on our signal yet?"

"Stupid Shartese garbage." Maurus flicked a screen. "I can't tell how strong our range is. I'm really fighting these flow levels."

Chase looked back to see Parker lying still, his head in Mina's lap, skin pale and damp. "What can we do?" he asked.

Mina just stared back at him with her implacable gaze, making it impossible for Chase to read whether she thought Parker would make it or not.

Chase looked out the window, but the stars visible

through the portholes seemed to barely move. The idea of getting stuck out here, an inconceivable distance from anywhere, made his skin crawl.

Maurus leaned back from the console and sighed. "The Federation was supposed to put more range extender stations out in some of these Naxos clusters, but apparently that's another project that got caught up in red tape."

The entire statement was made up of words that made no sense to Chase. "What exactly is the Federation?" he asked, knowing that the question would sound strange, but tired of always feeling like he was two steps behind everyone else. "I mean, I know who's in it, but what does it do?"

"What is the Federation?" Maurus repeated incredulously. "Chase, where are you from?"

Heat rose in his cheeks. "I don't know. I mean, I have amnesia."

"But aren't you and Parker related?"

"No, he kind of found me. He and Mina were helping me when the whole Trucon thing happened."

Maurus stared at Chase. "I had no idea." He paused. "So when we were in the Starjumper, Mina was incapacitated...?"

"Someone had been chasing us." Chase stopped, unsure how much detail to give. But it did seem that he and Maurus had a common enemy, and more than that, he *wanted* to tell him everything. "Soldiers from the Fleet."

Maurus narrowed his eyes. "What?"

A sudden series of strangled beeps came out of the console. With a shudder, the shuttle began to spin around in a slow arc. "No no no no no," muttered Maurus, leaning in to the controls, his face pinched with concentration. Gradually their gyration slowed to a stop, and he leaned back and smacked the console.

"Cursed Shartese! Vo didn't do the proper upgrades on his energy storage units. I overloaded the flow and we just lost three fusion chambers. Electrical systems are failing." His fingers flew over the screens. "We're going to lose all power very soon."

Cold horror crept over Chase. This was it. They were going to die stranded in the middle of the cosmos. "What do we do?" he asked in a small voice.

Maurus stared at a circular graph on the screen filled with dots and numbers. "There's a Zeta planet nearby. The atmosphere is a little thick, but there's plenty of oxygen and we should be alright if we can get there. Mina, is that okay?"

"Do what you can," she said quietly.

"What about Parker?" asked Chase.

Maurus's dark eyes were filled with anguish. "I'm sorry."

Chase turned his head away so Maurus couldn't see his expression. How had it come to this?

"I'm turning off every possible system to conserve energy, so it's going to get really cold. I'm turning off the gravity generator as well. Buckle yourself in." A moment later, the track lights along the walls of the shuttle blinked out, leaving only the dim bluish glow of the operating console as a source of light. Chase felt his body begin to lift off the seat, and his arms floated up alongside him.

The air inside the shuttle turned icy cold, and Chase tucked his hands into his armpits. His breath came out in white plumes.

Mina murmured something to Parker in the back and passed a silver insulation blanket to the front seat. "Chase, take this. I've got another one for Parker." Chase struggled to pull the floating blanket around himself. Maurus turned away from the console for a moment to help him unbuckle and wrap up.

"Aren't you c-c-cold?" asked Chase.

Maurus tugged the blanket tightly around Chase's shoulders. "Can't pilot if I'm all bundled up." Chase caught his eye for a moment. Maurus's face was intense, his expression unreadable.

The minutes inched past. Chase's hands and feet tingled with cold, then burned, then went numb. He grew drowsy and had trouble staying focused on Maurus's actions. His eyelids sank closed.

"Mina, I've had to decrease oxygen production," he heard Maurus say thickly. "You may need to take over for me."

Mina said something in reply, but Chase was drifting under again.

"We're getting close."

Chase forced his eyes open, and Maurus pointed out the tiny orb of the Zeta planet in the shuttle's portholes. Their approach to the distant clay-colored planet was agonizingly slow. Chase tried to force himself to stay awake and watch, but he had developed a fierce headache, and his numb feet ached.

"We're not going to make it, are we?" he slurred. Maurus glanced at him, then turned his attention to the console without speaking a word. A few exhausted tears hovered at the corners of Chase's eyes. The pain in his hands and feet was agonizing, and he slipped back into semiconsciousness to escape.

"Wake up." Mina's voice rang out from the backseat.

Chase opened his eyes to see the planet filling up their window. Beside him Maurus was blinking hard and lightly slapping his own face as he focused on the changing numbers.

"There's not enough power for a proper landing, but the shuttle has a parachute that'll slow our descent." He frowned at the console, looking worried. "Well, the sensor's broken, but it should have one. I'll try to put us down in water. I've got to divert all the power into the heat shields so we can make it into the atmosphere without burning up. Make sure you're strapped in."

Chase checked his belts and glanced back at Mina, who had wrapped her arms around Parker's torso. She braced her feet against the walls.

"Alright, here we go," said Maurus grimly. "This is going to be rough."

As the planet loomed closer and closer, Chase realized that they were not traveling slowly after all, that they were actually hurtling toward the planet's surface at a speed that would smash them into little more than gas particles when they hit the ground. A bright glow from the portholes illuminated the cabin, and the temperature jumped from freezing to terribly hot. Suddenly drenched in sweat, Chase clawed at the insulation blanket, but it was wrapped around him and secured under the seat belt, and he couldn't get it off.

Maurus gripped the edges of the console, watching shifting numbers, his lips moving silently. He frowned and touched the console. "Deploy," he said loudly. He began scrabbling at the console, his eyes wild. "Override!" he yelled. "Deploy! Deploy!"

With a mechanical clang, the shuttle jerked to a sudden stop midair, sending everyone lunging forward. Mina slammed into the back of the seat, and Maurus cracked his head against the console with a curse. Chase's head swam from the motion, the heat, and the low oxygen levels. His stomach felt as if it were trying to climb out of his throat.

"Everyone okay?" gasped Maurus. "We should land in water in less than a minute…I hope." Through the portholes, all Chase could see was a swirling, creamy-colored haze. He slipped in and out of consciousness, but when the haze finally cleared, what he saw below was not blue water, but something sluggish and brick colored. He cringed and braced for impact.

They hit with a hard jolt, but rather than crumpling, the shuttle plunged and then drifted slowly back up. Chase squinted out the window. "Nah water?" he slurred.

"Close enough," said Maurus, forcing out each word with difficulty. "Mina, open the hatch."

"I don't think that's a good idea," said Mina calmly. "The pressure change is too great, it will hurt you. Can you open a vent?"

"Not much…pressure," protested Maurus, but he lolled his head forward and made some changes on the console. There was a hiss, and moist, earthy-smelling air began to seep in, pressing from all sides like a leaden blanket.

They were alive, at least for a little bit longer. Too nauseated to feel anything close to relief, Chase leaned forward and threw up on the floor.

# CHAPTER SIXTEEN

Chase sat back in his seat and waited for his dizziness to subside as the external air slowly filled the shuttle. The planet had a thick, sticky atmosphere, and his forcing the moist air into his lungs felt like breathing syrup.

Maurus looked over at him, his face flushed and his eyes bulging slightly. Chase wondered if his own eyes looked that way. It certainly felt like it.

"Let's get out of here," Maurus wheezed. "Mina, open the door."

Mina unlocked the ceiling hatch and pushed it open. Maurus struggled to his feet to join her. Chase looked skyward as a blast of hot, humid air swirled through the cabin, blowing his hair across his forehead. He didn't have the energy to stand. He could hear them talking, but their words were swept away by the wind.

Mina hoisted herself out onto the roof, and Maurus sat

back down in the shuttle, heaving a deep breath. Chase rolled his head over to look at him. "And?"

Maurus attempted a wry smile. "Could be better. We're in the middle of some kind of mud sea. Might be this world's version of an ocean. Can't tell how far it goes, but it looks like a pretty thick soup out there."

Chase peeled himself off the seat and twisted around to look at Parker's still, pale form on the floor. He stared at Parker's chest until he could see its shallow rise and fall. "Aren't there any people living here?"

"Guidance systems indicated there were no colonies on the planet." Maurus leaned toward the controls. "We'll have to hope someone picks up our distress beacon."

Chase turned back around and looked at the flickering console screen. "Where are we?"

"This is a Zeta-grade planet. That means it can support organic life, but has no native civilization. Some Zeta planets are colonized, like Qesaris, or . . ." He hesitated, and said, "Or Trucon. But ninety-nine percent of the time they're deemed unfit for settlement—this one probably because of the thick atmosphere."

"Why was Trucon colonized if it was full of those monsters?" Chase asked. It seemed like years since the scaly creatures had attacked him outside Parker's house.

Maurus paused for a moment to catch his breath. "The

Zinnjerha? They were a threat, but I suppose the planet was very appealing for colonization because of its proximity to three other hospitable Zeta planets." A dark look crossed his face.

"What is it?"

"I should have known," Maurus muttered.

"Known what?"

"The mission my captain had sent me to investigate was a report of nighttime trafficking movement in the Truconian desert—Lyolians, of course, which is why it had to be me. But when I got there, none of it was true. The story wasn't even feasible. I wasted all my time trying to figure out how my captain got his information wrong, when he was the one who knowingly sent me on a fool's errand. I should have known something was wrong."

The bitterness and regret in Maurus's voice evaporated any doubt Chase might have had that he wasn't behind the Trucon attack. He was telling the truth—he'd been set up. "It's not like you could have known what was going to happen," Chase said.

Maurus shook his head. "No, but I should have questioned every possibility. You can respect authority without mindlessly trusting it."

Mina's face appeared in the open hatch overhead. "The shuttle is beginning to sink," she said.

A spike of adrenaline shot through Chase's stomach. "What?"

She climbed into the back. "It's gone down three centimeters in the last minute."

Maurus cursed. "We must have split a seam when we hit the ocean." He clambered out onto the roof. Chase struggled to follow him, but it seemed as if his body weighed twice as much as usual—just raising his hand felt like pushing his arm through water.

Taking a looped length of black cable from a storage compartment, Mina hopped out onto the roof of the shuttle. Chase hauled himself after her through the open hatch and looked outside at the strange world they had landed on.

All around them, for as far as he could see, was a wide expanse of flat, brick-colored ocean, rippling in a strong wind. The air was hot, moist, and earthy, and swirling clouds of pink- and cream-colored gases filled the sky. Mina tied one end of the cable around her waist and handed the other end to Maurus. Before Chase could ask what she was doing, she jumped off the sinking shuttle and without even a splash disappeared into the thick, murky liquid.

Chase looked at Maurus for an explanation, but he only studied the spot where Mina had gone under. A moment later, her head popped back up, glazed in viscous red mud.

She wiped her face. "It's very sticky, but I think I can swim in it." She began a lap around the vehicle.

"What's she doing?" Chase asked Maurus.

"She thinks she sees some trees, or land, far in the distance. She's going to try pulling the shuttle there."

Chase squinted. "I don't see anything."

"It's too hazy to see very far. She's the android; I'm taking her word for it."

"Are we going to sink?" Chase asked. "What if no one hears our distress call? How are we going to get off this planet?"

Maurus's mouth twisted, and he squeezed Chase's shoulder. "Come on. We've made it this far, haven't we?"

"Throw me the rest of the cable." Mina had completed her lap, and the head that poked above the surface was barely recognizable. She tied the free end of the cable to the shuttle and began paddling out in front, trying to pull the shuttle, but with no landmarks, it seemed like they weren't moving at all.

"This is useless," Chase said. "She's not going anywhere."

"Look behind you." A shallow wake, barely indented in the swampy surface, showed that they were making some kind of progress. "I'd imagine she'd burn her limbs out and wear them down to stumps if that's what it took to save Parker. Not that she will—I've seen androids similar to her take a lot tougher beating than this."

Chase still couldn't see anything in their hazy environment other than swirling hot gas, but he hoped Mina's senses were better than his.

Maurus gazed ahead, and then he gave his head a shake, as if to clear it. "I feel like I'm getting the hang of breathing this stuff, how about you?"

"I feel like I'm underwater," Chase admitted.

Maurus laughed. When he looked over, a stab of fear went through Chase. Maurus's face was crinkled up in a friendly grin, but a spot of bright red had bloomed in the white of his left eye. Chase felt the urge to touch his own eyes, wondering if the same thing was happening to him. He looked away, glancing down into the cabin, and shouted in alarm.

Below them, Parker lay in a shallow puddle of glossy mud that had formed on the floor of the shuttle. Maurus leapt down into the cabin and hoisted Parker's limp body so Chase could pull him out onto the roof.

"Mina!" Maurus yelled, pulling himself out and crawling down to the nose of the shuttle. "It's filling up inside, it's going to sink soon!" Mina didn't break pace, paddling resolutely onward toward a destination that only she could sense. Chase huddled beside Parker on the roof of the shuttle, wiping the mud from his face. Parker's eyes stayed closed, and his breathing sounded ragged, as though he were choking on something.

"Parker, can you hear me?" Chase said in his ear. "Just hang on, we're going to get you help." He was a liar. They weren't getting off this planet, and the only thing that awaited them was a horrific death by drowning in a sea of mud.

The shuttle was definitely sinking, and as the nose began to dip below the surface, Maurus scooted back toward the open hatch.

Chase squinted into the distance and blinked a few times to make sure he wasn't imagining things. "Hey, I think I see something!"

Rising from the maroon swampland was the hazy outline of an immense structure on the horizon. As they drew closer, he saw that it was organic, an interwoven network of stalks that sprouted densely from the water to form a towering pale jungle that stretched on for miles.

The shuttle slipped deeper beneath the surface, and Chase pulled Parker higher onto the tail section. Eventually Mina could pull it no farther, and she untied the cable from her waist and fought her way back to the tail section.

"Alright, we're going to have to swim from here. It's not as far as it looks. Loop Parker's arms around my neck and I'll pull him there."

"Can you swim?" Maurus asked Chase.

"I think I can," said Chase. Together, he and Maurus slid off the side of the shuttle and into the cold ooze. If he had found it difficult to move in the planet's air, the sea was a thousand times worse. He thrashed as hard as he could, until his entire body tingled, but he barely seemed to move forward in the sludge at all. He stopped to catch his breath, and immediately the sea began to suck him down.

"Hey!" shouted Maurus, bobbing in the distance. "Make it over here! You can make it to me!" Chase struggled through the mud, fixed on his goal, and was hyperventilating nearly to the point of blacking out by the time he reached Maurus's side.

"I can't do this," he croaked, clutching at Maurus's shoulder.

"It's okay, we'll do it together," said Maurus. "Put your arm around my neck, and I'll help you stay above the surface. See?" They kicked at the mud side by side, Maurus pulling Chase up every time he began to sink. Their progress was minuscule. Maurus heaved for air, and Chase knew he was slowing him down.

Mina and Parker vanished in the distance. Maurus made Chase pause a couple of times so they could catch their breath, and when Chase looked over his shoulder, he was dismayed to see how close they still were to the foundering shuttle. He began to wonder how much longer they would last before they gave up and surrendered to the swampy depths, when Mina's face emerged from the haze ahead.

"Hold on, I can take him," she called, and she paddled up

close so Chase could grab on to her firm shoulders. "I'll be back for you," she said to Maurus.

"I'll make it," he panted.

"I'll come back," she repeated, and took off toward the pale jungle. Chase appreciated the boundless strength in her android limbs as she moved them steadily forward, her legs churning effortlessly through the thick mud. The outcropping ahead drew closer. The stalks were actually some type of gnarled, leafless trunks that all grew together into one another. It was impossible to tell if they were individual plants, or one endless, knotty growth.

When they reached one of the trunks, Mina ordered Chase to hang on tight as she climbed up the intersecting branches. He clung to her neck, dripping sticky tendrils of mud. She took him up to a wide intersection of twisted branches, where she had left Parker tucked snugly in the fork of two large boughs.

"Keep an eye on him. I'm going back for Maurus."

Chase touched one of Parker's arms to let him know he was there and hunched on a branch beside him, shaking with exhaustion. Parker's skin was waxy pale and he looked like he was already dead, but his body was still scorching hot. Ahead of them lay only swirling haze—the shuttle was too far away to see and had probably sunk by now. Behind them stretched a never-ending forest of pale branches.

Hot winds dried the mud coating Chase, causing it to shrink and pull on the tiny hairs on his arms. Finally Mina appeared below with Maurus clinging to her shoulders. As Chase watched them scale the trees, Parker suddenly thrashed, hitting him on the cheek. He tried to hold Parker's arm down, but Parker began to shake uncontrollably. His eyes rolled back in his head, and yellow foam ran from his mouth and mingled with the mud on his chin.

"Mina!" Chase screamed. "Come quick!"

A second later she was leaning over Parker. "He's having a seizure. We have to turn him on his side so he doesn't choke."

Maurus clambered up beside them and shook his head, his face twisted with grief. "We're too late. The poison is starting to overload his brain."

"Do something!" Chase looked frantically back and forth at Maurus and Mina. "There's got to be something we can do!"

Lying on his side, Parker coughed, spraying thick yellow foam on the branch beside him. A sharp, acrid smell hit Chase's nose, overpowering the fetid stench of the mud sea.

"Don't let any of that touch you," warned Maurus.

The tree gave a tremendous shudder, and with a sharp crack, one of the branches supporting them broke loose.

"Move!" Maurus leapt up, grabbing a branch above them as the rest of the nest began to break apart. Chase scrambled for a branch, but the one he grabbed splintered away from the tree.

With a shout, Maurus reached out and caught his arm, hanging on to the tree with one hand and Chase with the other. The branch Chase had grabbed splashed into the mud.

"Hang on! Grab something!" Maurus pulled Chase higher, and Chase reached for a nearby branch. There was another sharp cracking noise above, and a shot of panic raced through Chase.

Then it happened again, out of his control: Although Maurus had a tight grip on his arm, Chase slipped through as though his arm had simply dissolved, and plummeted toward the sea.

He smacked into the mud hard enough to knock the wind out of him, and the sludge sucked him down deeper. Below the surface it was thick and silent. He wasn't even sure which way was up. His chest began to hitch for oxygen, and mud shot up his nose. His mind screamed incoherent thoughts.

So this was what it felt like to die.

A strong arm reached around his chest, and someone began jerking him upward. He gasped for breath as he broke the surface and wiped the mud from his face and eyes, coughing and spitting.

"Here," said Maurus, pushing him up toward the lowest

branch. Chase grabbed hold of it, but it peeled away from the tree and dropped into the mud. Maurus reached for the next branch up, but it pulled off as well. Tree limbs rained down around them, as though the tree were shedding them voluntarily, and with them came Mina and Parker, tumbling into the mud. Mina looped one arm around Parker and towed him to the next tree, but its low branches came off in her hands as well.

"It doesn't want us on it," called Maurus. "The trees are somehow all connected, and they don't want us to climb them. Parker must have poisoned them."

Chase clung to the wide trunk of a tree, but there was no easy handhold and he kept slipping. Finally he let himself sink a little, so only his nose and his eyes were above the surface.

"No! Hold on!" Maurus reached over and grabbed Chase under the armpit. "Don't let go!"

"I can't hold on forever," mumbled Chase, spitting out more mud. He tried to keep his grip, but he was hot and exhausted and couldn't breathe. Blackness crept into the edges of his vision again, and Maurus's face seemed to be getting smaller and farther away. At least Parker wasn't dead yet, because the sound of his retching carried over the mud, interrupted by the choked rattle of his breathing.

Chase knew he was nearing his physical limit as a

roaring sound filled his ears, growing progressively louder. Maurus screamed something, probably telling him to hold on, but he just couldn't anymore.

Maurus grew frantic, waving an arm wildly. He let go of the tree and splashed out, struggling to paddle away from the jungle. Was he trying to go back to the shuttle, to see if they could still climb back onto it? Chase used his last ounce of strength to turn and look.

A dark shadow passed across the mud, and a moment later, a narrow airship broke through the haze, skimming over the sea, engines roaring. Maurus waved his arms to get the ship's attention. The vehicle approached and hovered, as Maurus fought his way back and pulled Chase from the tree.

"Go get Parker," Chase mumbled as they swam back out to the airship.

"Mina's bringing him," panted Maurus. "Get in!"

A hatch on the airship opened, and a man in a bulky insulated jumpsuit and reflective helmet leaned out and reached for Chase, grabbing him under the arms and pulling him inside the ship. He dragged Chase into the middle of the cabin floor and crouched down in front of him.

"Were you the ones with the distress signal?" the man shouted, his voice muffled by the helmet. "An escape shuttle, NQR coordinates?"

Chase gaped stupidly back at his own distorted reflection on the man's visor. Of course—these people had followed the shuttle's distress beacon. He nodded, and the man turned back to the door and left him sitting in the dark interior.

When all four of them had been pulled on board, dripping mud everywhere, the man gestured outside to ask if there were any others, and Maurus made a cutting motion under his chin to indicate that there were not. The man went to the front of the ship, where a pilot sat at the controls, and the door sealed shut.

Parker lay with his head in Mina's lap, his arms and legs trembling. "This boy needs immediate medical attention," she said.

Maurus crouched by Parker's feet and held his ankles down. "He was exposed to Goxar poison almost twenty-four hours ago."

The man in the space suit pressed the barrel of a hand-blaster against Maurus's temple.

"It's the end of the road for you, Lieutenant Maurus," he said in a cold voice.

Chase looked up, and with a gasp he noticed the elliptical symbols on everything—the equipment, the walls, the space suit. The Fleet had found them.

Maurus reacted instantly, throwing his hand up to knock the blaster away and tackling the man to the floor. He landed a solid punch to the man's side before lunging for the pilot, who had already jumped up from the controls. Swinging an arm around, the pilot planted a taser into Maurus's back with a sizzle. He wavered for a moment and dropped to the floor.

"No!" cried Chase, jumping to his feet.

The pilot turned to him, pulling off a shiny helmet and flicking a long dark ponytail out from underneath. Her cheeks were flushed, and her eyes glittered. "You want to go next?" she asked, snapping the taser at him.

The man Maurus had knocked over removed his helmet, revealing a narrow, grimacing face. "I don't think that will be necessary, Vidal," he said dryly. He glared at Chase. "Sit down." The pilot returned to the controls, and the man pulled a set of shackles from a drawer and used them to bind Maurus's hands behind his back.

The cabin darkened as they zoomed out of the atmosphere and left the mud planet behind. Blue track lights illuminated along the floor. Chase sank to the floor, numb with despair. Their run was over; Maurus was a dead man. And whatever it was about Chase that had caused the Fleet to raid Dr. Silvestri's lab, he was probably about to learn.

Beside him, Parker arched into another seizure, his feet beating a staccato rhythm against the floor. Mina lifted his head up to keep him from choking.

Chase tried to hold Parker's feet down. "Help!"

The man came over and pressed two fingers to Parker's muddy neck, jerking his hand away when he noticed the crust of yellow foam around his mouth. He shook his head with a frown. "Kid's not going to make it."

"Come on, Parker, stay with us," pleaded Chase. Parker jerked violently on the floor, making horrible choked noises. This couldn't be happening—he couldn't just die like this.

On the other side of the cabin, Maurus began to stir, moaning and cursing when he realized that his hands were bound. "Forquera, you traitor," he hissed.

With a snarl, Forquera wheeled around on his heels and wrapped his hands around Maurus's throat.

"Say that again," he growled. "Try it."

Parker's feet drummed against the floor. Mina pulled him upright, trying to clear the thick foam out of his airway. A nasty odor hit Chase's nose as the bio-molding on her fingers began to dissolve.

"Stop!" Chase shouted at Forquera, trying to grab Parker's arms to keep him from hurting himself. "Please, help us!"

But Forquera ignored them, choking Maurus until his eyes rolled back in his head. By the time he took his hands off Maurus's throat, Parker's feet had stopped kicking.

Because Parker had stopped breathing altogether.

# CHAPTER SEVENTEEN

The next minute was a blur.

Forquera shouted orders and moved around them, but all Chase saw was Mina pumping Parker's chest and fishing in his mouth to try to clear his blocked airway. His own voice, shouting Parker's name over and over again, rang strangely in his ears, as if it were being shouted from the other end of a long hall.

Colored lights streaked past the front windshield as the airship decelerated and drew to a stop. Outside, the rhythmic stomp of approaching bootsteps grew louder. The hatch on the side of their vehicle cracked open, and soldiers streamed in, shouting and pointing their weapons at Maurus. He struggled to sit upright, his face set in a defensive snarl.

"On your feet!" yelled an officer.

"Where is the medical bay?" Mina demanded, her voice

nearly drowned out by the shouting and commotion around them.

Forquera waved his hand to get someone's attention. "Reyes! Take these two straight to sickbay." Without so much as a glance back at Chase, Mina scooped up Parker and jumped off the airship.

A pair of soldiers dragged Maurus to his feet and shoved him out the hatch. He shouted as he crashed to the floor. Chase tried to follow, but one of the soldiers cut him off with the nose of his weapon.

"Colonel, what do you want to do with this one?"

Colonel Forquera examined Chase, a frown darkening his lean face. "Keep him with Maurus for now. We'll let the captain decide."

The soldier prodded Chase toward the exit hatch. Their airship had parked in an enormous flight bay with a high white ceiling. Rows of other small spacecraft lined the floor— some similar to the one they had arrived on, others sleek black fighters—and soldiers in blue jumpsuits moved around the vehicles in a constant stream of activity. An empty pathway cut through the middle of the room, ending at a tall interlocking door.

Maurus had been shoved out to the middle of the floor. The activity in the hangar came to a halt as everyone stopped working to stare at him. Silence fell across the room. Maurus sat stiffly, his hands still bound behind his back, hair and clothes matted with dried orange mud.

"Murderer!" cried a thin voice from the back of the hangar.

Maurus locked gazes with Chase. His dark eyes boiled, though with fury or fear, Chase could not tell.

Something nudged Chase in the back. "Keep going," said the soldier behind him. Colonel Forquera pushed past, glancing around at the crowd as he stepped down out of the airship. Chase followed him across the hangar, feeling conspicuous in the cracked layer of mud, but hardly any of the soldiers bothered to look his way.

"We should just eject this traitor out the spaceway right now, Colonel," said a tall blond officer who stood closest to Maurus. "Never should have let this kind of filth into the Fleet." He looked down at Maurus and spat.

Maurus kicked out and tried to sweep the officer's feet out from under him. With a curse, the officer jumped back, reaching for his handblaster.

"Stand down, Lieutenant Derrick!" said Forquera angrily. The officer scowled and dropped his hand. "On your feet," he said to Maurus. "You still have to go through decontamination."

Maurus staggered upright, swaying to catch his balance without the use of his hands. A trickle of sweat cut a dark line through the mud caking his face.

A shout echoed across the bay: "Captain on deck!"

On the far side of the hangar, a set of doors flew open as Captain Lennard burst through. Chase recognized his pitted face from the transmission he'd seen on Vo's ship. The captain was barrel-chested, with close-cropped hair that might once have been brown but now was sprinkled thickly with gray. His pale eyes blazed as he charged toward them and stopped just short of Maurus, and his lip curled up in a snarl. "You..."

A tangible anticipation hovered over the hangar as everyone, including Chase, waited to see what the captain would say to Maurus. Someone in the back coughed, and Lennard glanced around the flight bay, anger twisting his face.

"What are you all doing?" he shouted. "Don't you have jobs to do?"

Noise surged as everyone rushed back to work.

Forquera snapped a salute. "Captain, I was about to take them over to decontamination. They were in some sort of swamp down on the Zeta, but there were no known reads on any possible toxins they may have picked up."

The captain turned his fierce gaze on Chase, whose pulse quickened as he stared back like an animal caught in a trap. "Who is this?"

Forquera paused. "He was on the surface with Lieutenant

Maurus, sir. There were two others, an android and a boy with Goxar poisoning. Ensign Reyes already took them to sickbay. It didn't look like the boy was going to make it."

Captain Lennard cocked his head. "Was the android poisoned too, Forquera? Send word to sickbay that it should be restrained. I don't need a rogue andy running around my ship."

"Sorry, Captain." Forquera ducked back and spoke into a device on his wrist.

The captain turned back to Maurus. "Move," he growled, pointing to a door. Maurus turned away from him and led the way, shoulders thrown back defiantly. Forquera gestured to Chase that he should follow. A soldier in a blue jumpsuit met the four of them at the door, swiping the door open with a badge hanging around his neck, and they entered a long room lined with shower stalls that would have seemed like a communal bathroom were it not for the strange medicinal smell in the air.

As soon as the door closed behind them, the captain whipped around and with a powerful backhand knocked Maurus to the floor.

"Scum!" he spat. "Your treachery has taken thousands of innocent lives."

Of course the captain had to keep up the façade of blaming Maurus for the Trucon disaster. His crew wouldn't know about his involvement in the sabotage—he certainly wouldn't admit to it in front of them. Chase waited for Maurus to reveal to everyone in the room that Lennard was the true criminal, but lying on his back where he'd fallen, Maurus only pressed his lips tightly together and shook his head.

Lennard continued. "If it weren't for the need to maintain the integrity of the Fleet, I'd execute you on the spot."

Maurus barked out a short laugh. "Integrity? I truly hope you don't believe that."

Before Lennard could act on the fury that crossed his face, the blue-suited soldier stepped between them, helping Maurus to his feet and leading him to an open stall. Maurus walked under a spigot and glared at Lennard, his arms still bound, as a hot shower washed over him, rinsing away most of the sticky red mud. The steam rising around him filled Chase's nose with a sharp chemical odor.

Lennard loomed on the side, his fists clenched, and continued his act. "I knew I was taking a risk, accepting an alien officer into my crew, but I never expected to wind up with a mass murderer. You'll be dead before the day is through, if I get my way." Maurus stepped out, dripping, and gave Lennard a dark look as the medical officer held a blinking device up to his arm.

"He's all clear, no sign of radioactivity or biological threat," said the medical officer.

Maurus shook the water from his hair. "Are you done? You don't have to put on a show for me. Let's be honest."

The captain smiled with a ferocity that made Chase's skin tingle. "Oh yes, please. Let's."

*Here it comes*, thought Chase.

Maurus took a step forward, and in a tense voice, asked, "How much of the plan were you aware of? Did you realize the scope of what was going to happen to Trucon?"

The captain narrowed his eyes. "Of course not. What do you take me for, Maurus? Don't try to place any of the blame for this disaster on me."

"None of the blame?" Maurus jerked his head back in mock surprise. "Take your share, Captain. You may not have known the entire plan, but you certainly deserve some of the credit for sending me to Trucon and letting the consequences unfold."

The captain grabbed him by the collar. "How dare you even suggest—"

"You know it wasn't me! I didn't plot the attack!"

Lennard pulled Maurus closer to him, and his voice dropped lower. "Are you trying to tell me that you're not intimately involved with the Karsha Ven?"

Maurus's face flushed red. "You can't use me like this!"

Lennard shoved Maurus away. "Use you? Why should I care if anyone uses you? You're just another extremist from a dying planet that shouldn't even be a part of the Federation!"

The medical officer ushered Chase into the shower just as Maurus spat at Lennard. The hot chemical water streamed over Chase's head, rinsing away the dried mud and blurring his vision. Captain Lennard threw a punch at Maurus, who bent over and rammed his head into Lennard's abdomen, knocking the air from him with a grunt. Forquera jumped in and pushed Maurus to the floor, and Lennard drove a boot into Maurus's ribs. It connected with a sharp crack, and Maurus screamed.

"Stop it!" Chase jumped out of the shower, water cascading down his face. "Let him go, he didn't do anything!"

Lennard and Forquera turned and looked at Chase, and for a moment, everyone froze. Lennard took a step toward him, his face suddenly as gray as his hair.

"Maurus, what is this?" the captain croaked. "What have you done?"

"I—what?" Maurus looked confused.

Chase took an uncertain step backward, and Lennard whipped out a handblaster, pointing the barrel straight at Chase's forehead. "On the floor! Get down!"

Chase sank to his knees. His insides turned to ice. The coating of mud had been protecting him—now he was fully exposed.

"Don't you touch him!" shouted Maurus. "He's got no part in this!"

"Captain?" asked Forquera, arching his eyebrows. He looked at Chase again, but showed none of the recognition that the captain did.

"Get me a set of shackles now and cuff this thing up!" yelled Captain Lennard, spraying Chase's face with spittle. *Thing?* His eyes were wild in a way that made no sense, as if Chase were somehow terrifying. "Take them to the brig."

"Both of them, Captain?" asked Forquera, waving over a soldier to shackle Chase's hands behind his back.

"Yes, both of them! Now!" Lennard backed away, his wild eyes glued on Chase. Without another word, he turned and bolted from the decontamination room.

Pointing his blaster, Forquera herded Maurus and Chase from the flight deck and into a large hallway. Maurus marched in front, glaring straight ahead and leading the way down a series of corridors. Chase followed behind him, so dazed that he barely noticed all the soldiers who stopped and stared at them.

What he had feared most of all had come true. He was a captive of the Fleet, exactly where Dr. Silvestri had warned him not to end up. But worse than that, how did Captain Lennard recognize him—and why did he seem so shocked to see him?

The brig was a long, narrow room with a desk station at one end, and four windowed doors spaced along the side wall. A young soldier sat behind the desk. "Colonel!" he barked, snapping to attention. His eyes immediately went to Maurus.

"Is number three open?" Forquera asked.

"The new one's in number three," said the soldier, looking curiously at Chase. "Two is empty. A child, sir?"

Forquera shook his head brusquely. "Captain's orders. Put them in two."

The young officer badged open the holding cell and ushered Chase and Maurus inside. The door slid shut behind them. The small room was lined with a bench, and Chase sat on one side, facing Maurus, both of them with their hands still secured behind their backs.

Maurus tipped his head back against the wall and closed his eyes. "I'm finished," he said softly. He opened his eyes again. "Chase, I'm so sorry you've gotten wrapped up in this."

"I'm sorry too." Chase tried to focus his thoughts on Maurus's predicament, to avoid thinking about his own. What came was guilt: If he and Parker had never followed him into the Shank, if they'd never ended up on Vo's ship, Maurus would have made it to Lyolia. "You could have gotten away."

"We were never going to survive down there on the Zeta," Maurus said.

"But if you still had your silver case . . ."

"It doesn't matter anymore. Lennard would have just thanked me for returning it to the Fleet before he tossed me out the airlock. This is my fate—my life has been forfeit since this whole mess began."

"They have to let you contact your people, right? You can still ask them for help. Make them call the Lyolian president or whatever."

Maurus exhaled and looked at the ceiling. "Chase, when I said *my* people, I never meant the Lyolian people."

"But you're from—"

"I'm Lyolian, yes. But I'm talking about *my* people." He frowned at Chase, as if deciding how much to say. "The Karsha Ven."

The information was slow to sink in—Maurus was admitting that some of the accusations were correct. That he was a member of the reviled Karsha Ven rebel group. "You mean . . . you *are* a terrorist?"

"No!" Maurus's voice was harsh. "The Karsha Ven is not a terrorist organization. It's a group of Lyolians trying to get the best choices made for our world. Some branches have used violence and tarnished our reputation, but at its core, it is not a violent movement."

"How can a member of the Karsha Ven become a Fleet soldier?"

Maurus shook his head. "You can't. I had silly ideas about

unity and leadership. So many of the Karsha Ven leaders are too stubborn, too reactionary, but I thought I could be the one to make a difference. I thought I would bridge the disagreements and bring peace to my homeworld. So I lied, I hid my connection to the Karsha Ven and climbed the ranks of the Lyolian military, and when the opportunity to participate in the officer interchange program appeared, I jumped on it. Or at least I thought I had, when in fact it seems I was stepping into a well-planned trap, delivering myself as the perfect scapegoat for this attack. Clearly the captain knows— he probably knew all along. I'm a fool!" He kicked at the wall and lay down on the bench.

Chase didn't speak, still trying to reconcile this information. He thought he knew Maurus by now—persecuted soldier from a troubled planet who had stolen from Chase and Parker, but also protected them. But if part of the accusation against him was true, if he had lied his way into the Fleet, then what else had he lied about?

The door to the cell slid open, and Captain Lennard walked in. He stared at Chase for a moment. "Where did you find your companion, Lieutenant Maurus?"

Maurus cracked one eye open and glared at Lennard.

"How do you know this boy?" Lennard asked.

Maurus swung his legs over the edge of the bench and hoisted himself upright, looking suddenly alert. "How do *you* know him, Captain? It certainly looked like you recognized him."

A thundercloud crossed the captain's face. "We're not talking about me here, Maurus. Answer me."

Maurus took a quick breath, as if he were about to say something, and then he clamped his mouth shut and shook his head.

Lennard turned to Chase. "What is your name?"

Chase hesitated. "Corbin Mason."

Lennard narrowed his eyes. "Where are you from?"

"I don't know."

"Of course you don't," spat Lennard. "What is your mission?"

"My . . . mission?" Chase asked. "I'm just trying to find out who I am."

"Who you are is no one. You shouldn't even exist!" The naked hatred in Lennard's eyes made Chase feel like the man might try to strangle him at any moment. "How do you know Lieutenant Maurus?"

Chase stared at him for a moment, stunned. "We found—"

"Shut up!" hissed Maurus.

Lennard leaned over so that his flushed, raging face was all Chase could see. "I don't know what you're doing here, but I will figure out what you've got planned! Whoever sent you here won't get away with any of this!"

The captain raised his hands as if to strike Chase, who jerked away in surprise. A sharp tingle ran up his arms as his wrists slid right out of the shackles. He pushed his hands farther behind his back, hoping the captain wouldn't notice, but the captain had already turned his attention back to Maurus.

"You'll be tried for your crimes later today, Maurus. Your sentence will be carried out immediately following judgment."

Maurus lurched to his feet. "No. I'm allowed a representative from my people."

"Your people! You think the Karsha Ven's going to waste any time fighting for you? They don't care. To them, you're already dead."

"They won't abandon me! You Earthans have no concept of what we're truly about."

Lennard paused. "So you admit, you *are* Karsha Ven?"

His eyes flashing with horror, Maurus pressed his lips together for a moment. "I'm allowed a representative," he repeated.

"Not for a court-martial. This is military law."

"You can't do this to me." Maurus's voice grew frantic. "I need more time. This isn't—" He ran at the captain, who shoved him hard in the chest. Maurus stumbled backward, unable to catch his balance, and fell against the bench.

"You should have considered that a long time ago. Someone will be down shortly to escort you to the court-martial." Lennard stalked out of the cell, and the door slid shut behind him.

Maurus lowered his head, breathing raggedly. His chin-length hair hid his face.

Maurus had revealed the truth about himself. It was time for Chase to give up his secret as well. He stood up and crossed the cell.

"He's right, you know," Maurus said in a broken voice. "The leaders of the Karsha Ven will believe I did this. They're not going to come anywhere near me."

Chase held out his bare wrists. "Look at me."

"Let me be, Chase!" Maurus's voice was strained. He looked up through the curtain of his hair and paused. "How did you get your shackles off?"

A twinge of excitement kindled deep within Chase. "There's something you don't know about me."

Maurus's gaze rose to Chase's face. "Why does the captain know who you are, Chase?"

"I don't know. There's a lot I don't understand. But I know I'm . . . different."

Before Chase could continue, the door slid open, and he whirled against the wall, pressing his hands behind his back again.

A pair of blank-faced soldiers entered. "Lieutenant Maurus, come with us."

Maurus looked up at Chase. His dark eyes were wild, but there was a focused intensity that hadn't been there a minute ago. "It's too late to help me. But get yourself out of here. Make sure the truth gets out with you. Make sure the universe knows what's happening." The soldier reached under his arm and yanked Maurus toward the door. "Get off the ship! Go to—" His last words were cut off as the door slid shut.

Alone in the cell, Chase hunched in the corner and attempted to put the shackles back on so that no one from the Fleet would wonder how he got them off. He jammed the metal cuffs against his knuckles, but no matter what he tried, he couldn't force his hands back into them.

He had no idea how to control whatever it was he could do—how could he help Maurus, let alone himself? How did he think he would get off an enormous battleship in the middle of the galaxy, when all his allies were either locked up, or dead? Not even when he'd woken up in utter confusion at Parker's home had he felt this lost. The reality was this: The enemy had him.

There was no way he was going anywhere.

# CHAPTER EIGHTEEN

Chase lay on the hard bench in the holding cell, unable to sleep. The lights never went off, and he had no idea how much time had passed since they'd arrived on the *Kuyddestor*—at least two days, maybe three. A soldier had removed the shackles lying beside him on the bench without comment, probably assuming Lennard had taken them off, and had entered his cell several more times to deposit a tray of food and retrieve it again, untouched. No one would answer Chase's questions about Parker or Maurus.

Parker was dead. He had to be. There was no way he could have survived. Chase's mind kept replaying his last memory of Parker as he writhed on the floor, choking on thick gobs of acrid foam that dribbled from his mouth. And then the terrible stillness when he stopped. Chase mashed his hands against his eyes and rolled toward the wall, his face contorted with misery, but no tears came.

He was too angry with himself to cry. Why hadn't he prevented this from happening? Sure, Parker was smart—annoyingly so at times—but Chase was the special one. He should have been able to protect his friend, to save him, but he'd failed. And now Parker was gone. He'd never again ridicule Chase for not knowing something, never give him that easy grin and friendly slap on the back. He ceased to exist. The thought made Chase feel hollow with grief.

The door opened. Chase lifted his head and saw a soldier standing outside his cell.

"Come with me," the soldier said.

Chase sat up quickly. This was the first time anyone had spoken to him since Maurus was taken away. "Where to?"

The soldier frowned and stepped back, motioning for Chase to exit his cell. Chase followed him out into the hallway.

"Is my friend alive?"

The soldier stared straight ahead as he marched, ignoring the question.

"His name is Parker. He came here with Goxar poisoning. What happened to Lieutenant Maurus? Where are you taking me?" Chase's irritation grew as the soldier kept walking, blank faced, and he fell into a sullen silence.

They came to an elevator and took it up several floors to a long gray corridor. A wild range of possibilities flickered through Chase's head, but deep in his gut he feared it was one of two options: He had been called to witness either Maurus's trial or Parker's funeral.

They finally stopped in front of a pair of double doors. The soldier waved his badge, and they walked into a room full of people.

Sitting in a chair in the middle of the floor was Parker.

"You're alive!" Chase rushed forward but stopped short of giving Parker a hug, standing awkwardly in front of him with an enormous grin plastered across his face.

"Retrieved from the brink of death, they tell me." Parker returned an embarrassed smile as he pulled himself to his feet. His color was still waxy, with unhealthy brown circles under his eyes and shiny new skin around his mouth, but he seemed okay—a world of difference from the last time Chase had seen him.

"How did they—what did they—?" Chase stammered. He reached out and gave Parker's arm a squeeze, just to make sure he was really there.

Parker shrugged. "Oh, you know, pumped me full of synthetic blood, restarted my heart a few times. I guess they had to replace some of my veins and skin with grafts. The ship's doctor is really good." He rubbed his chest at the spot where the Goxar's spike had hit him, wincing a little, and sat down again with a wan smile.

Mina looked on placidly over Parker's shoulder. Behind her were a team of soldiers, and a scowling woman sitting at a console. One side of the room was empty, and there was a row of metal disks stamped into the floor. Chase realized they were in a teleport chamber.

"What's going on?" he asked.

"They finally let Mina contact Asa," said Parker. "He's coming to get us."

"Us?" Excitement thrilled down Chase's spine.

"I told them we're not leaving without you."

Chase was filled with a flood of overwhelming gratitude. Finally, this nightmare was about to end. Asa was coming to free them from the Fleet, bringing with him all the answers for Chase's questions. Giddy with relief, he felt as if he were floating above the floor, but a wary thought jerked him back down. "What about Maurus? Do you know what happened to him?"

Parker grimaced and shook his head, but before he could answer, Captain Lennard entered the room. He frowned at Chase as he walked over to the console, and Chase froze. Dread crept into the back of his mind—he couldn't believe that Lennard would let him go this easily.

"Alright, Corporal Lahey—are we set?" asked the captain. The sour-faced woman nodded. "Soldiers, keep your weapons at the ready. Start the transit." Everyone stared expectantly at the floor disks, and Parker rose to his feet again.

A moment later, a man in a tan suit materialized in one of the circles. He had a slight build and thinning blond hair, and he stepped forward with a smile and a bow. For all the secrets that surrounded Asa Kaplan, he looked about as mysterious as a piece of toast.

"Captain," he said respectfully. Chase could feel Parker straining at his side to get a good look at him and realized that he was doing the same.

Lennard snorted. "Are you kidding me? Tell Mr. Kaplan that if he expects me to hand over anybody, he'd better show up in person—not send one of his androids to do his dirty work."

The man said nothing, scanning the room slowly before he stepped backward onto the circle. If the man was indeed an android, he was of the same high caliber as Mina, because he looked human to Chase. He decided it was the man's exaggerated stillness that helped Captain Lennard recognize that he was not human. A second later, the man disappeared.

They all stood for a few minutes, waiting. Finally the corporal at the console spoke. "Here he comes."

The man who materialized on the teleport circle this time was very tall, with broad shoulders and a slim waist. His dark hair was slicked back severely, and he had intense blue eyes set deep in his pale face. He looked younger than Chase had expected, but just his stance gave off an air of power.

"Captain." His tone was more challenging than respectful.

"Mr. Kaplan," replied Lennard.

Asa Kaplan looked at their group. "Mina," he said in greeting. His gaze flickered over Parker, who stared at Asa as though he were trying to gobble him up with his eyes, and landed briefly on Chase. The look was piercing, but it gave away nothing—Chase couldn't tell if Asa recognized him. What he could tell was that under his cold guise of control, Asa Kaplan looked either furious, or terrified.

Asa turned to Captain Lennard. "I would like to thank you for caring for my ward in these troubled times," he said in measured tones. "I don't know how I can repay you. I'll be glad to take him off your hands now."

"Not so fast, Mr. Kaplan," said Lennard, matching Asa in intensity. "I'm afraid we have a problem."

Chase's heart sank. Of course it wouldn't be this easy.

Asa leveled his intense stare on the captain. "I don't understand."

"It seems that the boy in your care refuses to leave without his companion." Lennard stepped over and put his hand on Chase's shoulder. Chase flinched before he could stop himself. "Do you know this boy?"

Asa regarded Chase with a long stare. "Not personally. My android informed me about him. I'm willing to take him into my care." Chase looked away to hide his disappointment. Asa wouldn't have any answers for him. "Is he an orphan?"

"One could say that," said Lennard. "Are you sure you've never seen him before?"

"If you're trying to make a point, Captain, your directness would be appreciated," said Asa harshly.

"What I'm trying to deduce here, Mr. Kaplan, is if you can tell me what this creature is."

Asa frowned. "A boy?"

"He does claim that. He tells me his name is Corbin Mason, although that is a lie. He believes his name is Chase Garrety," said Lennard.

Chase opened his mouth to deny this, but Asa locked eyes with him, and a tiny, almost imperceptible shift in Asa's gaze froze the words in his throat. "And why do you believe he is not what he says?" asked Asa, his eyes never leaving Chase's face.

"I happen to know, Mr. Kaplan, that the real Chase Garrety died several weeks ago," said Lennard.

*Died?* Chase felt as though an electric jolt had been sent through his body. His mind began to reel. He'd been called dead before. Did this mean it was true?

"And if I may ask, how did the real Chase Garrety pass?" asked Asa.

"It was a home invasion. The boy was killed along with his parents."

The words struck Chase like a hammer. He felt dizzy, and his eyes lost focus for a moment as he absorbed the meaning. He had no parents. They were dead. He was dead. How could he be dead? Parker put a hand on his arm, bringing him back to the present.

"I saw the scene myself," Lennard continued. "There is no doubt."

"You saw proof?" Asa asked.

Lennard inclined his head. "There is no doubt," he repeated.

After a moment's hesitation, Asa stepped off the teleport circle and crouched down to come face-to-face with Chase. Chase gazed back blearily, sweating. He felt like throwing up on the man's shoes. *Help me*, he thought. *Help me figure out who I am.* But Asa only stared back with his cold blue eyes, examining Chase with no more emotion than if he were purchasing merchandise.

After a minute, Asa stood up, saying, "There must have been a mistake, but I'll take the boy with me. I certainly have the means to care for another orphan."

Lennard nodded. "I thought you might say that." He crossed the room to the transport console and turned on his heel. "This boy isn't leaving my ship, and neither are you."

Asa's eyes narrowed. In a pinwheel of motion, the captain and every soldier in the room reached for their weapons.

Asa leapt backward onto the teleport circle, grabbing at his wristband.

"Freeze!" shouted Lennard.

But Asa Kaplan had already vanished.

"No!" cried Parker, lunging at the empty space. "Come back!"

Chase stumbled backward against the wall, staring ahead with glazed eyes. After hungering for so long to know who he was and what had happened to him, this answer was more than he could stomach.

He had no family. No parents were looking for him, because they were dead, and because he wasn't even Chase Garrety. He was no one at all.

Mina held Parker from throwing himself on the teleport floor, and Lennard shouted orders into the console for the bridge to hold Asa's ship with threat of fire.

"I'm sorry, sir," came a woman's voice from the console. "They're already out of range."

"There's no civilian ship with engines that powerful," Lennard snapped. He glanced around until his eyes came to rest on Chase. Before Chase could react, the captain crossed the room and grabbed his collar. Chase reached for Parker, but Parker stood dazed in Mina's arms, looking shocked at being left behind by the one person who was supposed to care for his well-being.

"Lahey, gather as much data as you can on Asa Kaplan," said Lennard. Swiftly he led Chase from the teleport chamber and down the hall, and shoved him into an elevator.

"I *will* get to the bottom of this," Lennard threatened, stepping in after him.

Chase stared back defiantly. His initial fear of the captain was fading, and in its place came anger. Captain Lennard had just provided him with more information about himself than anyone else—he certainly knew more about Chase than Asa Kaplan did. And he probably knew more than he'd said. But this whole time, instead of trying to help Chase, he'd been trying to force information from him.

They marched back to Chase's empty cell in the brig, and Lennard sealed the door behind them. They locked eyes, and the room was silent but for the captain's loud breathing. Chase opened his mouth to demand answers, but the captain spoke first.

"Where is Lilli Garrety?"

"Who?" Thrown by the unexpected question, Chase tried to keep a straight face while his mind raced. *Lilli Garrety?*

Lennard pressed his fingertips against his temples. "The boy you are impersonating had a sister. She's gone missing, and I need to find her."

A memory flitted through Chase's mind: a small, angry girl wielding a knife.

*Chase is dead.*

*I saw it happen.*

Puzzle pieces began to fit together, and Chase struggled to keep his expression blank. It was his sister. The girl who tried to kill him on Qesaris was his sister. He shook his head.

"She's a very special girl, and I think someone created you to find her first," Lennard continued. "I can't let that happen. Do you know where she is?"

*I'm being held by the one who led the end.*

It was only a clue, but she'd tried to tell him where she was. How stupid was he to just ignore her plea and leave her stranded! Chase needed something to distract the captain, to keep his reeling emotions from playing out too plainly across his face. "Did you kill them?" he asked recklessly. "Did you kill Chase Garrety and his parents? She got away from you, didn't she?"

Lennard sucked in his breath, and his face turned a boiling, furious red. "I will grind the truth out of you if I have to tear you limb from limb to do it," he growled, leaning in close. "I'm going to find her first." He exhaled a long, rancid breath in Chase's face, and left the cell.

A million thoughts battled for attention in Chase's mind, but one stood out above all others, filling him with hope. With sadness. With rage.

*Please, Chase.*

*Guide the star.*

Those were the words she'd spoken, same as the first ones he remembered saying. Whether his were from a real memory or an implanted one, whether he was actually Chase Garrety or a man-made replacement, he knew there was a little girl who needed his help. A little girl who held the answers to who he was, and what had happened to him. A resolution formed in his chest, hard as a diamond. He would get off this ship, and he would rescue her.

But he had to find her before Lennard did.

# CHAPTER NINETEEN

Chase stared at the door of his cell.

He had a plan. It wasn't a great plan. It wasn't even a good plan, and it depended on his belief that he had the ability to evade grabbing hands, blaster shots, and whatever else might await him in the halls of the starship.

But first he had to get through that cell door.

Mina was in one of the two cells to his left. He'd seen them bring her in not long after Captain Lennard had left him. Parker wasn't with her, so Chase guessed he was back in the medical bay, wherever that was. He hadn't heard anything about Maurus and wondered with a sick feeling in his gut if he'd already been tried and executed. He knew if he was able to break Mina out, they wouldn't have time to look for Maurus. He hoped they'd be able to find Parker. His plan didn't extend much further than that.

He pressed his hands flat against the door. It certainly felt solid. Impulsively, he knocked his head against the metal surface. It bounced off with a dull thud. "Ow," he muttered, rubbing the tender spot.

He was crazy for thinking he could escape. He had no idea how to control his phasing, if that was what he could do. Nibbling doubts crept up, questioning his memories. Maybe there had been a weak spot on that container door. Maybe the hand shackles had been left open. Maybe the blade the girl had plunged into his neck was a fake, a gag knife that retracted into the handle. He closed his eyes and thought of the horrible coldness he'd felt when she stabbed him, and remembered her pale, furious face. No wonder she'd been so shocked, seeing her own brother strolling around on Qesaris after she'd witnessed his death. She had to be terrified.

She couldn't be more than ten years old. He imagined her, crouched alone in some dark corner, scavenging for food.

He couldn't let Lennard get her.

Chase opened his eyes and positioned himself so he could just barely see out of the cell door's window to where the guard sat behind a console, looking bored.

It was time.

"Hey!" he shouted. The guard didn't react—the cells were nearly soundproof. Chase tried again, yelling and pounding on the window.

The guard looked up from his desk and frowned. As soon as Chase caught the guard's eye, he staggered away from the door, groaning. He dropped onto the bench, clutching his stomach with one hand and his head with the other.

The soldier's face appeared in the window. Chase shook his head frantically and wailed. The guard began to step away from the door, back toward his console, probably to call for help. Not good.

Chase screamed at the top of his lungs, slid from the bench, and flailed on the floor.

It worked. The guard waved his badge at the door and rushed to Chase's side. The door slid shut behind him.

"What's the matter?"

Still thrashing, Chase eyed the soldier's badge hanging on a cord around his neck. Could he snap it? Probably not. He wiggled and contorted himself into position, knees drawn to his chest, and launched his feet into the soldier's stomach.

With a surprised *oof!* the soldier doubled over and fell back against the wall, stunned. Chase sprang to his feet, yanked the badge up from around the soldier's neck, and waved it against the door's sensor.

Nothing happened.

"Nice try," wheezed the soldier. "Drop it and put your hands out where I can see them."

Chase glanced back at the door, clenching the badge in

his hand. It was now or never. He would have to try jumping through the door. He wasn't sure if he'd be able to take the badge with him, but his clothes seemed to make the journey every time, so it was worth a try.

Pressing the badge tight against his chest, Chase closed his eyes and ran at the door.

A wave of stinging numbness washed through him, and Chase tumbled to the floor outside his cell. Nausea curdled his stomach, and he curled up in a ball, waiting for the horrible tingling on his skin to go away. When he opened his eyes, he saw the soldier staring, dumbfounded, through the cell-door window. Feeling the hard edges of the badge in his hand, he pounded his fist on the floor in victory.

He'd done it. He could run through doors. He could phase.

Chase staggered to his feet and looked in the window of the next cell. The lights inside had been turned off, but he could see a shape of about Mina's size sitting in the corner of the room. He waved the badge at it, hoping it might work from the outside, but the soldier was right—in his hands it was useless.

He gritted his teeth and leaped at the door, grimacing as the same awful sensation passed through him. He fell to his hands and knees and coughed to stop gagging as his numbness began to subside.

"What on Hesta's seven suns?" asked a hoarse voice.

With a gasp, Chase looked up. It was Maurus, not Mina, who slouched on the floor, one leg extended out, both hands pressed to his side. His face looked scruffy and bruised, but his gleaming eyes were wide-open.

Had he been in the next cell all along? "I thought they killed you!" Chase blurted out.

"Not yet," Maurus said, sitting up and wincing. "Though not for lack of trying. Lennard's been, ah, encouraging me to record a confession. How did you get through that door?"

"This doesn't work," said Chase, holding up the badge.

Maurus shook his head. "Of course not. All Fleet badges are DNA-coded. How did you get it?"

Chase stood up, ignoring the question. "Tell me how to open the cell doors."

Maurus stared at him for a moment, and then got to his feet, hands still pressing tightly against his side. "Use the console at the desk. Access code 0990 should open the screen—it should be easy to figure out from there. What are you doing?"

Chase faced the door, taking a few quick breaths to prepare himself. This was getting easier. "Getting us out of here."

He ran at the door and jumped. This time, knowing what to expect, he landed on his feet. He leaned over for a second and gave his head a shake. Maurus stared out the window in shock. In the other cell, the soldier he had trapped was shouting and pounding on the door. If he had a communicator, he might have already called for help. Someone could walk in at any second and stop them.

Chase ran to the console and touched the screen, where a number pad blinked into view. Carefully, he touched the digits, 0-9-9-0, and the screen changed, filling up with a jumble of buttons and commands.

Chase looked at Maurus's cell window, panicking. "Which do I press?" he shouted. For once, he wished Parker were there. Chase forced himself to calm down and analyze the entire screen. Finally, on the right side he spotted a section marked Units, with buttons marked 1 through 4 underneath. Maurus and the guard were in the middle two cells, but which of those was 2 and which was 3? He couldn't risk opening the wrong door.

After a moment's contemplation, Chase pushed the button marked 1. Mina had to be in either 1 or 4, and once he knew which was which, he'd know the number to Maurus's cell. Another screen popped up with a list of commands, and Chase pressed Open Door.

The cell closest to him opened up. So that was cell number 1.

"Mina?" Chase called. Nothing. Quickly he opened cells 3 and 4, and Maurus rushed to the console. A moment later, Mina walked out of cell 4, calm and collected as ever.

"Good job, Chase," she said.

He stepped out from behind the desk. "How do we get off this ship?"

Maurus checked the console. "If we can make it to the lower flight deck, I'll get us out of here. We have to move fast—as soon as anyone realizes we've escaped, they'll lock everything down."

Chase turned to Mina. "Do you know where to find Parker?"

Before she could answer, a low groan came from cell number 1. Everyone turned and looked at the open door.

"Parker?" Chase dashed for the cell door, his pulse spiking. If that was Parker, he didn't sound good. What he saw inside the cell stopped him in his tracks.

Vo sat slumped on the bench. There were several crusted gashes in his face, which was mottled with green and yellow bruises, and one of his eyes was swollen shut. He bared his teeth and made an ominous rattling sound in the back of his throat.

Behind him, Maurus cursed loudly and pushed past Chase. "What happened? How did you get here?"

Vo glared at Maurus. "After you leave, another attack," he croaked. "No escape shuttle. Namatan shipper rescue me, call Fleet for help. And I tell them where to find you."

"Where is the silver case?" asked Maurus. "The one you took from me?"

"Gone. He took it."

"Who? Was it Captain Lennard? Tell me!" Maurus grabbed Vo's shoulders and pressed him against the wall.

Vo gave a hideous scream that cut off in a wet coughing fit, and Maurus backed off. When he recovered, Vo eased himself off the bench and onto his feet. "You wanna know who took case? Same person that took these," he hissed.

Shuffling on his long haunches, Vo turned around. To Chase's horror, on Vo's back, instead of his four long golden limbs, there were now four bandaged stumps. Vo looked over his shoulder, glaring at Maurus. "He came for *you*, make *me* suffer."

"Who?" Maurus shook his head, his mouth agape.

Vo glowered as he shuffled back around to face them, and then the folds of his face curled up in a malicious smile. "Rezer Bennin." He spoke the name slowly, enunciating every syllable, while giving a pointed look at Maurus. "Come to take his revenge for you stealing his money and android. *He* took case."

Maurus brought his hands to the sides of his face and groaned. "Cursed suns of Hesta, I can't go back and face that man. He'll kill me on sight."

"Cut off *your* arms." Vo's voice grew vicious. "I hope he cut off every one of your limbs, worthless Karsha swill!"

Maurus spat a few incomprehensible words at Vo and turned away. "Let's go, Chase."

"What about him?" Chase gestured at Vo, who, although obviously in a great deal of pain, leaned against the wall with a strangely contented smile on his face.

"Don't feel too bad for him," Maurus said coldly as he turned to leave. "He's Shartese. Those limbs will grow back." Taking one last look at the smuggler, Chase followed him out of the cell.

Maurus slipped behind the desk and typed something on the console, and Vo's cell door slid shut. Mina stood by the door. "Do you know where to find Parker?" he asked. She nodded, reaching for the handle.

"Try not to attract any attention," said Maurus. "The standby fighters are staged in the reserve hangar on level J. You've got five minutes, or we're leaving without you."

Mina walked out the door.

"Alright, let's move fast," Maurus said to Chase. He rifled through the guard's desk and withdrew a slender black baton. "Just stick close to me."

"But I'm not a soldier," said Chase. "They'll spot me in a second."

"This ship has a small civilian population—you'll be fine. I know a back hall where we probably won't run into anyone. Keep your head down and walk fast." He opened the door, sticking his head into the hallway before exiting the room.

The hall outside the brig was empty, and Maurus quickly cut across and into another quiet corridor. They walked swiftly for a minute, heading toward a recessed doorway. Maurus reached out for the handle, but the door opened before he could touch it. He jumped back with a salute, dropping his face toward the floor.

The young soldier who came through the door began raise his arm in return, but then he gasped, "You!"

"I'm sorry." Maurus whipped out the black baton and pressed it against the soldier's neck. It made a sizzling sound, and he tumbled to the floor.

Chase stared at the fallen soldier. "What did you—?"

"Stunned him. He'll be fine." Maurus led Chase down several flights of steep metal stairs and into a narrower, curved hall where the right-hand wall was lined with doors. He stopped at the first one and entered a numbered code to open it. As they stepped into a dark hangar, Chase could see the sleek lines of the fighter parked inside.

Maurus approached the Khatra quickly and opened the side door. "Get in."

"We have to wait for Mina and Parker."

"We can't," said Maurus. "There's no time to wait."

"But—"

"They'll be fine. The Fleet isn't after them, they're after

you and me. We need to get out of here right now." He grabbed Chase by the upper arm and began to pull him toward the craft.

"We can't leave them!" Chase yanked his arm, wincing at the sharp tingling as he phased through Maurus's grip.

Maurus looked at his hand, then at Chase. "How did you do that? What on Taras are you?"

"I'm not leaving Parker behind!" Chase repeated.

"No worries, you won't have to," said a voice behind him. With a wry smile on his face, Parker stepped into the docking chamber with Mina, his eyes already on the vehicle. "We're stealing a Khatra?" he breathed, reaching out reverently to touch it.

Chase exhaled with relief and stepped aside to usher Parker toward the Khatra.

"Everyone in, *now*," barked Maurus.

With a boost from Mina, Parker climbed up into the fighter, peering over the vehicle's one seat. "Are you joking? We'll never all fit in here."

"You don't have a choice," Maurus said. "Hurry up!"

The crawl space behind the Khatra's seat was barely big enough for one person. They wedged themselves in shoulder to shoulder with their knees drawn up to their chins. Chase had to incline his head at a sharp angle to avoid hitting the metal hull. Maurus jumped into the seat and closed the hatch. He drummed his hands against the manual controls as the vehicle powered up.

"Come on, come on, come on," he muttered. The seconds stretched on, and finally Maurus hissed, "Yessss." They lifted off the deck.

"It worked?" Chase asked. He strained to look over the back of the seat and caught a glimpse of star-spattered space through the front window.

"We're out!" said Maurus. "We're as good as—"

"Lieutenant Maurus!" interrupted a furious voice from the front console. "What do you think you're doing?"

Maurus veered the fighter out and away from the *Kuyddestor.* "Sorry, Captain, looks like you lose this round."

"All weaponry is pointed right at you, Lieutenant—you have ten seconds to surrender," said Lennard.

"And kill my hostages? I think that's against Fleet regulations, isn't it?"

"Are you insane?" Lennard roared. "Do you realize what you're doing?"

"Yes, I do," said Maurus. He was quiet for a moment, tapping at the console. When he spoke again, his voice was low and hard. "Just like you knew what you were doing when you sent me to Trucon on that bogus mission. You won't get away with any of this."

There was a pause. "Don't—" came the captain's angry voice over the console.

At that moment, Maurus launched the fighter into a fold, and they passed out of transmission range.

# CHAPTER TWENTY

They reappeared in a quiet segment of space, and after a tense second, Maurus released the breath he had been holding. "We did it!" he said, sounding fiercely pleased. "Hang on a minute while I plot out our course."

Parker leaned toward the front, unintentionally jamming his arm into Chase's side. "Where are we going now? What's the plan?" He was ghostly pale, and the occasional deep wheeze made it sound like he still had some difficulty breathing.

"Are you sure you're up for this?" Chase asked.

"Of course," Parker scoffed.

"Because you look terrible."

Parker made a face. "It'll take a lot more than a full dose of Goxar poison to keep me down. So what's the plan?"

As Chase twisted away from Parker's sharp elbow, he realized he hadn't given much thought to where he might find his sister. Qesaris was the only place he had seen her, so it seemed only natural to go back and look for her there. When Maurus didn't answer, he spoke up. "I have to go to Qesaris to find my sister."

Parker shifted to look at Chase. "Your *what*?"

"Don't worry," came Maurus's low mutter from the front. "Qesaris is where we're headed."

Chase paused. He had expected Maurus to want to go straight to the safety of his homeworld. "You're not planning to go after the case, are you?"

"Why wouldn't I?"

"You heard what Vo said. Rezer Bennin is out for revenge—he'll kill you. You'll never get the case. Just leave us on Qesaris and go back to your people."

"Go back to my people? Is that an order?" Irritation crept into Maurus's voice. "If I can get that case, I still have a chance to clear my name. And not just that—I can expose whoever it was in Fleet command that orchestrated the destruction of Trucon. This is my duty as a soldier of the Fleet."

Chase shook his head. How could Maurus still think of himself as a Fleet soldier after all that had happened?

Parker jabbed him in the shoulder. "I'm sorry, your *what*? Can you say that again? Sister?"

It was useless to argue with Maurus, so instead Chase turned to Parker. "Yes, my sister. You remember when I told you about that girl in the bathroom, when you told me I was crazy?" He proceeded to repeat what Lennard had said to him about Lilli Garrety. "That must have been my sister— that's why she was so upset when she saw me," he finished, trying to contort himself into a more comfortable position against Mina, who sat as still and inflexible as a statue.

"Because she thinks you're dead, just like the captain said." Parker was silent for a moment. "How do you think she found you in the first place?"

"I don't know." Chase had gone over the memory so many times in his head that he was able to recite their entire conversation to himself. "Wait, there was one thing. She mentioned a name, something like, 'Dornan didn't see you, but I did.'"

"Dornan?" Maurus's voice rang out sharply. "As in, Colonel Eileen Dornan?"

"You know who that is?" Chase asked.

"She's the chief medical officer of the Naxos Vector Command. What does she have to do with you?"

"I have no idea—" Chase began to say.

"Of course! Don't you remember, dummy?" Parker interrupted. "She was the officer running things at the medical center. She put the lasobind on my forehead after I split it open."

The older female officer with the baby-doll face! Chase gaped at Parker. "Do you tinik—?"

"Hold that thought, Chase," Maurus said, sitting up from the console. "I've got our course entered. Lennard's going to be right on our tail, so I'm giving it the full push. Things might get a little rough—we're going to get to Qesaris in record time. Prepare for fold."

Before Chase could utter another word, the universe collapsed around them, and the fighter tore across the galaxy in a dizzying rush, completing each fold nearly on top of the last. Bright objects flashed in the windshield, nearby planets and colored swirls of distant nebula. After an hour or so, Chase began to get a tight headache from all the folding, and his entire body ached from being cramped up for so long. It was still infinitely better than riding in Vo's decrepit shuttle.

Then the flashing images stopped, and they were enveloped in darkness again, with only the glow of the console to see by. The vehicle's gravity generator kept them seated, but Chase could feel that the Khatra was zooming downward. Gray light filtered in through the front window as they entered the atmosphere of Qesaris.

"I'm sure Lennard put an alert out on this fighter, so I can't land in any standard docking stations," said Maurus. "I'm going to land us at the port in the Shank. This will put us close to Rezer Bennin's lair, so we can get in and out with the case in a hurry."

*We?* Chase pushed the question out of his head, and instead tried to think of how he would go about finding his sister. Her final clue, *I'm being held by the one who led the end*, was not terribly helpful, and a planet was a very large place to be hidden on. Was it possible that she was still in the café where she'd jumped him? Unlikely, but maybe it was the best place to start.

Maurus slowed the vehicle, and after a few gentle turns, they settled to a stop. Almost immediately the hatch popped open. "Alright, everybody out—quick, quick," said Maurus, exiting the Khatra with a fluid jump and leaving Chase and Parker to pull themselves out of their cramped positions and scramble after him. Mina landed beside them with a heavy thump.

They walked swiftly through the hectic port, weaving through the tangle of parked vehicles and steaming vents and drawing stares from the raggedy men and creatures who worked there. Fortunately, the contingent of Fleet soldiers who'd been monitoring the port when they left was no longer there. Maurus rested one hand near his hip, where he carried the black baton he'd taken from the brig. They took a lift up to the street level of the Shank, and Maurus began to lead the way down a dark alley.

Chase stopped. "Hang on. Where are we going?"

Maurus glanced back at him with an impatient frown

and ushered the group into a recessed doorway. He scanned the three of them. "Okay, we need a plan. Mina, you should take Parker out of the Shank, somewhere safe."

"Don't you—" Parker began to protest.

Maurus turned to Chase. "You come with me. We'll deal with Rezer Bennin."

"What?" asked Chase, raising his voice over Parker's noisy objections. "No, I came here to look for my sister."

Impatience crossed Maurus's face. "Lennard is already on his way here, and it's only a matter of time before Vo cracks and tells him about the case. I have to get to it before he does."

"But I need to find her," said Chase, wrinkling his brow.

Maurus's voice dropped low. "I don't know if I can do this without you. We'll go look for the girl once we've taken back my case."

"You mean if we're still alive. If we're not being chased halfway across the galaxy." Chase's temper began to rise. "This may be the only chance I have to save her."

"You don't even know if she's really your sister!" Maurus said through gritted teeth.

"Captain Lennard said—"

"You told us he said *Chase Garrety* had a sister, and he also said Chase Garrety is dead. Look at you! You're not human, you pass through solid objects! How can you think you're really that boy?"

Chase felt his face growing hot as a tight, angry feeling knit together in his chest. "I am. I know it."

"You realize it's possible you never even saw the girl? Nobody else did, did they? Parker, did you see her? Her image could have been implanted in your memory as a way to control you."

Chase paused, uncertain. Could that be possible?

"Shut up!" Parker stepped forward and shoved Maurus in the chest. "Stop trying to manipulate him. We saved your life once already, or did you forget that?"

Maurus knocked Parker's hands away. "And I'd be back with my people by now if it weren't for you!"

Parker snorted. "You still can—go back and get the Khatra. Get out of here."

"Don't tell me what to do." Maurus grabbed Parker's shirt, and instantly Mina's hand was clamped on his shoulder. He let go, hissing in pain.

"Stop!" Chase shook his head at all three of them, fighting over what was his decision. "Parker, I can take care of this."

Maurus shook Mina off and turned all his attention on Chase. "I'm asking you to trust your gut. Yes, you're special. There's no one like you in the universe. But you have to realize that you can't really be that boy. You're probably walking into a trap." He placed his hands on Chase's shoulders, his dark eyes blazing with purpose. "Let's go get that case and tell the universe who was really behind the Trucon attack."

Chase put his head down to avoid Maurus's fervent gaze. On the *Kuyddestor*, he'd been so certain he needed to save his sister, but now Maurus was messing with his head and that certainty was crumbling. It felt incredibly selfish to ignore Maurus's noble goal in favor of his own possibly imagined one, and for a moment it seemed almost like he had no choice.

But he was so close to getting the answers he needed. How could he reach them if Maurus made him change his plans? He closed his eyes, and the girl's terrified face flashed before him. Anger pulsed in his veins. Chase raised his head and squared his shoulders. "Maybe I'm not Chase Garrety," he said. "But I know what I saw, and that girl needs me. If you wait, I promise I'll help you afterward."

Maurus's face tightened, and with an angry huff he dropped his hands, backing away. "I won't make it to afterward. But I won't waste any more time trying to convince you. Good-bye, Chase." He turned and stalked down the alley, shoulders taut, quickly disappearing into the gloom.

Chase turned to Parker. "Did I do the right thing?"

"Do you really believe you have a sister out there?" Parker asked.

Chase bit his lip. Maurus had told him to go with his gut

on this, and his gut told him that the frantic, desperate girl he'd seen needed his help. He nodded, and then asked, "Do you really think I'm Chase Garrety?"

"Pssht, of course! Did you not have a Chase Garrety chip in your head when I first met you?" Parker smiled. "So, how are we going to find this sister of yours? Tell me exactly what she said to you, every word."

"Parker," said Mina. He ignored her.

Chase racked his brain. "She said . . . I should know the safe place, and I should go there and ask for help."

"And I don't suppose you remember this safe place, do you?" Parker looked at him hopefully. "No. That would be too easy. What else?"

Chase dug deeper into his memory. "She said 'guide the star,' like I did—"

"Would be useful if we knew what that meant." Parker squinted. "So I guess we go look for this Colonel Dornun?"

"Parker," Mina repeated.

He turned to her. "How do we find the Fleet medical center again?"

Mina shook her head. "It's time for us to go. I'm going to contact Asa now so he can come and pick us up."

"Absolutely not." Parker narrowed his eyes. "You can tell him to come and get us afterward, but first we get Chase's sister. Then we can all go live happily ever after with Asa."

Mina frowned. "This is not up for debate. We have to leave now."

"No!" Parker raised his hands as if he were about to shove her, but he stopped himself. "Look, I'm giving you an order. My life isn't in any danger, so you can't override me. I know you have a map of Qesaris somewhere in that positronic brain of yours, so let's go find this Dornan lady and see what she can tell us about Chase's sister. Or tell Asa to come join us, if you think he'd like to help."

Mina shook her head. "He won't come to Qesaris himself. It's too dangerous for him."

"Of course it is!" shouted Parker. "And we all saw for ourselves on the *Kuyddestor* that Asa Kaplan puts Asa Kaplan first."

There was an awkward pause.

"Parker, they were going to arrest him," said Chase. "He had to get out of there."

"Oh, he had to, huh?" snapped Parker. "He had to abandon me there, then, did he? Just like he's abandoned me my whole life? Why did he even agree to be my guardian? Why didn't he just throw me in an orphanage?"

"He wanted to keep you safe," said Mina quietly. "You're very important to him."

"And he shows that by leaving me stranded on a Fleet ship in the hands of a madman. Come on, Mina, you're going to have to try harder to sell me on that one." Parker turned and threw his arm around Chase's shoulders. "Let's go find your sister." Without a glance back at Mina, he raised his voice and added, "You're welcome to come along. But you're not stopping me."

Parker started to lead Chase down the alley, and when Chase looked over, Mina was already walking at his side. "The Fleet medical center is in the Meolon District," she said calmly. "We can take a jettaxi."

✳   ✳   ✳

Chase, Parker, and Mina stood in the shadow of a warehouse across the street from the looming hulk of the Fleet medical center, watching the soldiers that marched in and out of the main entrance. "So, that's a pretty big place," said Parker. "How on Taras are we going to find Colonel Dornan in there?"

Chase considered this. "She's a doctor. Pretend that we're sick?"

"You'll end up in an exam room," said Mina. "And in deep trouble when they realize you're faking."

Parker looked around at the ground. "Find something to hit me in the head with. I'll tell her the lasobind didn't hold."

Chase rolled his eyes. "She said something about wanting to send you over to recruiting."

"That's right!" Parker snapped his fingers. "She wanted to recruit all the orphans into the Fleet."

Chase flinched at the word *orphan*, thinking of what Lennard had said about his parents, but a sly smile had spread across Parker's face. "We'll go in and tell them we're new recruits, here for our physical exams. And we'll tell them we were instructed specifically to ask for Colonel Dornan."

"What about Mina?" Chase asked.

"What about you?" Parker turned to face her. "What's your story?"

Mina shrugged. "I'm your personal property."

"Good enough." Parker started to walk toward the entrance.

"And once we're inside, how do we get back out?" Chase asked, jogging after him.

Parker flashed him a grin. "I'm counting on you to figure that part out. Hey, so your sister—she can do what you do? Jump through walls?"

Recalling how she'd vanished right in front of him, Chase shook his head. "I don't think so. She was just there, and then she wasn't."

Parker gave him a strange look as he pulled open the main entrance door. "Whatever, mystery man. Let's do this."

The first thing that hit Chase when they walked through the entrance was the noise: chattering, shouting, wailing.

The lobby was even more packed than it had been a few days earlier. The majority of the crowd was still humanoid, but now mixed in was the occasional glimpse of dangling tentacles or glossy black fur. Stressed mothers chased bawling children while scowling seniors hunched on chairs, giving everyone the evil eye.

Parker edged his way through the crush to the front desk, where the soldier on duty looked up and narrowed his eyes. Following on jittery legs, Chase didn't know how he was going to pull off lying to the guard. Luckily, he didn't have to.

"Brother, we are so late! You've gotta help us," trilled Parker in a high, funny accent.

Chase had to stop himself from turning to stare at him.

The soldier shook his head. "I'm sorry, I don't—"

"Your old lady officer, I can't remember her name—Dobbin? Domain?—she helped us out with some wound control back on T-day and said we had to come here and report to her—I guess it was yesterday? Day before? I don't know, brother, time has gotten so mixed up since this whole thing went down, and today somebody found my android—can you believe it? My freaking android, in all this! But, man, we're so done because we totally missed the appointment for our physical, and your lady Doskin seemed really interested in recruiting us, and—"

"Shut up," snapped the soldier. Chase blanched as the

man whipped out a handheld console and scrolled through the screen. He was probably calling for security to come and take them into custody. He nudged Parker on the arm, preparing to turn and race for the doors.

The soldier looked up again with a sour expression. "Physicals are taking place on the eighth floor. Elevators are over there. You can find the way yourselves."

"Oh, brother, thank you so much!" said Parker, taking a step away from the desk. "And this officer lady, Dalton—"

"Dornan," said the soldier.

"Yes! Where can we find her to apologize?"

"If she wants to see you, she'll find you." The soldier turned to the next group and started barking orders.

They backed away and headed for the elevators. "This place is a mess," said Parker in a low voice.

"Are all these people refugees from Trucon?" asked Chase.

"The news said three million people were displaced." Parker shook his head. "And Qesaris isn't big enough to handle them all."

They took an elevator up to the eighth floor, where Chase approached a tired-looking orderly and asked where they could find Colonel Dornan. The orderly told them her facilities were on the twentieth floor before heaving himself to his feet and plodding away.

The elevator would only take them as far as the sixteenth floor, but they had Mina break open a stairwell door and climbed the last four floors. They hung back by the stairwell, scoping out the situation. The halls on the twentieth floor were white and sterile, and only a few hospital staff patrolled this level.

"Stay here," whispered Chase, stepping out into the hallway.

"Forget it," said Parker. They slipped down the hall with Mina following like a guard dog, pressing themselves into doorways to avoid crossing paths with any of the hospital staff. In the end, Colonel Dornan's office wasn't hard to find.

It was the one she was standing outside of.

Chase recognized her broad, rosy face and bobbed blond hair from their brief interaction at the refugee registration. She was discussing something with another officer, waving her hand around as though she were describing something large. Another soldier approached them and said something in a low murmur.

"What?" Dornan's sharp voice echoed down the hall, carrying her evident displeasure with it. Chase pulled his head back slightly, his heart pounding. Had someone spotted them? A moment later, she led the two officers away and they vanished around a corner.

Chase waited for a few moments and turned back to Parker and Mina. "Come on!" he whispered, and ran down the hall to Dornan's office. The door was locked.

Without a word, Chase lowered his head and jumped through, shaking off the tingling sensation with a shudder. It was a sleek room, lined with tall cabinets and a console-topped desk square in the middle. He unlocked the door for Mina and Parker, who stared at him in awe.

"Just start looking for anything you can find about a girl," Chase urged. "Her name is Lilli Garrety."

Chase began sifting through all the cabinets, finding mostly books and medical supplies. He wasn't even sure what he was looking for. Mina sorted through objects in a storage room in the back of the office, while Parker tried to hack into the desk console.

"Shh!" Mina stepped out of the supply closet, her head cocked. A second later Chase heard the voices approaching in the hallway.

"Hide!" he whispered.

Mina pulled Parker into the storage room, but there was no room for Chase. He climbed inside a cabinet, leaving the sliding door cracked just enough so that he could see out.

The hallway door opened and Colonel Dornan entered, her face twisted into a furious scowl. "How dare you come here! What were you thinking?"

Chase frowned when he saw the towering man-beast who entered behind Dornan. Tawny, ratty knots of hair hung around a face that was covered with a jumble of tattoos. Chase's mind raced, trying to remember where he'd seen the man before. A heavy musk scent filled Chase's nose. He'd smelled this somewhere else, he was certain.

"I told you, he couldn't be reached and I had nowhere else to bring this. I'm not carrying it around any longer." With an animal snarl, the man pulled something from a satchel slung across his chest and slapped it down on Dornan's desk with a crack.

"Drad it, Fersad, would you be careful?" said Dornan. She picked up the object and rubbed her sleek desktop. "Tell me you at least found the Lyolian."

A rushing sound filled Chase's ears as he stared at the slim silver object in her hand.

Vo had lied. Rezer Dennin didn't have Maurus's case.

The Fleet did.

# CHAPTER TWENTY-ONE

A chill trickled down Chase's spine like ice water as comprehension settled in. This was Vo's revenge. Angry about losing his ship, he'd lied about who attacked him, setting a trap that they'd all blindly believed. He had sent Maurus right into the hands of Rezer Bennin, a man who wanted him dead.

With this realization came the memory of where Chase had seen the tattooed man, Fersad: in the Shank port, where he'd been looking for Maurus. He, not Rezer Bennin, had attacked Vo's ship, stealing the case when he couldn't find Maurus.

Maurus was walking into a trap. Chase wished he could contact him somehow to stop him from going, but all he could do was stay silent and watch as Fersad tried to explain to Dornan why he still hadn't caught the AWOL pilot.

"The Shartese smuggler had the case, but he told me that

Lieutenant Maurus had already escaped, and by the time I tracked him down to a Zeta planet, there was no trace. It's possible that he drowned on the planet."

"Possible? Is that what we're paying you for, Fersad? Possibly dead?" As she spoke, Dornan removed two identical disks from the silver case and laid them on her desk. She slid her fingers across the console. "At least you managed to get these back." She turned and walked directly toward the closet that Chase was in.

Chase leaned back from the door, and with a gut-twisting wave of nausea, rolled sideways through the side and into the next cabinet. The burning, tingling sensation didn't subside, and he realized with a start that his body was divided up into three pieces by the low shelves inside the cabinet. When he heard the door slide shut a moment later, he rolled back into the first cupboard and pressed his eye against the crack again.

Dornan was emptying a bottle into a plastic bucket.

"Don't you think he'll want to see them?" asked Fersad.

"I think he'll take my word for it that the disks have been destroyed, don't you?" snapped Dornan. "It was his foolish idea to make a hard copy in the first place."

She dropped the two disks into the bucket and stepped back, covering her mouth as a thick column of vapor rose from the bucket. The acrid tang of disintegrating compounds reached Chase in the cupboard, and his heart sank even further. She was destroying the disks. Now Maurus had no way to prove his innocence. Not that he would need to, once Rezer Bennin got hold of him.

Dornan coughed and opened a compartment on her wall, setting the bucket inside and pressing a button that resealed the compartment door. She turned on her heel. "Now I suggest you go out, find Lieutenant Maurus, and end this catastrophe of an operation. Are we understood?"

Fersad grunted and turned to leave.

"Oh, and Fersad? Don't ever come back in this building unless you want a gaping blaster hole in your chest in lieu of payment."

The mercenary stomped out the door, and Dornan took a seat behind her desk.

Chase's mind raced. Could he stop Maurus from falling into Vo's trap? It was probably too late to stop him from contacting Rezer Bennin, although there might still be time to help him. But Chase's sister was still out there too, possibly in just as much danger as Maurus. And only she could give Chase the answers he needed about who he was and what had happened to him.

He looked around the cupboard for a weapon and saw only papers. There was no motion from Parker or Mina in the supply closet. Chase looked back at Dornan. A black baton rested on her desktop.

Quickly counting to three, he jumped out of the cabinet and snatched the baton from her desk.

Dornan whirled around in her chair, her hand flying to the blaster at her waist. When she saw Chase, the color drained from her face, and her mouth fell ajar.

"What are you doing here?" she croaked.

Chase took a step toward her, noticing the slight movement she made away from him. "Where is my sister?" he asked in a trembling voice.

"This isn't happening. You can't be here," said Dornan. The hand that wasn't gripping the blaster gun crept across her console.

She recognized him. Chase stared at her in disbelief. Yet another person who said things that made no sense, who knew more about his past than he did. The truth was right there in the officer's stunned blue eyes. All the frustration and fear Chase had felt in the last weeks boiled up in a rush, spilling over.

"*Why* can't I be here?" he exploded. He swung the baton with all his strength at the console. She jerked her hand away with a cry and the baton slammed into the screen, shattering its glass top into a thousand crystals. He raised the baton to strike again. "What!" *Crash!* "Am!" *Crash!* "I!" *Crash!*

"You're dead!" cried Dornan. "You were . . ." She trailed off, her mouth hanging open like the last word was stuck in her throat. Chase raised the baton threateningly. "Dispersed!"

Chase stopped, arm hanging over his head. "What?"

The words began to rush out of her. "It wasn't supposed to happen like that. The soldiers went beyond my authority."

"You were there?" A nasty feeling had started to snake its way up from the pit of Chase's stomach, and he clenched the baton tighter. "You were there when they killed my parents?"

Dornan pinched her lips together. Her eyes were wide and terrified. "It was necessary for the defense of the Fleet."

Chase gaped at her, feeling like he was going insane. Here was someone who knew exactly what had happened to him—happened to Chase Garrety, at least. He pointed the baton at her neck. "You're going to tell me everything that happened, or else I'm going to—"

"Whoa there, Chase," said a voice behind him. Parker had stepped out of the supply closet, with Mina right behind him. His gray eyes were cautious as he reached for Chase's shoulder. "We're here about your sister, right?"

Mina took the baton from Chase's hand in one smooth movement. She tucked it under Dornan's chin, pressing it to her throat as she reached down and removed the blaster from her hand. She tossed it on the floor. "Chase won't hurt you because he's human, but I'm a machine. Tell us where to find Lilli Garrety."

Dornan lifted one shaky hand and pointed toward the hallway.

"She's here?" asked Chase incredulously. When his sister said, *I'm being held by the one who led the end,* had she meant Dornan?

"Why don't you take us to her?" suggested Mina, pressing the baton harder against Dornan's throat. She hid the weapon as they moved out into the hall and held the woman's hand as if they were old friends. Dornan led them down the antiseptic corridor to a small, inconspicuous door guarded with a three-part locking system.

What Chase saw on the other side of the door knocked the breath out of him like a punch to the gut. The room was filled with various blinking machines, with a long table in the center, and laid out on the table like a tiny corpse was the girl from the café.

Thin cables from a few of the machines ran to her body, connected to her with tape and bandages. Her blond hair stuck out in all directions, and the deep circles under her eyes stood out like purple crescents in her pale skin. She wore the same light blue pajamas that he'd seen her wearing before. How had she ended up like this, when he'd seen her so alert and aggressive in the café?

"Wake up," Chase whispered, laying his hand on her arm. He half expected her eyes to open when he touched her cool skin, but they remained closed. Her chest rose and fell with shallow breathing. He pinched her arm lightly. "Hey? I'm here. I'm sorry it took me so long to come get you." He wanted to pick her up and carry her out, but didn't know where to begin with all the cables that ran from her body.

Behind Chase, he heard Mina ask Dornan, "What did you do to her?"

"She's under heavy sedation," said Dornan slowly. "She's an extremely dangerous child."

"She's just a little girl," said Chase.

Dornan made a harsh noise. "You, of all people, should know exactly what she is."

Mina stepped forward and began systematically detaching the lines by removing the bandages and tape strips that held down the flat metal disks on the end of each cable.

"Do you have any idea what you're doing?" asked Dornan. "You'll kill her, is that what you want?"

Chase's heart pounded in panic. "Mina?"

"Check the medications," said Dornan. "It's ganglaphin, the strongest sedative available. You can't just take a patient off without a step-down protocol, especially at this dosage."

Mina frowned and looked at the IV machine, and Dornan quickly reached for the communicator at her belt. Parker leapt forward to tear it from her hand. They struggled over the device for a moment, and then Dornan wrested it free, smacking Parker across the face with it. With a grunt, he fell backward, but before he even hit the floor, Mina had seized Dornan by the wrist. She wrenched the woman's arm behind her with such force that she dropped the communicator with a shriek.

Parker climbed back to his feet, holding the side of his face. "Take that," he mumbled.

"Chase, take your sister off the table," said Mina.

He went to the girl's side and hesitated. There were still three lines attached to her. "I don't know which one to take off first."

"Just take them all off, it doesn't matter," said Mina. "You can do it. You're not going to kill her." Warily, Chase pulled at the edge of a tape strip on the girl's skinny arm and lifted off the metal disk.

"You may not kill her, but she'll never wake up again," said Dornan.

"Shut up," said Mina. She wrenched Dornan's arms higher up her back, and the officer squawked and buckled to her knees.

Chase paused, looking at the frail girl. Mina wouldn't lie to him about this, would she? He wasn't even sure if she could lie. With trembling hands, he pulled off the three pieces of tape and lifted the metal disks from the girl's skin. Her eyes remained closed.

"Shouldn't she wake up now?" he asked.

"No, not right away," said Mina. "You'll have to pick her up."

Gently Chase slid his arms behind her shoulders and under her knees and lifted her from the table. She felt as light and fragile in his arms as a little bird. He stared at her in wonder. Behind those closed eyes was all the information he craved so badly.

Mina forced Dornan to take a few steps, so that they were standing alongside the table.

"Parker, come over here and tape these lines on her arm."

"With pleasure," said Parker. Dornan began to struggle as he reached for her arm.

Mina tightened her grip. "Colonel, I can break your arm in ten places before you even feel the first snap—but believe me, you will feel it."

Dornan ceased fighting, and Parker taped one of the disks to her arm. For a moment, nothing happened, and then her head began to droop forward and she folded toward the floor. Mina caught her and hoisted her limp body up onto the table.

"Put everything you see on her—every line we took off the girl," said Mina. "We'll try to knock her out deeply enough so that she can't send anyone after us right away."

As Parker applied the lines to the unconscious woman, he looked over at Chase, who held the delicate girl as if she were made of glass.

"This lady knew what happened to you," Parker said.

Chase looked at Dornan's slack face. There would be no getting answers from her now. "Once my sister wakes up, she'll be able to tell me."

"It might take a few hours for these sedatives to wear off," said Mina. "Dornan was right about one thing—they had her on an extremely high dosage of a very powerful sedative." Seeing Chase's nervous expression, she added, "But she'll be fine."

Parker slapped the last line on Dornan. "Have a good sleep, you old bat." He looked at Mina and Chase. "Now, how are we going to get out of here?"

Mina cocked an eyebrow. "I'd say we just take the stairs. Quickly, before someone finds Colonel Dornan and raises an alarm."

The hallways of the twentieth floor were mostly empty, but as they walked toward the stairs, an older man in a lab coat stepped out of one of the offices. Chase's pulse sped up. He glanced up long enough to see the man giving them a funny look, but he didn't try to stop them. When they reached the stairwell, Mina stopped and lifted the girl out of Chase's arms. He opened his mouth to protest, but she cut him off, saying simply, "Run."

Chase rushed down the stairs two at a time with Parker at his side, Mina right behind them. At about the tenth floor, a door crashed open somewhere above them, followed by a man's shout: "We'll head down, you go to the roof!" The sound of their footsteps gave Chase a surge of adrenaline, and he started taking the stairs three at a time. Beside him, Parker was clutching the railing, and at the next landing he missed a step and skidded down onto one knee. Chase whipped around to help him up, and gasped at Parker's glassy eyes and the sweat coating his pallid face. "What's wrong?"

Parker shook his head, pulling himself quickly to his feet. "I'll be fine," he wheezed, pushing Chase's hand away.

Chase ignored him and looped his arm under Parker's shoulders. "Two at a time. Come on, we can do this." They ran in sync down each flight, pausing for a moment on the landings. The men's steps grew louder as they closed the distance. Their angry shouts echoed down the stairwell. Chase focused on the flights remaining. *Three to go. Two to go.*

Finally they reached the ground floor, bursting through an outside door onto the street. Chase glanced backward and caught a glimpse of two soldiers directly behind them, almost within grabbing distance as the door began to swing shut. His view was cut off as Mina grabbed the handle with one hand and pulled with all her strength, buckling the metal door and wedging it securely in its own frame.

Parker was already staggering out toward the street, where he quickly hailed a jettaxi. The driver, a small creature completely covered in dark, glossy fur, barely looked at them as they tumbled into the vehicle and ferried them away from the military building and up into the streams of traffic.

"We need to get to a communication hub so I can contact Asa," said Mina. Parker nodded and leaned back against the seat, breathing slowly.

"Are you okay?" Chase asked.

"I'll be fine." Parker closed his eyes. "Just give me a sec."

Chase leaned over his sister and brushed the chunks of blond hair from her face, willing her to open her eyes, but her long lashes lay closed against her cheek. There was nothing he wanted more in the world than for her to wake up and tell him everything he needed to know about himself. He smiled, imagining how happy she would be once she realized he had come for her.

Another thought gnawed at the back of his mind: Maurus. His thoughts produced a horrible image of the doomed Lyolian, strung up and tortured in Rezer Bennin's lair. He pushed the image away. Maurus was probably already dead—there was nothing that anyone could do for him. And it had been his decision not to flee to his homeworld. Chase leaned in toward his sister and whispered in her ear, "Wake up."

They had the jettaxi drop them off in an abandoned alley, and Mina broke into a closed warehouse. Chase carried his sister, keeping an eye out for somewhere to set her down, and followed Mina and Parker while they located an office with a communication console.

"How do you even contact him?" Parker asked, sinking into a chair and watching her fingers fly across the console.

"I ping him first with a series of code fragments inserted at specific intervals into a shifting order of public bandwidths based on forty-three algorithms." She glanced at Parker's baffled face. "It's complex."

Chase laid his sister on a cot in a corner of the office and crouched beside her. The connection he felt to her was so strong, he made a decision at that moment: He was Chase Garrety, not a clone, nothing man-made. He had to be. And he had saved his sister, and soon Asa would come, and she would wake up, and everything would be right.

Only it wouldn't. Because Maurus was still out there, and maybe he was alive, and Chase would never know if he could have saved him too. Now that all the answers were right at his fingertips, walking away would be the hardest thing he'd ever had to do. But he couldn't leave Maurus to his fate without knowing that he'd tried to help. Maybe

Chase didn't completely understand the rules of the galaxy—which species he could count as allies, who not to trust—but he knew in his gut that Maurus was one of the good guys. He couldn't just leave him to his fate.

Chase touched his sister's cool temple as he whispered good-bye and promised to return, and then he stood and turned to the others at the console.

"I'm going to look for Maurus," he announced.

Parker whipped around. "What? No."

"Parker, I have to."

"Then I'm coming with you."

"You're in no shape to go anywhere, and you know Mina won't let you." She didn't even glance up from the console. "Besides, I need you to stay here and make sure my sister is safe."

"You'll get yourself killed."

"Come on. It's me." A quiet confidence had been building in Chase ever since he'd broken out of the brig on the *Kuyddestor*. "I don't know what I am, or what all I can do, but I don't think there's anything that can hurt me. I'll be fine."

Parker laughed and shook his head, but he looked angry. "Sure, you're special. You can do things that make no sense. I've been trying to come up with a rational explanation for how you jump through doors, but I can't. It's insane.

So you're magical, whatever. But you're not invincible. Remember when you first showed up at my home, how you were wounded? Bleeding? You don't know what can hurt you, but obviously something can. And if that Rezer Bennin guy catches you, he'll keep trying until he figures out what that is."

Chase considered this. He'd survived being shot at, stabbed, and locked up, but his phasing ability hadn't kept him from almost drowning in the mud sea—Maurus had. So he wasn't immortal, but if he played it smart, he knew he had a chance. "I have to go. I can't just leave him there. You know that. Promise me you'll keep my sister safe."

Parker gave him a long, troubled look before he nodded.

Mina said something in a low voice, and Chase turned around to see that she had pulled up a screen on the console. It was silver for a moment, and then Asa Kaplan's face materialized.

"Thirty-second window, Mina," he barked.

"I've got Parker. We're on Qesaris in a district called Nano City. I'm sending you the coordinates right now."

"Is the Garrety boy there?"

"Yes, and his sister," said Mina.

Asa's brow furrowed. "I'll pick you up in twenty minutes."

"I won't be here," said Chase, stepping in front of the

screen. "I have to go help a friend first. He's being held by a man named Rezer Bennin."

"No," said Asa abruptly. "Stay put. Who is your friend?"

"He's a Fleet soldier. Well, he was—"

"Don't go anywhere," Asa interrupted. "I'll be there in twenty minutes."

"I'll be fine—I can do this. I'm different."

"I know you are," said Asa in a harsh tone. "Just stay with Mina."

The words almost slipped past Chase. *I know you are?* If Asa Kaplan knew about Chase's ability, maybe he actually knew more about Chase than anyone else. Maybe he'd just been pretending not to recognize him. "What do you mean? Do you know who I am?"

"I'll be there in twenty minutes. *Do not leave.*"

"No!" shouted Chase. "Tell me! Do you know who I am? Did you know my parents?"

Asa's face had gone red. "I will not discuss this over a comm feed!"

"Then I'm going." Chase crossed his arms. "You can find me in the Shank. I'll probably need your help by then."

"You can't do this! Not for a Fleet soldier," Asa yelled, grabbing the sides of his screen. "Don't—" The transmission cut out and the screen went blank.

Chase looked at Mina with a questioning frown. Had she

turned off the communication, or had something happened to Asa? "Thirty-second window," she said with a shrug. "I can't stop you from going."

"Come on, just wait for Asa to get here," said Parker. "Let him help."

"I have to go now. If Rezer Bennin hasn't killed Maurus, Lennard will find him soon anyway." Chase didn't speak his other thought—that after seeing Asa's reaction, he doubted the man would let him go after Maurus once he'd arrived. "Mina, tell me how to get back to the Shank."

Mina gave Chase a simple list of directions and money for a jettaxi, and wished him luck. Parker looked pained as he squeezed Chase's arm. "Be careful. We'll come help you as soon as we can."

Chase nodded and looked over at his sister lying motionless on the cot. *I'll come back for you*, he promised her in his thoughts. He headed for the door before he could stop himself.

Taking the jettaxi was easy, and the silent driver pointed Chase toward the shadowy alleyways of the Shank. Evening settled over the district as he wandered, lost in the maze of corridors, but it wasn't intimidating to him this time. He wove his way through the crowds, catching glimpses of translucent aqua skin, golden limbs, silver eyes, and deep maroon hair. Outside an eatery he spotted one of the large, pale men with the wide-set eyes. An Ambessitari.

"Take me to Rezer Bennin," he told the man, using the boldest voice he could muster.

The Ambessitari looked down at him and scoffed. "Why should I?"

Chase flashed a confident smile. "Tell him I already escaped from him once, and I'd be happy to do it again." The man's lip curled up in a sneer, and Chase raised his chin in challenge.

It was only a tiny flicker of the man's eye, but Chase realized a moment too late that someone was coming up behind him. Then all he saw was darkness as a cloth bag came down over his head.

# CHAPTER TWENTY-TWO

Chase sat in blind oblivion, knees smarting from where he'd been shoved to the floor. People shouted around him in a strange, coarse language. They'd left the bag over his head, but he could tell he was inside somewhere by the way the voices echoed off the walls.

The Ambessitari men who captured him had shackled his hands behind his back and shoved him into an open vehicle. Cool wind rushed by as they veered through the streets of the Shank. He'd had to fight down panic with the reminder that he was *letting* himself be taken this way, that he could easily break free and run away, and no one would be able to stop him.

The voices around him rose to a chorus of shouts that cut off abruptly, like someone had clapped a hand over everyone's mouths.

"Enough," said an imperious voice. "Take it off."

With a snap, the cloth bag was yanked from Chase's head. He blinked a few times as his eyes adjusted to the dim light. They seemed to be in a small storage room with only one window and stacks of crates lining the walls. Three Ambessitari men stood beside Chase, one of them holding the limp cloth bag, all facing the other side of the room. Chase turned his head.

Rezer Bennin sat at the end of a long table, an unfinished meal before him. His flat Ambessitari face looked as hard and mean as before, and there was no emotion in his beady eyes.

"I do remember you. One of the little Earthan boys that got away." He took a sip from a gold cup and cleared his throat. "I suppose you came here about your friend."

Chase hesitated. Was Bennin talking about Maurus? How could he know that they'd been traveling together?

As if he'd heard Chase's thoughts, Bennin said, "I *know* how you got out of the port." He set the cup down and rested his cold gaze on Chase. "I know the Lyolian helped you escape, right around the same time the android he'd sold me was breaking my arm and sprinting out the door. What I cannot figure out is why you're all returning to me now? The smart move would have been to stay on the opposite end of the galaxy, wouldn't it?"

Chase sat up straighter. "Where is he?"

Bennin wiped his mouth with a red cloth and continued, ignoring the question. "Are you looking for a silver case as well? I don't have it, whatever it is. But the timing works out brilliantly for me." He touched a raised comm panel on the table. "Maurus, would you come in?"

The door at the back of the room opened, and Maurus walked through, taking his place by Bennin's chair. He looked straight ahead as though Chase weren't even in the room.

"Maurus?" Chase asked, confused. There was something strange about the way Maurus moved, a mechanical stiffness in his joints. Chase lurched to his feet, taking care not to slip out of the shackles on his wrists, and moved into Maurus's line of view. There, deep in the Lyolian's dark eyes, he could see the struggle that proved Maurus was still there, still himself. As soon as he saw Chase, anguish filled his eyes, and Chase could practically hear him asking, *Why did you come here?*

"What did you do to him?"

Rezer Bennin's lip curled with cold humor. "I recently took receipt of a special delivery of . . . toys. Show him your collar, dog." With jerky movements, Maurus reached up and pulled aside his jacket, revealing the silver gleam of a metal band pressed tightly against his neck.

Bennin lifted his gold cup and drained it. "Now, take this chalice," he said softly, "And use it to break your own nose."

Every muscle in Maurus's face stood out as he grasped the cup. He paused for a moment, and Chase hoped he would resist, but with a violent swing Maurus smashed the cup into his face, where it connected with a sickening crunch. Blood ran down his face and dripped off his chin, and only his wild eyes showed his agony.

"Now jump out the window," said Bennin quickly.

Maurus turned on his heel.

"No!" cried Chase, stepping forward.

Bennin barked out a laugh and called Maurus back to his side. "You're right. This is too much fun to have it end so quickly. And besides, I have another new toy to try out when this one grows tiresome."

A chiming sound came from somewhere. Bennin glanced at the comm panel and frowned, pressing a finger to the screen. "Saleh, this is true? When did we receive word?" he asked. A soft voice came from the panel, saying something that Chase couldn't understand. Bennin stood and placed his napkin on the table, still talking to the console. "Interesting. No, I was about to step out for a minute to check on a misplaced munitions shipment one of my men came across. Well, he's the one who wants the meeting. He can wait."

Bennin headed toward the door, saying something to his henchmen in their coarse language. He looked over his shoulder at Chase.

"Don't go anywhere," he said with a scary grin, and left, taking two of his hulking henchmen with him. The third positioned himself beside the door.

Chase hesitated for a moment and went to Maurus's side. He glanced over his shoulder to see if the Ambessitari would try to stop him. The man didn't move, his beady eyes staring dully at the wall. Still, Chase kept the shackles on his wrists for the moment so he could speak to Maurus without any unnecessary interference.

"Let's go," he whispered. "I, um, I command you to come with me."

Blood still trickled from Maurus's nose, cutting a fresh course through the brick-colored splash already drying on his chin. His eyes rolled around in their sockets, though the rest of him remained stock-still. Chase had no idea what he was trying to communicate, but guessed that *That's not going to work* was at least part of it. He examined the collar, which bit deeply into the skin around Maurus's neck, all smooth, thick metal but for one tiny hole on the side of the band.

"Get away from him," came the henchman's growl from the doorway.

"Do you really think we're going to escape?" snapped Chase, showing his shackled hands.

Maurus stared at him helplessly, and guilt rushed over Chase for abandoning him in the alley. He'd thought that maybe the Lyolian would be locked up here, trapped somewhere that Chase could break into, like on the *Kuyddestor*. This collar was much worse than he'd expected.

"Mina and Parker have my sister," he whispered. "We found her, and Parker's guardian is coming to get them. We also saw . . ." He looked down, regretting what he had to say next. "There's this guy with tattoos all over his face—we saw him last time in the port. He's the one who had your case. He brought it to Dornan while we were there."

Through his broken nose, Maurus's breathing grew fast and slushy.

"She destroyed the disks inside. They're gone."

Maurus made a choking noise, and tiny drops of fresh blood spattered from his nose. His eyes rolled up to the ceiling, and his skin grew ashen.

"Can you let him sit down?" Chase asked the henchman. He tried to push Maurus toward Bennin's chair with his shoulder, but Maurus's muscles locked up, and although it looked like he was close to passing out, he remained standing where Bennin had left him.

The door opened and Chase turned, preparing to confront Rezer Bennin and insist that he release Maurus.

Instead, Asa Kaplan walked through the door. Exhilaration passed through Chase in a rush and he began to smile, but his mouth froze at the look of intense fury on Asa's face as he stalked into the room. He turned back toward the door, where a slender, maroon-haired woman batted her eyelashes.

"He'll be back shortly, if you could just wait here a minute," she said in a silky voice, closing the door.

Chase stared at Asa's back for a moment, relief at his arrival mingled with dread at how angry he looked. But if Asa was here, that meant the others were safe, and he'd come to help Chase and Maurus escape. Chase glanced at the henchman, who still watched him but ignored Asa entirely, and turned sideways so that the guard couldn't see his mouth. "Help me get this collar off him," he whispered in as low a voice as he could manage. "I can't figure out how to open it."

Asa turned around and shook his head slowly. The anger in his hard blue eyes was unsettling. Was he really that mad that Chase had left against his wishes?

Beads of sweat were forming at Chase's temples. "I'm not leaving him. Parker said you'd help—"

Asa crossed the room in two long strides to stand directly beside Chase. "Shut up," he hissed. "Tell me where they went."

"Who?" A cold bolt of fear shot through Chase, and his voice faltered. "Parker, my sister . . . they're with you, right?"

Asa shook his head, just a tiny, deliberate tilt.

Chase's heart began to race. "Why not?" he whispered. "You were supposed to get them at the—"

"They weren't there," Asa said through gritted teeth.

"What?" All the blood drained from Chase's head, and he started to feel dizzy. "Then what are you doing here?"

Instead of answering, Asa whirled away and stepped toward the door. A second later, it opened and Rezer Bennin walked back in with his henchmen. A smile curled across his face.

"Jonah Masters, my old comrade," Bennin purred. "What a pleasure!"

Chase opened his mouth, about to ask Bennin to take off the collar, but confusion stopped the words from coming out. They knew each other? Who was Jonah Masters?

Asa gestured back at Maurus. "I see you're enjoying your new playthings."

"I did wait an eternity for them to arrive, but the collar is delightful."

Asa nodded, his face cool and unreadable. "If I'm not mistaken, you've got a rather high-profile guest here today."

Bennin gazed at Maurus for an uncomfortably long time.

"Just settling a debt. Was there a particular reason for your visit, Jonah?" he asked, his voice light.

"Bennin, you're one of my best customers. I just wanted to ensure personally that you were satisfied with this latest delivery."

Chase looked back and forth between the two men, trying to make sense of their conversation. The collar choking Maurus had come from Asa? Did he and Bennin work together? Why was Bennin calling him by a different name? In another corner of his mind, a greater worry was gathering like a thunderstorm: Where were Parker, Mina, and his sister? Chase looked to Maurus, desperate for an ally, but the Lyolian was still locked in place, his dark eyes reflecting the turmoil that Chase himself felt.

"I'm more than satisfied," Bennin answered. "These items were well worth the wait. In fact, I was about to try out the particle disperser next. Would you like to stick around for the demonstration?"

*Particle disperser?* Where had Chase heard this term before? Something to do with teleportation—wasn't this the illegal vaporizing weapon that Mina had told him about?

"Indeed I would," said Asa. "What were you planning to use it on?"

Bennin tilted his head with a sarcastic laugh. "Not what.

Whom. I didn't spend all that money on a particle disperser to use it for clearing shrubs."

Asa gave him a tight smile. "On whom, then?"

Chase knew what the answer was going to be, but his heart burst into a sprint when Rezer Bennin pointed across the room and calmly said, "As a warning to all who would try to swindle me, I'm going to disperse the Lyolian."

# CHAPTER TWENTY-THREE

*D*isperse. This was the word that Colonel Dornan had used to describe what had happened to Chase. This had to be the same kind of weapon that had been used on him and his parents.

A hoarse, stifled moan started deep in Maurus's throat and stayed there, trapped behind tightly sealed lips. There was pure terror in his dark eyes—frozen in place by the controlling collar, Maurus had no chance to defend himself. Chase stepped forward between Maurus and Rezer Bennin.

"I won't let you kill him," he said.

Bennin raised an eyebrow. "Excuse me?"

"I won't let you do it," Chase repeated. Behind him Maurus made frantic, unhappy noises.

Bennin's cold eyes flickered thoughtfully over Chase. "Keep this up, and I'll use the device on you instead."

The shackles bit into his wrists and caused a painful

tingle that Chase knew meant he was about to phase through them again. He had to focus all his concentration to keep them from sliding off. When he looked up, he saw Asa watching him with a strange, piercing gaze, but still the man made no move to help.

"I suppose you were hoping to find this?" Bennin took something small out of his pocket and held it out, pinched between his forefinger and back thumb—a tiny metal cylinder that looked like it would fit in the hole in Maurus's collar, obviously the key. Bennin tossed it on the floor. "Go on, get it," he said in a taunting voice.

Chase stared at the key and nearly gave in to the temptation to pull his wrists through his shackles and dive for it. But he glanced at Asa, who gave another tiny, deliberate shake of his head, with a look so menacing that Chase wasn't sure if he was more scared of Bennin or him.

The comm panel chimed again. With an impatient sigh, Bennin stalked across the room and thumbed the panel. He tapped his many fingers across the table as a soft voice mumbled something. A sudden expression of sheer delight broke out on his face.

"Bring them up," he purred, and turned to Asa. "What an unexpected treat! We have more guests."

Asa nodded. Chase tried to catch his eye again, but Asa ignored him. Anger began to cloud Chase's thoughts as he stared at Asa's straight profile, his expression utterly calm, as though Rezer Bennin hadn't just threatened to disperse Chase. Was this really the man they'd thought would be their savior?

The door opened, and the maroon-haired woman led a small group into the room. As each person entered, Chase's heart plummeted.

Mina, carrying the slack form of Chase's sister in her arms.

Parker.

And the mercenary, Fersad. Pointing a blaster rifle at all three of them.

For Fersad to capture them so quickly, he must have been tracking them since they left the medical center. Chase strained to get a look at his sister. Mina shifted her onto her hip, and one of the girl's arms flopped down at her side, making it look like she was still unconscious—or worse.

A large, fresh bruise was forming on the side of Parker's face. His eyes traveled from Chase's shackles to Maurus's bloody nose, and then widened when he noticed Asa. "How the—"

In a flash of movement, Mina clamped her hand onto Parker's shoulder. His words cut off in a gasp as he nearly buckled to the floor. Oblivious to this, Rezer Bennin had already turned to Fersad, a smile stretching across his flat face. "Fersad, I don't know how you do it. As a tracker, you are a true virtuoso. How ever did you find her?"

Fersad's tattoo-marbled face bent into a frown as one of Bennin's henchmen relieved him of his blaster. "Spotted her coming out of a Fleet medical center. She was holed up in a warehouse in Nano City with these kids." He glanced nervously around the room and paused when his eyes reached Asa. "Hello, Jonah," he muttered in acknowledgment.

Asa returned a thin, irritated smile, giving no sign that he recognized Fersad's captives.

"Welcome back, my dear," Bennin crooned to Mina. He looked down at the girl in her arms and prodded the child's neck. "What's this, is she dead?"

Chase's heart jumped up in his throat.

Mina shook her head. "She needs to see a doctor immediately."

"I see. Thank you, Fersad. I appreciate you returning my property to me."

Fersad gave an awkward half nod and stayed where he was.

Bennin paused for a moment, and made an inauthentic noise of surprise. "What am I thinking? You're expecting a reward." He went to the comm panel. "Saleh, bring up a—"

Fersad coughed. "Actually, I'd like to make a trade. For him." He raised a clawed finger toward Maurus.

Of course it hadn't been hard for Fersad to track him down. The whole population of the Shank probably knew Maurus had come here, just like they knew that Bennin was looking for his missing android. Chase glanced at Asa, who watched the exchange dispassionately. It took all his self-restraint to keep from screaming at Asa to step up and tell Bennin that he was Mina's true owner.

"Ah. The Lyolian." Rezer Bennin stood for a moment with his head inclined, and then whirled around, his long coat flaring out around his knees. He opened one of the containers along the wall and removed a long cylinder of black metal, dotted with a few levers and fitted with a strap. "Do you know what this is, Fersad?"

"I can't say that I recognize it," said Fersad nervously.

"No, you probably wouldn't. It's a particle disperser."

Chase stared at the device. This was the creation that had, if he could believe what Dornan said, supposedly blasted him into nothingness. It didn't look like much more than a metal tube, but the simplicity of the device somehow made it more ominous. He couldn't take his eyes from it.

"Fersad, do you know what this device does?" Bennin asked.

Fersad hesitated, and nodded quickly. "Vaporizes."

"Well, yes, that's the fool's answer. 'Disperses' is the technical term, but more precisely, it blasts a stream of evanescent energy at its target—for the sake of this explanation, let's say it's you." He paused to flash a vicious smile. "This energy dissolves your body down to the very molecular level and flings those molecules out across the galaxy. A slight trace of you will remain, a biological smudge to show your final standing point, but that's all. Isn't that fascinating? I'm just aching to try it out."

Fersad's eyes darted nervously at the weapon. Chase felt as tense as a drawn wire, waiting to see if Bennin would pull the trigger. Hovering at the edge of his subconscious was a small, morbid curiosity to see the device in action. Would Fersad just vanish? Would he explode? With a start, Chase realized that the shackles were slipping off again and pushed his wrists closer together.

When Bennin spoke again, his tone was silky. "Now, Fersad, I have only one question for you. How high is the bounty?"

"The what?"

"For the Lyolian, Fersad. I'm no simpleton. To me, he is simply the man who wronged me. But, I realize, to the rest of the universe he is a destroyer of worlds, the most-wanted man in existence. So what's the going rate?"

Fersad narrowed his feral eyes. "I brought you the android," he growled.

Bennin leveled the particle disperser at Fersad's chest. "And your reward will be your life. I think it's an excellent bargain. Anyone else I would have killed without asking, but you're an outstanding tracker and I may need your services again. My offer will expire shortly. I suggest you take it."

Fersad reached for Mina's arm, and Bennin pulled a lever on the back of the particle disperser. The weapon responded with a surging hum and a crackling film of orange sparks danced along the black cylinder. Two of the henchmen stepped on either side of Fersad.

"Get out." Bennin's voice was as flat and hard as his eyes.

With a snarl of frustration, Fersad turned on his heel and stalked out of the chamber, followed by the two Ambessitari henchmen.

Bennin smiled as the door closed behind Fersad and turned to Mina, staring with an intensity that would have made any human uncomfortable. Mina stared blandly back.

"That's quite a high-caliber android you've got," Asa commented.

Rezer Bennin turned slowly to face him. "We can stop the charade now." His voice had gone low and dangerous.

Asa said nothing, a hint of a smile playing around his mouth.

"You've been supplying me with your goods for, what, twelve years?" Bennin said. "But I'll admit I know next to nothing about you, other than the fact that you appeared out of nowhere—despite my efforts, I haven't been able to find a shred of information about you prior to our first transaction."

"You mean when I outfitted your men to help you over-throw the previous Rezer?" Asa asked, arching an eyebrow.

Bennin smiled. "Correct. You're an enigma, Jonah. But it's never really mattered, since you produce the most advanced weapons available on the black market."

Twelve years? Black market weapons? This sounded to Chase like someone very different from the owner of a tech corporation.

Asa inclined his head. "I appreciate the compliment, Bennin—*Rezer* Bennin—but I don't quite see what this has to do with—"

"Stop," Bennin interrupted in a derisive tone. "Rumors have been circulating for years that you have any number of other high-tech endeavors outside the weapons field. You think I didn't immediately suspect that she might be one of yours? That I didn't check for your mark before I had her reanimated?"

Asa's features hardened, and in a threatening tone he said, "Then I'm sure you're pleased that I'm giving you the opportunity to return my property to me."

At last Asa had finally claimed what was his, but instead of satisfaction, all Chase felt was more anger. Was this just about his property—about getting Mina back? He hadn't even looked at Parker since he entered the room. Chase wrestled with disappointment as he watched Asa. This cold-blooded weapons dealer, whatever his name was, wasn't anything close to the hero he'd hoped for.

Bennin arched an eyebrow and looked down at the weapon in his hands, running his fingers over the levers, adjusting one of them by a few notches. "What's your relation to the children?"

Asa shrugged noncommittally. "No relation."

Bennin tilted his head with a smirk. "No? Then you won't mind if I just—" He pointed the particle disperser at the girl in Mina's arms.

"No!" Chase's hands flew up automatically, reaching for his sister. The shackles clattered to the floor.

Rezer Bennin turned, swinging the crackling weapon toward him. Staring down the barrel of the disperser, Chase froze down to the very last hair on his head. Bennin looked down at the empty shackles lying on the floor, and his eyes narrowed.

"What remarkable children. Or should I say, experiments?"

Asa's cool expression broke, and anger flooded into his face. "They're *not* experiments. I'm their guardian. Let them be."

"I'm not sure I believe you. Maybe if you have to start

from scratch—" Bennin hoisted the disperser into firing position, still pointing at Chase.

Chase sucked in a gasp. It was all he had time to do.

In the corner of his eye, he saw Mina shove his sister into Parker's arms and throw herself at the henchman guarding the door. Asa dove across the room, tackling Bennin at the waist. A brief blast of the orange disperser beam skimmed just over Chase's head and hit the ceiling, sending down a rain of concrete chunks.

The disperser flew free and skidded across the floor.

"How dare you!" cried Rezer Bennin, who lay on his back with a look of stunned fury.

Asa crouched at Bennin's ankles. "Don't make me hurt you, Bennin. Just let us walk out."

"So the children do matter," Bennin spat, teeth bared.

"If you hurt any one of them, I'll kill you," Asa promised.

Chase took a step toward the fallen disperser. Bennin yanked a handblaster from his coat and pointed it at Parker, who stood wide-eyed, clutching Chase's sister to his chest.

"No!" Asa's voice rose in panic, and he leapt at Bennin as he fired. The red blast hit Asa square in the chest, and sent him flying backward. He rolled across the floor and lay still.

Holding the handblaster out in front of himself, Rezer Bennin got to his feet. His flat features were disfigured with rage. He walked over to pick up the disperser, looping it around his shoulder, and pressed the comm panel.

"Saleh, send up the men!" Bennin paused and, when no answer came, slapped at the panel again. "Saleh! Where are you?"

He primed the disperser using the hand that was still holding the small blaster. The weapon crackled and spooled up as he brandished it at everyone. "I've had enough of this." He pointed it at Asa's body. Then he cocked his head, frowning.

A rumbling noise sounded outside the room and deepened, joined by a sound like grating steel. Rezer Bennin reached for the comm panel again.

And then the door exploded off its hinges.

A tall, imposing figure stepped through a cloud of smoke into the chamber, blaster raised. Behind the helmet visor were familiar craggy features and pale wolf eyes.

Despair struck through Chase like a deep chord. It had taken Captain Lennard less time than he had expected to catch up. He'd almost forgotten that the captain was pursuing them. But with Bennin on one side, Lennard on the other, and Asa possibly dead, they'd never be able to escape.

Five more armed soldiers slipped through the door behind the captain. "Rezer Bennin, on behalf of the Federation of Allied Planets and the Federal Fleet, I order you to surrender!" Lennard shouted.

"I don't think so!" Bennin brandished the disperser. "Do you know what this is, officer?"

"That is illegal contraband," said Lennard. "Under section 427 of the Fleet charter, I order you to surrender your weapon and come peacefully."

"Fool! This weapon? You don't stand a chance—I can disperse this entire room before anyone takes their next breath. Do you want everyone here to die?"

An orange beam burst from the end of Bennin's particle disperser, and Lennard dodged, narrowly missing the shot. The beam hit the wall behind him, leaving a gaping hole. "Rezer Bennin, put down your weapon!" he thundered.

Maybe there was still a chance. Taking advantage of the distraction, Chase dropped to the floor and scrambled over to where Bennin had tossed the collar's key. Someone from the Fleet took a shot at Bennin, who ducked and fired off another blast of the disperser. Keeping close to the floor, Chase dashed back to Maurus and with fumbling fingers stuck the key in the tiny hole. The collar broke apart and tumbled away.

Maurus dropped to his knees, hands limp at his side. His dark hair fell across his face.

Bennin grabbed Chase by the arm, and for a second he

resisted, letting the man's hand start to slide through his arm. But Maurus looked like he could barely lift his head, let alone run away. He would need the extra time that a diversion could provide.

"Get them out of here," Chase hissed at him, climbing to his feet.

Rezer Bennin wrapped his arm around Chase's neck, still gripping the disperser with his other arm. "If you want this boy to live, you'll let us go." He took a step toward the back of the room, wrenching Chase along with him.

As he stumbled backward in Bennin's grip, Chase kept his eyes on Lennard. "Take the shot!" he yelled, not sure if he meant Bennin or Lennard, half hoping they would both fire on each other at the same time. The captain's snarl deepened, but he didn't fire.

Movement on the right—somehow Parker had slipped across the room to Maurus's side, still balancing Chase's sister on one hip. He was trying to help Maurus stand, but the Lyolian fell back down, his muscles too exhausted from the strain of the collar. Chase's heart sank. There was no way Maurus would be able to escape. By the defeated look in his eyes, it was clear that Maurus knew this too.

"Run, Chase," he said hoarsely.

And in a microsecond, it happened. Chase could feel the

tension running through Rezer Bennin's body and down his right arm as he turned the weapon, and he knew Bennin was going to fire the disperser at them all, Maurus and Parker and Lilli Garrety. He had to stop him.

If he was really Chase Garrety, he'd already survived the disperser once, and he could do it again.

If he was Chase Garrety.

Chase phased through the arm wrapped around his neck and spun around, grabbing the nozzle of the disperser with both hands. He pressed it against his own chest.

"Chase, no!" screamed Parker.

There was an explosion of orange light and, in the background, more screams. Chase's vision narrowed to a pinpoint as his body was overtaken with violent, uncontrollable trembling. For a moment, he was filled with a strange feeling of thinness. The room began to fade away.

Barely there, he could feel himself jittering away to nothing but a shadow. He screamed, but he couldn't tell if he was actually making the noise or if it was only in his mind. In waves he slipped away, dissolving and retracting in a painful tug-of-war. His hands on the weapon were almost transparent, melting outward.

A piercing sound caught his attention, a high-pitched, keening wail. Chase tried to see who it was and in that moment had the strange sensation that his eyes were everywhere, that he could see the entire room through the orange haze.

The girl, his sister, was finally awake. She was pushing away from Parker, who struggled to hold her, and her mouth was torn wide with a continuous scream. She slithered free and sank to the floor, her eyes huge and terrified, filled with the nightmare she had awoken to.

*It's okay*, Chase wanted to tell her. *I can do this*. But he couldn't speak. He wasn't even sure his mouth was there anymore.

Shapes moved around the room, activity that he couldn't distinguish. Chase focused on Rezer Bennin as he stopped to prime the weapon again. A burst of light fanned out behind Bennin like a halo, and the furious expression on his face melted into a blank stare. He fell forward, into and through Chase, landing on top of the disperser.

"Move! Move! Move!" screamed a voice.

With a colossal *snap!* like a hard bolt of electricity running down his spine, Chase came flying back to himself—his whole, present, focused self. He stumbled backward, his vision blurry and indistinct. He needed to find his sister, but he could barely see. A pair of wiry arms caught him, helping him stay upright.

"Hold on there, buddy," came Parker's voice. "I've got you."

"Is he alright? Don't touch him—he might be unstable," said Lennard's voice.

"Shut up," snapped Parker. "He's fine. Chase, do you need to sit down?"

"No. Maybe." Chase wasn't even sure if the words were making it out of his mouth, but with Parker's help he sank to the floor, breathing deeply and trying to focus.

Figures moved around him, disjointed voices swimming around and between the movement.

"Tie Bennin up, get him to the brig."

"You got her? Get her out."

"Where's Kaplan?"

"How soon until Dietz gets here?"

"Looks like an escape passage."

"Get your hands off me!"

The last one was Maurus, and Chase blinked until he could make out the shape of the Lyolian, kneeling at the center of a circle of soldiers.

"Lieutenant, on your feet. You're coming back to the ship with us," said Lennard, stepping into the circle.

Maurus spat at his feet. "I'm not going anywhere with you. Kill me now if that's your plan. The truth will come out in the end."

Lennard exhaled loudly. "Don't make this harder than it needs to be. We can—"

Shouting by the door drowned out the rest of the captain's words. Fersad entered the room, trailed closely by two soldiers.

"I need to leave," growled the Kekilly mercenary. "I played my part, so pay up."

"Sorry, Captain, we couldn't stop him—" said one of the soldiers.

"Fersad, step outside and wait," interrupted Lennard. "I'll be finished here in a moment." There was a tense stare down for several seconds, and finally the rangy mercenary turned and stalked out of the room.

"He's been working for you all this time!" said Maurus, his voice rising hysterically. "You sent him after me on Trucon—"

He staggered to his feet, swinging his fists at the soldiers surrounding him. With a frustrated roar, Captain Lennard whipped around and shot Maurus in the chest.

This Chase saw clearly: The Lyolian's eyes turned sightless as he fell backward, shock still written across his face. He hit the floor hard.

"No!" screamed Chase. He staggered to his feet and charged the captain.

Lennard raised his hands, but Chase swung right through them. The captain tried to outmaneuver him, to grab his arms, but Chase was a blur of motion and rage. He couldn't be restrained, and his fists connected where he wanted to connect, landing punches on Lennard's ribs and chest. For a moment, he felt himself reaching a level of control over his ability that he didn't know he had.

Lennard tried to push Chase away and stumbled backward, holding a hand protectively in front of himself. He looked shaken. "Take him to the ship," he told his soldiers.

"I'm not getting on your ship!"

"Yes, you are. If you want to stay with your sister, you'll get on the ship."

Chase whipped around. The spot where the girl had been was empty. Parker had vanished too—even Asa and Mina were gone. Rage boiled up inside him. "Where did you take them?"

"Chase, will you please cooperate?" A cautious tone crept into Lennard's voice, as though he were talking to a wild animal. "I can explain more later, but for now I need you to do as I tell you."

Chase looked at the back of the room, where a team of soldiers was loading Maurus's body onto a stretcher. A sob started to build in the back of his throat.

"You killed him." His voice broke on the words.

Lennard glanced at the door and made a signal to one of

his soldiers. "No, Chase, I stunned him. He'll be fine. It was the only way I could get him to come easily, but you know I can't do that to you."

Something loosened in Chase's chest. Maurus was alive. But confusion bloomed and swelled, taking the place of his anger. "You're helping him now?"

Lennard took a step toward Chase, his hands still lifted in a defensive way. "I made a mistake," he said in a low voice. "About him, and about you. Maurus said something that made me take a second look at everything that happened. And then the brig officer told me how you jumped through doors, and I realized that by some miracle, somehow, it was really you. I've been trying to find you ever since. And now I need to get you both away from here as quickly as possible."

The soldiers carried Maurus out, leaving only Chase and Lennard in the empty room. Parker, Mina, Maurus, his sister, Asa—everyone was gone. His choice had been made for him, but still Chase couldn't bring himself to trust Captain Lennard. "Why? What's going to happen?"

A soldier leaned in the door. "ETA two minutes, Captain."

Lennard nodded in acknowledgment, but he kept his eyes on Chase. "Because others from the Fleet are coming and this is the only way I can keep you all safe from them. Please, Chase, come back to the *Kuyddestor* with me."

*Kuyddestor.* Hearing the word spoken in Lennard's drawl, a distant connection formed in Chase's mind. He frowned. *Kuyd-de-stor.* Could that be the answer?

He spoke hesitantly. "Guide . . . guide the star?"

Relief broke out on the captain's weathered face. "Yes, Chase. Guide the star. Thank the heavens—it's really you."

# CHAPTER TWENTY-FOUR

The gray horizon of Qesaris fell away as the transport shuttle shot out of the atmosphere. Chase gripped his armrests and looked around at the soldiers who filled every other seat. Lennard had told him that Parker and his sister had been sent ahead of him, but he still felt a gnawing apprehension in his gut. He was exhausted, sore, and hungry, and wanted desperately to trust the captain's promise that they were safe now, but a distrustful side of him knew that Lennard could easily turn back into a tyrant once they were all stowed away on his ship.

"We'll be there in ten minutes," said the raven-haired officer sitting next to him.

"My friends are already there, right?"

"Everyone's safe, don't worry." She gave him a warm smile.

Through a sliver of front windshield, the hulking form of the *Kuyddestor* loomed ahead of them, far bigger than any building Chase had ever seen. Their transport airship slid neatly into the gaping maw of the entry spaceway, and multicolored lights shot past as they skidded down a tunnel into the docking bay.

They exited the airship into a bright, bustling crowd. The cavernous hall was abuzz with activity, but the atmosphere was completely different from the last time Chase had arrived there—still intense, but the people on deck now seemed focused with an upbeat, positive energy.

The officer put a hand on Chase's arm. "Just wait here. I'll send someone over to take you to a debriefing room." She turned and left him standing alone by the airship.

Chase waited approximately two seconds before slipping into the crowd to find everyone on his own. He weaved through the row of vehicles, keeping his distance from the jumpsuited mechanics running through the bay.

"Hey there, stop." Chase turned toward the low voice and saw Colonel Forquera ducking under the wing of a fighter to reach him.

"Where are they?" he demanded. "Where is my sister?"

"Relax, they're here. Come with me."

Still crawling with anxiety, Chase let Forquera lead him out of the commotion of the docking bay. They passed through a doorway into a quieter hall, and Forquera glanced at him. "How are you doing?"

Chase shook his head. "I don't know." His hands trembled, and he knew they wouldn't stop until he was sure this wasn't a trap.

They stopped in front of a door that opened on a room with a long table. At the far end sat Parker. Alone.

"Chase!" He jumped to his feet, pushing his chair back with a scrape. "Are you okay?"

"Where did they take my sister? Where's Maurus?"

Forquera ushered him inside the room and allowed the door to close behind them. "They've both been taken up to medical bay. They're fine."

"Let me see her," he insisted.

"You can see her when she's stabilized."

"She's okay," said Parker. "I saw them taking care of her."

Chase frowned uneasily. He trusted Parker's word, but it still wasn't the same as seeing her himself.

Forquera stood beside the door. "When Captain Lennard gets back on board, he'll want to talk more with each of you. For now, I'll need you to stay in here until I can get the quartermaster to assign you some space. I'll have someone bring you some food as well."

"One question," said Parker, holding up his hand to stop the colonel from leaving. Forquera nodded. "How did the captain figure out that Maurus's mission was a setup?"

Forquera looked surprised, and an amused smile touched

the corners of his mouth. "Because the report the captain received, the one he sent Maurus out to investigate, described a Lyolian slave trafficking ring delivering new shipments in the Truconian desert at night. The captain realized that someone had given him a falsified report, because—"

"The Zinnjerha had already been coming out at night for two weeks before that," finished Parker.

"Exactly. There was no way anyone could have been moving anything."

"Is that why the Zinnjerha were acting funny?" asked Parker. "Did they sense the attack was coming?"

Forquera frowned. "I don't see how they could have. The thermodetonators weren't installed until the day of the attack. As far as I know, nobody knew why the Zinnjerha were acting up—and now we probably never will." He waited a second to see if Parker had any more questions, and then he left.

Chase sat down in a chair and put his fists on his forehead.

"What's wrong?" asked Parker.

"I keep thinking this is going to be a trap. Last time we were here, Lennard hated me, and he wanted Maurus dead."

Parker shook his head. "Yeah, but last time we were here, he thought you were a clone. Surviving that disperser was proof enough to everyone that you're really Chase Garrety. That, and the microchip you had under your scalp."

Chase touched the back of his head. The microchip, Dr. Silvestri... everything on Trucon seemed like it had happened ages ago. "Too bad the chip got destroyed."

"But that wound you had there, you probably got that before you were dispersed. It left a bit of a scar, right? No clone would have that. It's proof of who you are. As for how the captain knows you, that's something you'll have to find out from him."

"What about Maurus? Last time, Lennard was pretending not to know anything about the Trucon attack and setting Maurus up to be executed. Did he change sides?"

Parker dragged a finger across the table, and a console illuminated in its shiny surface. He started flipping through screens, frowning as he spoke. "Lennard wasn't pretending. He was never involved in the plot against Trucon. He was set up, just like Maurus was—he sent him out on a falsified report, and he believed everything that happened afterward was Maurus's fault. After we escaped, I think he realized this. When Maurus called the mission bogus, he must have taken a second look and figured it out."

"But he was working with Fersad. I saw it myself—he was going to pay him off."

Parker grinned. "I bet he did. Apparently you weren't watching the newsfeed in your transport. Check this out." He scrolled through a few screens, and landed on a video feed of a blond reporter standing in an area that looked like the Shank.

"And it's no surprise the Karsha Ven's response to this news has been abject denial," she said. "I'm Parri Dietz, here on Qesaris with a surprising turn of events in the story of the millennium, the attack on Trucon—if you've been watching, you'll know that I was just speaking with Captain Lionel Lennard, commander of the *IFF Kuyddestor*, who has stepped forward to exonerate his officer Lieutenant E. Maurus, previously the prime suspect in the attack."

The screen switched to a recording of Captain Lennard glaring at the camera, his eyebrows drawn in a fierce frown. "We had attempted to maintain cover in order not to ruin the months of undercover work that my soldier did posing as a Karsha Ven militant, but recent events have made it necessary for me to take this information public. I can vouch that Lieutenant Maurus was *not* involved in the Trucon attack—he had nothing to do with it, and was acting under my orders to investigate a Lyolian trafficking ring in the Ganthas colonies. It was simply a case of being in the wrong place at the wrong time. I've pulled him from the field, and he's currently recuperating in an undisclosed location."

The image flashed back to the reporter. "Supporting this statement is the taped confession we recently received from a Kekilly mercenary named Fersad who claims to have knowledge that the Karsha Ven was in fact behind this attack, and that he provided them the means to their advanced weaponry by linking them with a black-market weapons dealer named Jonah Masters."

Chase looked up from the screen. "Asa?"

Parker touched the image to pause it and nodded. "When Lennard's team caught Fersad leaving Bennin's hideout, the captain must have bribed him to say that Asa was the one who helped the Karsha Ven get their hands on the thermodetonators—the ones that someone in the Fleet actually gave to their own soldiers."

"But . . . Asa couldn't have agreed to this. Now they'll be after him. What did he say?"

Parker stared Chase in the eyes for a moment. "He didn't say anything. He's gone."

Chase gasped. "He died?"

"What? No—while you were letting yourself get blown to smithereens, Mina helped him up and they booked it out Bennin's escape passage."

"They just left?" After all that Mina had done to protect Parker, Chase couldn't imagine she'd abandon him in the heat of battle.

Parker made a wry face. "I'm sure it wasn't personal. Mina was created to protect me, but Asa's her true owner, not me. Apparently in her settings, 'Asa in mortal danger' overrides

'Parker in mortal danger.' Anyhow, his not being there to defend himself gave Lennard an easy scapegoat to put in Maurus's place."

"But it wasn't Asa or the Karsha Ven that attacked Trucon," Chase said. "It was someone in the Fleet. They'll know, and come after Maurus."

"Not likely," said Parker. "Whoever planned this wanted it to look like an attack by the Karsha Ven, right? So in effect they got what they wanted. Now they can't step forward without identifying themselves."

"But now they know that Lennard knows the truth . . . ," said Chase.

Parker nodded and leaned back in his chair. "Which means that Captain Lennard, and Maurus, and basically everyone on this ship are going to have to watch their backs."

※    ※    ※

Chase stared at the metal walls of the tiny room that the quartermaster had assigned him, picking at a plate of rehydrated beans and noodles. It was a space of his own, but it was far from comforting—it looked like someone had thrown a bed and table into a supply closet. And although he knew he wasn't a prisoner on the *Kuyddestor* this time, he jumped every time he heard a noise in the hallway outside his room.

He'd been on the ship almost a full day and still hadn't

been allowed to see his sister, and it was driving him crazy. Parker had finally told him she'd fallen back into a coma during transit to the *Kuyddestor*, and Forquera said she was being treated in an isolation unit of the medical ward. Chase thought that if he was able to see her, to squeeze her hand, maybe that would speed her recovery. He wanted more than anything to look her in the eyes and feel a connection with her again.

The door to his room slid open, and Captain Lennard stood in the doorway. His presence was as imposing as ever, but his pale eyes looked weary. "Hello, Chase. I'm sorry it's taken me so long to come talk with you." He pulled a chair up to the table. "How are you doing?"

Chase set down his fork, feeling like he had so many questions that he might explode. He started with the biggest one. "What am I?"

Lennard ran a hand over his face. "I wish I knew. We never saw any signs that you had inherited anything."

"What do you mean?" Chase asked, growing agitated. "How do you know so much about me?"

"Chase, I've known you since you were a baby. I knew your parents long before you were born."

This still wasn't an answer. Chase wanted to scream with frustration. Instead he repeated slowly, "What do you mean?"

Lennard nodded and cleared his throat. "Let me start at

the beginning. I met your parents nineteen years ago, when I was a lieutenant on the DR-Explorer *Roscommon*. I found them hiding in the cargo hold—they were stowaways. At first I thought they were just a pair of regular Earthan teenagers running away from home, but they were more than that.

"They told me how they had just escaped from some sort of genetic modification program, that their lives were in danger. I should have turned them in to the master-at-arms, but they begged me not to. They were so frightened—even though I suspect they could have snapped my neck if they needed to—and from the way they acted, it seemed as if something very traumatic had happened to them. So instead of reporting them, I helped them find a place to hide, and we formed a friendship that lasted . . ." He trailed off and closed his eyes.

Chase absorbed the information hungrily, building a rough image of his parents in his head as the captain spoke. As the pieces of his past began to fit together, he was filled with a strange combination of relief and melancholy. Finally, here was the answer to where he came from, why he was different—but he knew these explanations wouldn't have a happy ending.

"What kind of genetic modification?" he asked quietly.

"They never explained that to me, though it was clear that they were different because of it. From the outside, they looked like normal Earthans, but they were light-years smarter than anyone I've ever met, and their senses seemed . . . heightened. I swear they could communicate with each other without saying a word, just like the Falasians do. I knew they were afraid of the consequences their modifications would have on any children they might have, but they were in love. And you were born, and you were so normal. And then came Lilli.

"Even when she was a baby, your parents started to notice strange things. They would lay her down for a nap in her bedroom, then walk out into the living room to see her sitting on the floor, playing with an orange. But they'd turn around, and there she was, lying in her crib. We called what she does 'traveling.' She can be in one place and produce an identical copy of herself anywhere else. At first it was fascinating, but then we began to see the possible dangers of her ability—we had no control over where she goes, what she sees, who sees her. If she receives a cut on her traveling copy, the same cut manifests itself on her original body. That was when your parents placed a special sort of tracking chip under her scalp, and for safety's sake they gave you one as well."

So that was how Lilli had attacked him in the café—she'd sent a traveling copy of herself—while the whole time her real body had been strapped down on a hospital gurney, a captive of the Fleet. Trackable by the same technology that Chase had carried. Asa's technology.

"Do you know where they got the chips from?" he asked.

Lennard shook his head. "They never told me. I'm sure they had contact with more people than just me, but you grew up hidden in a deep corner of the galaxy, isolated from the rest of the universe. Your parents wanted nothing to do with the outside world."

It was possible Chase's parents had simply bought the microchips on the black market, looking for a dealer who could keep their transaction confidential. But then how would Asa have known that Chase was different? If he was a friend of the family, wouldn't he have claimed Chase as soon as he saw him on the *Kuyddestor* instead of pretending not to know him? Chase's mind turned to another, darker possibility—that Asa, with his shady connections, had somehow been involved in the Garretys' eventual downfall. Maybe he was the one who led their attackers to their home. It would take time for Chase to sort out all his suspicions, and he wished he'd had more time to demand everything Asa could tell him about his parents.

"So what happened to them?" he asked, his stomach tightening with dread at what he knew would come next.

Captain Lennard sighed heavily. "Everything was fine until about four weeks ago, when I tried to contact your parents and got no response. That had never happened before." He lowered his head and massaged his temples with his thumbs, pausing for a moment before he continued.

"By the time I was able to get to your home, it was clear that whoever your parents had escaped from had finally found them. Your house was empty, and there were signs that there had been a struggle. I took a molecular readout, and found biotraces of your mother, your father, and you. Hard evidence that all three of you had been killed with a particle disperser."

Although he already knew most of this information, Chase watched his own hands tremble as the captain spoke. He remembered something Parker had said to him once, when they first met: *Maybe what happened to you is so horrible, once you find out, you'll wish you never knew.*

"Why not Lilli? Why did they keep her alive?"

"They must have known about her ability, and I'm sure there were people who wanted to learn more about what she could do. You, they eliminated, because they thought you were just a normal boy. We all did." Lennard was looking at Chase with a strange, almost pleading expression on his face. "Can you imagine my shock at seeing you, who I *knew* was dead, turning up on my ship over three weeks later? I was completely consumed with my search for Lilli. It was impossible that you'd survived, and with everything that had just happened on Trucon, I assumed someone was setting a trap for me. How could I have known?"

"So why did I survive? What am I?"

"Chase, the combination of your parents' altered DNA must have given you a genetic advantage we couldn't see. Whether or not your phasing ability existed before the incident, I can't say, but my ship's doctor thinks that when you were dispersed in your home, it triggered a change in your molecular makeup. Your particles were spread far and wide, which should have killed you, but instead they managed to find their way back together. Unfortunately it seems that your memory didn't rejoin the rest of you."

"So I'll never remember my life before this? I remember everything that happened before Bennin tried to disperse me. Isn't there a chance I'll get my memory back?"

Lennard frowned. "When you turned the disperser on yourself yesterday, you got kind of blurry but stayed in the room with us. Your body came back together quickly. But the first time you were dispersed, it was completely different." He gave Chase a cautious, sad look, as if he were trying to soften the blow of bad news. "After you were attacked at home, two weeks passed before you reappeared on Trucon. It's possible your body just didn't know how to reassemble itself yet. Dispersal is violent, sudden—and the brain is such a complex organ, it's not really a surprise that yours sustained a serious injury. You're lucky to be alive."

Chase stared at the half-eaten food on his plate. His parents were gone, and he might never even know who they were, what they sounded like or looked like. An idea occurred to him.

"Do you think my parents could have had the same ability as me? Maybe they just reappeared somewhere else, the same as me?"

Lennard shook his head. "I really wouldn't hold out any hope for that idea, Chase. They were special, but they weren't like you. You're a completely new evolution."

Chase nodded, but resisted this answer all the same. He knew the chance his parents were alive somewhere was basically nonexistent, but it made him feel better to imagine that one day he still might find them. And maybe that would unlock his memory, and everything could just go back the way it was supposed to be. He looked around at the metal walls of his room. "What happens now?"

"Right now we're headed to a mining colony in the Movala system. We need to lie low for a while, so in advance I grabbed an assignment that would take us as far into deep space as possible. We're essentially going to hide out there until we can figure out who's behind this."

Suddenly Chase realized he had potentially helpful information. "It was Colonel Dornan. I saw her talking with Fersad, and she destroyed the disks—"

"I've already talked with Parker about that. She mentioned someone else, didn't she?"

Chase thought back to what he'd heard Dornan say. *It was his foolish idea to make a hard copy in the first place.* At the time, he'd assumed she was talking about Lennard. He nodded.

"There's a bigger conspiracy behind this. Right now, I can't fathom what possible end could have been served by destroying an entire planet. I'll be investigating that along with my team, but while we do, I have to make sure I'm protecting the crew of the *Kuyddestor*."

Hearing the ship's name again, Chase looked up. "'Guide the star.' It's the only thing I remembered when I woke up on Trucon."

Lennard leaned toward him. "And that's a testament to how diligently your parents trained you for what to do in case of an emergency. I can't tell you how many times they repeated, 'If anything ever happens, get to the *Kuyddestor*.'"

"But, 'guide the star'?"

"Is what Lilli called it when she was a toddler. It was a family joke. So, in a way, you remembered her too." Lennard smiled, letting his gaze rest on Chase for a moment. "Well, I should let you get some rest. I know it'll take some time for you to adjust, but I'll do anything I can to help. You have no idea how glad I am—"

A low beep from the door interrupted him, and it opened on a soldier Chase didn't at first recognize. In the gray uniform of the Fleet, Maurus looked like a different person. His nose had been mended, and his hair was secured in a tight knot at the base of his skull. More noticeable, though, was that the hunted, desperate look was gone from his face. He stood tall and confident, eyes gleaming with energy.

"Captain," he said, snapping to attention.

"Lieutenant Maurus, how can I help you?" said Lennard. Chase stared in disbelief at the respectful exchange.

Maurus dropped his salute. "I came to see if Chase wanted to come down to the officer quarters for supper this evening, so I can introduce him to some of the crew. If that's alright with you, Captain?"

"I think that's a fine idea, as long as Chase wants to."

The idea of sitting down with a roomful of soldiers sounded intimidating, but Chase knew Maurus's intent was to help him get settled on the ship. "Yeah, thanks. That sounds good."

"I was just leaving," said Lennard, rising from his chair. "I'll let you two have some time together." At the door he stopped and turned back to Chase. "Not many of the crew know the real details of who you are. I'm telling everyone that the three of you were orphaned after Trucon and the Fleet is taking you in as future cadets. If anyone starts asking a lot of questions about who you are or where you came from, you have to tell me."

Chase nodded assent. "When can I see my sister?"

"Maybe tomorrow." Lennard furrowed his eyebrows. "We need to take it slow, okay? Lilli's had a very traumatic experience."

"But if I can just—" Chase began.

"I know you want to see her, and I understand. But you don't remember Lilli. She was a difficult child before any of this happened. I just want to make sure she's . . . ready for you."

Biting back the protest that rose to his lips, Chase nodded, but his thoughts swirled with fresh worry. What did the captain mean, a difficult child? Did she not want to see him?

Maurus saluted as Captain Lennard left. When the door slid closed behind him, he grinned at Chase. "Well, just look at us."

Chase returned the smile shyly. Maurus was still the same guy who'd traveled with him from one end of the galaxy to the other, who'd saved his life and whose life he'd saved, but things felt different now. He was a soldier again, and Chase was just a boy. "So everything's . . . okay?"

Maurus nodded. "The captain and I had a very long

discussion. We've worked out the details of the story that I was operating deep undercover—everyone on the crew believes it now. I've been returned to active duty on the expeditionary squad, and the captain and I will be working together to figure out who set us up."

"You talked about everything? Even . . . ?" Chase was hesitant to repeat Maurus's jail cell confession.

"You mean my connection with the Karsha Ven?" Maurus smiled. "Yes, we talked about that too. He was very upset about my deception, but I think he believes that my intentions were only good. He's agreed to keep it secret, but he had me re-swear allegiance to the Fleet, and I agreed to a little additional surveillance for a while. It's only fair, given what I kept from him."

"You re-swore allegiance to the *Fleet*?" Chase asked in surprise. After everything that had happened, he'd almost expected Maurus to be on the next flight home to Lyolia, not recommitting to the organization that had tried to kill him.

Maurus placed a hand on Chase's shoulder. "Despite what's happened, there are still many good people in the Fleet. Captain Lennard is one of them. Just like there are bad members of the Karsha Ven, those who would happily claim responsibility for what happened to Trucon, and others, like me, who only want the conflict on my homeworld to end. I still believe I can do good for both sides."

The elliptical badge on Maurus's uniform flashed red, and Maurus raised a hand to his ear. "Yes, right away," he said, answering a voice only he could hear. "Sorry, Chase, that was the chief of the exped squad—she'll have my hide if I don't attend debriefing. See you at seventeen-hundred hours, okay?" He gave Chase a squeeze on the arm before leaving.

Chase lay on his bed for a while, allowing the ocean of information to wash over him. So many things made sense now—his amnesia, his ability, Captain Lennard's first reaction to him. But he still had as many questions, and not just about Asa Kaplan. Colonel Dornan, for one: She admitted she'd been present when his family was attacked, but she was also involved in setting up Maurus to take the fall for Trucon. He felt crazy for even thinking it, but he wondered if the two attacks were somehow related. Maurus and Captain Lennard were planning to hunt down whoever had set them up, but if Chase was going to be living aboard the *Kuyddestor* for a while, he'd have to take every opportunity to do his own investigating as well.

It occurred to him that Dr. Silvestri had sent him down the wrong path—if he'd managed to stay far away from the Fleet like the doctor had warned him to, he never would have learned what "guide the star" meant. He didn't think the doctor had led him astray on purpose—he worked for Asa, after all. Avoiding the Fleet was part of his job. But what if Maurus hadn't stolen Mina on Qesaris? Would they have just called Asa for help and let him imprison them both in another comfortable compound? Chase would never have learned the truth from Captain Lennard, never would have found his sister.

Lilli. He turned the name around in his mind, examined it, but it brought up no memories. He wanted to go seek her out. At the same time he was afraid to finally talk to her. Who was this strange little person, this girl who had spent her whole life being different? What could she tell him about his life, their parents, about their deaths?

Chase climbed out of bed and padded barefoot to the door. Before he got there, it slid open. Parker pushed past him and sat down on his bed.

"Chase, this place is amazing," he sang. "I was just down on the flight deck, and I think I persuaded one of the pilots to let me have a go in the Khatra simulator."

Chase shook his head, smiling. "Settling in pretty quickly, are we?"

Parker grinned, kicking at a bedpost. "I already feel at home here, like this is where I'm meant to be. Not locked up in some remote compound with an android."

For the first time, Chase could appreciate how lonely Parker must have been when he first met him. "It was wrong of Asa to keep you isolated like that. Even if he was just try-ing to keep you safe."

Parker's grin vanished. "Safe? He didn't want to keep me safe, he wanted to keep me his prisoner." He planted his feet on the ground, suddenly agitated. "All my life I was told he was the owner of a tech corporation, and it turns out he deals weapons to criminals? What else was a lie? Did my parents really work for him? Were they criminals too? I may not have lost my memory, but I know just as little about my past as you do. Maybe less. Asa stole it all from me."

Chase frowned. "I still think he cared about you, even if he didn't always do the right thing." The terror on Asa's face when Rezer Bennin aimed his blaster at Parker had been unmistak-able. "He tried to protect you—he took a blaster hit for you."

Parker raised an eyebrow. "Are you sticking up for him?" His tone grew aggressive. "He never even looked me in the eyes, not once. Maybe some criminal code obligated him to keep me alive after my parents died, but don't you dare say that he cared about me."

Chase dropped his head, nodding. He knew he wouldn't change Parker's mind about Asa—Parker was too angry. But he needed to share the suspicions that were brewing in his mind, and so he continued in a low voice, "I think he might have known my parents. I haven't told Captain Lennard, but Asa knew about my . . . ability."

"Are you sure?" Parker gave him a doubtful expression. "I don't know how he could have. *You* didn't even know about your ability."

"Well, maybe he didn't know about the phasing exactly, but you heard what he said to me. 'I know you're different.'" Chase hesitated, fearing the reaction Parker might have to his next confession. "There's something else I never told you about my microchip. When Mina took me to Dr. Silvestri's home, he told me it was the same as yours. He said Asa designed it. I think maybe it's why I rematerialized at your compound."

Parker was quiet, and for a moment Chase was afraid he'd angered him by withholding this information. Then Parker looked up with a grim smile. "I guess we both have a good reason to hunt him down, don't we?"

"I need to know how my parents got that microchip from him, and what he knows about them," said Chase. "Maybe he can tell me why the Fleet sent people to kill my family."

Parker's eyes took on the faraway look of deep thought. "The ship's doctor is removing my microchip tomorrow. There might be a way for me to reverse it, to use the trace ping..." He looked at Chase with a fierce expression. "We'll find him, and we'll take him down. Him and his stupid android."

Chase felt an unexpected twinge of sadness when he

thought of calm, reliable Mina. "Don't you miss her though? You spent your whole life with her."

"Her?" Parker rolled his eyes. "You don't get it, Chase—you never got it. There is no *her*, she's an *it*."

"She saved your life."

"A program saved my life," said Parker. "She was never my mother, never my friend. She's just a machine."

Chase was silent, considering this. Despite what Parker said, he still sort of missed Mina. "Do you think Dr. Silvestri died on Trucon?"

"Didn't seem like he had much of a chance, did it?" Parker looked solemn for a moment. "It's a shame. He was a pretty okay guy."

Something in the corner of the room caught Chase's eye. Standing against the wall and staring at him was a blond girl in blue pajamas.

It took a second to get past his shock. "Hey," he said softly.

She vanished, blinking out like a light.

"Whoa," whispered Parker. "I think she wants you to come visit her."

Chase lifted his hands, frustrated. "Captain Lennard won't let me. I don't even know where they're keeping her."

"Oh, I can show you." Parker slid off the bed and headed for the door.

"How do you know where she is?"

"I've been doing a little exploring." One side of Parker's mouth tilted up.

A jealous twinge rose in Chase's chest. "Did you see her?"

"No, they've been keeping the door locked." Parker gave him a theatrical wink. "Not that that'll be a problem for you."

They slipped into the hallway, and Parker led the way down a maze of corridors and stairs. Soldiers passed by, most preoccupied by their own business, but some smiled at them or nodded acknowledgment. By the time they'd traveled at least three floors down, Chase was completely disoriented. He wondered how long it would take him to feel at home on the *Kuyddestor*, or if he ever would.

Halfway down a long, white hallway, Parker stopped and gestured at a closed door. Chase hung back a few feet.

"What is it?" Parker asked.

"I don't even know her," whispered Chase. "I don't remember anything."

Parker gave him a smile. "It'll be okay," he said. "Just go in and talk to her."

Chase hesitated, and then he bowed his head and, with the uncomfortable tingle that he was starting to get accustomed to, walked through the door.

# CHAPTER TWENTY-FIVE

The tiny girl sat in her bed and stared at Chase, although he couldn't tell if she was surprised by his unconventional entry. Even in a narrow hospital cot she looked so small, engulfed in blankets. Her skin was no longer as pale, but her eyes were dark and huge, and there were still violet crescents under them. Her short blond hair stuck out in all different directions.

"Hi, Lilli," said Chase. The name felt foreign in his mouth.

"Hi, Chase." Her voice was high and slightly hoarse, as though she hadn't used it in a long time. She watched him carefully and did not smile.

Chase took a hesitant step and crossed the room to her bed. His mind raced with questions. Should he hug her? A high five? Did he have a nickname for her?

"I'm glad you're okay," he said lamely.

Lilli nodded, but the words hung in the air between them.

Chase raced through his mind, trying to think of something else to say.

"Last time we met, you, uh, tried to kill me," he said with a nervous laugh.

Lilli looked down at her bed. "I was following Dornan around. When I saw her talking to you, I thought I was going crazy. I thought someone had cloned you."

"I guess that's what Captain Lennard thought too," said Chase.

Lilli gave him a strange look. "Yeah, that's what he told me," she said slowly. "It's not like anyone thought you'd still be alive. I was the family freak, not you."

"Yeah, I guess I survived . . . everything."

Lilli looked back up, and her dark eyes pleaded with him. "Do you really not remember anything?"

It was Chase's turn to glance away. He couldn't look at her desperate face. "Nothing," he whispered. "Not even my own name. I woke up a week ago out of nowhere, with a big wound in the back of my head." He reached back and touched the spot, long since healed. "I haven't even been able to get hurt since then," he realized aloud.

Lilli was silent for a minute, and when she spoke, he could tell that she had to force each word out. "It was because you tried to run. They were going to shoot at you, and

Dad told you to run, and when you did, they fired at the back of your head."

"Then what happened?" asked Chase.

His sister stared past him at the wall. "They said some mean stuff to Dad. And then they dispersed you. Only it wasn't like this time, where you were able to stay. You were just . . . gone."

Chase gulped. He knew he should stop here, but he needed to know more. "And then?"

Lilli continued to stare at the wall, and after a minute Chase thought she wasn't going to answer. Finally she spoke. "Then they dispersed Mom and Dad," she said in a barely audible voice. "And then it was just me."

She sounded so miserable that Chase decided to share the minuscule seed of hope he'd tucked away. "Maybe they're still alive somewhere, like me."

"No," said Lilli flatly. "They're not. They weren't like me— like us."

Chase lowered his head. "I'm sorry."

Lilli raised her eyebrows. "Sorry for what? It's not your fault. You fought back. You told Dornan you'd hunt her down and kill her yourself."

"What did our parents do? Did they try to stop it? What did they say?"

Lilli closed her eyes and said nothing, and after a few minutes it was clear that she was not going to speak any more about the attack.

"I wish I could remember them," said Chase.

Lilli's head jerked up. "How can you *not* remember? They were our parents!"

"You think I don't wish I could?" asked Chase hotly. "I'd give anything to have my memory back! You have no idea what it feels like to have no idea who you are."

"And you have no idea what it feels like to watch people murder your whole family, and be left all alone."

Chase raised his hands to his temples. How was he already arguing with her? Did they always fight like this?

"Neither of us is alone anymore," he said, sitting down on the bed beside her. "We have each other again."

Lilli gave him a guarded look and lay back down. "But I still feel alone," she whispered.

Chase sucked in his breath. "How can you say that?"

"Do you remember the time I fell in the creek and you pulled me out? Dad's stupid jokes? The special cake Mom made every year for your birthday?"

Chase dropped his head. It was painful to listen to the list of memories he knew were probably lost to him forever. "I'm sorry," he whispered.

"For what?" Lilli asked. "Because our lives got wrecked?"

"We've still got each other," Chase repeated. "Captain Lennard said we can live on the *Kuyddestor* with him."

"*Uncle Lionel* can't replace Mom and Dad," Lilli snapped.

"Uncle Lionel," Chase repeated, embarrassed. The name felt terribly wrong coming out of his mouth.

Lilli stared at him. "He's not our real uncle."

"Of course." Chase kept his eyes on the floor.

A few silent seconds dragged out between them. "We've known him our whole lives, but he's a stranger to you now," said Lilli quietly. "Just like me."

"You're not a stranger," Chase protested. "You're my sister. We share the same blood. And I need you."

She gazed at him for a minute with a tight, indecipherable expression, then turned her head away and rolled toward the wall. "I need to sleep," she mumbled.

Chase sat beside her, waiting. He had not expected such bitterness from this tiny girl, and her rejection stung like nothing else he had experienced in his short new life. *It's not fair, I lost everything too!* he wanted to scream. He stood up and started toward the door.

"Chase." Her voice sounded strangled. "Please don't leave."

"What do you want?" The question came out more harshly than he'd intended.

"Will you stay here until I fall asleep?" she whispered.

He sat for some time on the side of her bed, trying to sort out his thoughts. The adventure was over, but he recognized the long journey that still lay ahead of him. He knew he would have to be patient if he was going to uncover the person he had once been.

He laid a tentative hand on her shoulder. "I'll be here when you wake up."

# ACKNOWLEDGMENTS

I would be deeply remiss if I didn't thank the people whose support, encouragement, and effort contributed to the making of this book. My heartfelt thanks and appreciation go out to:

My spectacular agent, Joanna Volpe, whose tireless hard work allows me to keep playing around in my imagination. I am so, so grateful to have you on my side. Gigantic thanks also to Danielle Barthel, Kathleen Ortiz, Pouya Shahbazian, and the rest of the awesome team at New Leaf Literary.

My wonderfully supportive editor, Liz Szabla, and my publisher, Jean Feiwel, for their enthusiasm for this book, as well as Anna Roberto, Allison Verost, Mary Van Akin, and everyone else at Macmillan/Feiwel and Friends who worked on the words, design, artwork, production, marketing, and promotion. I'm so thrilled to be working with all of you, sometimes I have to pinch myself.

My reader numero uno, accomplice, and dear friend, Elizabeth Briggs, for keeping me sane and never sugarcoating. I'm fairly certain none of this would have happened if I hadn't met you.

Fabulous beta readers Karen Akins and Cortney Pearson, and the rest of my indisputably awesome support system: Jessica Love, Dana Elmendorf, Kathryn Rose, and Amaris Glass.

My dearly disbanded DFWs, Avi DeTurenne, Kelly Boston, and Deborah Blum, the critique group that kept me going and helped me wrangle my earliest draft.

My parents, Ken and Ruth Searles, who patiently let me keep them in the dark about my closet writing until things really started to pick up. Thank you for making our visits to the Bayliss Public Library a frequent and beloved part of my childhood, and for letting me grow up with the support and love that made me believe there wasn't anything I couldn't do.

And finally, my husband, Bülent Altan, for his unwavering and enthusiastic support, and for transitioning with good grace when his wife's creative side suddenly came out of hibernation.

Thank you for reading
this FEIWEL AND FRIENDS book.
The Friends who made

# THE
# LOST
# PLANET

possible are:

**JEAN FEIWEL**, *Publisher*

**LIZ SZABLA**, *Editor in Chief*

**RICH DEAS**, *Creative Director*

**HOLLY WEST**, *Associate Editor*

**DAVE BARRETT**, *Executive Managing Editor*

**NICOLE LIEBOWITZ MOULAISON**, *Production Manager*

**LAUREN A. BURNIAC**, *Editor*

**ANNA ROBERTO**, *Assistant Editor*

Follow us on Facebook or visit us online at mackids.com.

## Our books are friends for life.